"Camie feels safe here," Felicity said. "Perhaps if thy daughter is allowed to stay here, she will be able to get past her fears."

Ty knew he should go get Camie and carry her home. What would people say when they heard that he had left his only child at an orphan's home?

He didn't care. He recalled how happy Camie had been at dinner.

A hand came through the darkness and rested on his arm. "Thee has been carrying a heavy burden, friend. I will pray that the God who loves us will show us the way to help thy little one."

Her kind, unreproachful words reached him and soothed him like no others. He rose, his exhausted body aching, but with hope and peace flickering like a candle flame inside him. "I will go home now. My mother will come tomorrow. Thank you for your understanding."

Ty forced himself to walk away from her comforting presence. Miss Felicity Gabriel was different than any other woman he'd met. Her smile dazzled him. Love flowed from her. Why should it surprise him that Camie had been drawn to her? She had drawn him, too.

Books by Lyn Cote

Love Inspired Historical

†*Her Captain's Heart*
†*Her Patchwork Family*

Love Inspired

Never Alone
New Man in Town
Hope's Garden
*Finally Home
*Finally Found
The Preacher's Daughter
**His Saving Grace
**Testing His Patience
**Loving Constance
Blessed Bouquets
  "Wed by a Prayer"

Love Inspired Suspense

††*Dangerous Season*
††*Dangerous Game*
††*Dangerous Secrets*

††Harbor Intrigue

†The Gabriel Sisters
*Bountiful Blessings
**Sisters of the Heart

LYN COTE

Lyn Cote and her husband, her real-life hero, became in-laws recently when their son married his true love. Lyn already loves her daughter-in-law and enjoys this new adventure in family stretching. Lyn and her husband still live on the lake in the north woods, where they watch a bald eagle and its young soar and swoop overhead throughout the year. She wishes the best to all her readers. You may e-mail Lyn at l.cote@juno.com or write her at P.O. Box 864, Woodruff, WI 54548. And drop by her blog www.strongwomenbravestories.blogspot.com and read stories of strong women in real life and in true-to-life fiction. "Every woman has a story. Share yours."

LYN COTE
Her Patchwork Family

Steeple
Hill®

Published by Steeple Hill Books™

STEEPLE HILL BOOKS

Steeple
Hill®

Recycling programs
for this product may
not exist in your area.

ISBN-13: 978-0-373-82825-8

HER PATCHWORK FAMILY

www.SteepleHill.com

Printed in U.S.A.

Trust in the LORD and do good.
                    —*Psalm* 37:3

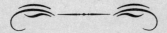

To my fellow Love Inspired authors—
you are a blessing to me!

Chapter One

Gettysburg, Pennsylvania
May 1867

Keeping to the line of fir trees rippling in the wind, Felicity Gabriel tiptoed to the rear of the dark clump of mourners at the memorial service. There she attempted to hide behind a bulky man. A strong gust tried to snatch away Felicity's Quaker bonnet and lift her gray skirt. She held on to the ribbons tied at her throat and pushed her skirt down. Ahead, she glimpsed the pastor holding on to his hat while reading from the Bible.

Her emotions hopped like crickets within her, distracting her from the familiar scriptures of victory over death. Then the man shielding her moved. She caught sight of the brand-new limestone marker. All that was left to show that Augustus Josiah Mueller had lived. Seeing Gus's cold stone marker with the dates 1846-1865 took her breath. She drew in damp air. *Gus*.

The war had lured Gus away and then cruelly abandoned him in an unmarked grave somewhere in Virginia. The cannons were all silent now, but when would the consequences of this war end—one generation? Two? More?

"Why are you here?" The voice Felicity had dreaded hearing snapped like the sharp tongue of a whip.

She looked at the mourners and murmured, "I'm here to show my respect to Gus, Agnes Mueller." Felicity lowered her eyes, not wanting to linger on the woman's red-rimmed, hate-filled eyes.

"I'm surprised that you had the gall to show your face here today." Each word was delivered like a blow.

"Agnes, please," Josiah Mueller pleaded, tugging at his wife's elbow.

"Our Gus is gone forever and we are left without consolation. And here you stand!" the woman shrilled, her voice rising.

There was a rustling in the crowd. Felicity knew there was nothing she could say or do that would comfort this woman who'd lost her only child. Or end her groundless grudge against Felicity. So she kept her eyes lowered, staring at the soggy ground wetting her shoes.

The tirade continued until the woman became incoherent and was led away, sobbing. As the mourners followed, many nodded to Felicity or touched her arm. They all knew the truth.

When everyone else had gone, Felicity approached the stone marker. Tears collected in her eyes. She knew it was human foolishness to speak words to a soul at a grave site, but she still whispered, "I'm leaving Pennsylvania, Gus, but I won't forget thee ever." And then removing her glove, she spit on her palm and pressed it—flat and firm against the cold stone.

Altoona, Illinois
September 1867

Amid the bustling Mississippi wharf, Ty Hawkins eased down onto the venerable raised chair. The chair was now his daily refuge where he got his shoes shined. Afterwards, he would catch a bite to eat at a nearby café. He rarely felt hungry these days even though he was several pounds lighter than he'd ever been as an adult. He would have liked to go home for lunch, sit on his shaded back porch and cool off. But he couldn't face home so soon again.

I'm home but I'm not home.

This dreadful fact brought a sharp pang around his rib; he rubbed it, trying to relieve the pain. *What am I going to do about Camie?*

Jack Toomey had shined shoes here as long as Ty had worn them. Ty smiled and returned Jack's friendly good day. The shoeshine man's dark face creased into a grin. "It's going to be another scorcher."

"'Fraid so, Jack."

"When is it going to realize it's fall?" As Jack blackened Ty's shoe, he gave him a long, penetrating look. He lowered his eyes. "Coming home's not easy. Takes time. Patience."

Jack seemed to be one of the few who understood Ty's suffering. The shoeshine man's sympathetic insight wrapped itself around Ty's vocal cords. Jack glanced up. Ty could only nod.

Jack's gaze dropped to Ty's shoes. "It'll get better. It wasn't easy going off to learn how to shoot people and it isn't easy to put down the rifle and come back."

Ty managed to grunt. No one said things like this to him. Everyone seemed to overlook how hard it was not to jump at any loud noise, or to walk out in the open without scanning his surroundings for people who wanted to kill him. Ty wondered for a moment what Jack would advise if Ty told him about Camie's dilemma.

The thought of discussing this private trouble with someone other than family only showed how desperate he was becoming.

Two urchins had come up to a woman on the street begging. She turned from the wagon and stooped down so her face was level with the children's. Through the moving stream of people on the street, Ty watched the unusual woman. The ragged, grimy children—a little girl who held a younger boy by the hand—nodded. "What's she up to?" Ty muttered to Jack.

"She don't look like the kind who would hurt a child," Jack said, looking over his shoulder again as he continued polishing Ty's shoe.

The woman started to help the little girl up onto the wagon.

Then it happened.

A towheaded boy of about ten or eleven ran by the woman. He snatched her purse, throwing her off balance. With a shocked outcry, she let go of the girl's hand and fell to the dirt street. Ty leaped up to go to the lady's aid. He shoved his way through the crowd. As he reached her and offered her his hand, Hal Hogan, a town policeman, appeared from the other direction. Red-faced, Hogan had his beefy hand clamped on the thief's shoulder. The boy cursed and struggled to free himself in vain.

Ty helped the lady up. "Are you all right, miss?"

She ignored his question, turning toward the caught thief. She very obviously studied the child's smudged and angry red face.

Hogan handed her back her purse and said in his gravelly voice, "I usually would have to keep the purse as evidence but since I witnessed the theft that won't be necessary. Would you tell me how much money you are carrying, miss?"

The young woman hesitated, then said, "I think only around five dollars." She looked into the thief's face and asked, "If thee needed money, why didn't thee just ask me? I would have given thee what I could."

The boy sneered at her and made a derisive noise.

Hogan shook the boy, growling, "Show respect, you." His expression and tone became polite as he said to her, "I saw the robbery and can handle this. No need for a lady like you to get involved in such sordid business." Hogan pulled the brim of his hat and dragged the boy away.

"Please wait!" the woman called after him and moved to pursue Hogan.

"Hey, lady!" the wagon driver demanded. "Are we going now or not? I've got other people who are waiting for me to get you delivered and come back to the station."

Ty had watched all this, his jaw tight from witnessing the theft and her fall. He touched the woman's sleeve.

She looked into his face, her large blue eyes worried. How could this woman say so much with only her eyes? This near-theft troubled her. Again, Ty nearly offered his protection, but why? The thief had been caught. He tightened his reserve and asked in a cool, polite tone, "May I help you up into the wagon?"

With one last glance in the direction where Hogan and the miscreant had disappeared, she nodded. "If thee would, please."

Then she gave him a smile that dazzled him. She was a pretty woman—until she smiled. Then she was an extraordinary beauty. Was it merely the high caliber of the smile that made the difference?

After he helped her up onto the buckboard seat, she murmured, "I thank thee." She was barely seated when the drayman slapped the reins over his team and with a jerk, the horses took off.

The lady waved her thanks once more and over her shoulder sent him another sparkling smile. He found himself smiling in return, his heart lighter.

Dalton watched from the shadowy doorway across the busy road. One problem taken care of. That kid wouldn't be making trouble for him anymore. But he didn't like that woman in the gray bonnet. What was she talking to those two little beggars for? He'd been watching them for days, waiting till they were ready. He frowned. No use looking for trouble. As soon as Hogan had appeared and nabbed the kid, the two had disappeared. But they wouldn't go far and soon they'd be ready for the picking. He smiled. The dishonest life was good.

Felicity turned forward, distinctly unsettled. The two hungry children had been frightened away and the boy arrested. This was not how she had envisioned starting out here. Would she be able to find the little pair again? She sighed. Her eyes threatened to shut of their own accord. Traveling by train for miles and days had whittled her down to nothing. She forced her eyes wide open, stiffened her weary back and folded her hands in her lap.

What she needed was a long hot bath, a good night's sleep. But those would be hours away. "Just a few more miles to tote the weary load"—her mind sang the old slave lament. But that was deceiving. In spite of her fatigue, uncertainty and hope tugged at her like impatient children. Here in Illinois, her work, the work God had given her to help the children, would begin, not end. She had planned on arriving a month earlier, but her sister Verity had needed help after the delivery of her first son in Virginia. Felicity smiled, thinking of how proud Verity's husband, Matt, had been of his son.

Then the recent touch of the man's strong hand on her arm intruded on her thoughts, the sensation lingering. She inhaled deeply. The man who'd leapt to her aid was not one to be taken lightly. And the red welt on his cheek could be nothing but the mark of a saber. A veteran like so many others. And with such sad eyes.

The wagon turned the corner. And there were the little girl and boy. The little girl was waving frantically, jumping up and down. "Lady! Lady!"

Felicity grabbed the reins. "Whoa!" The team halted, stomping, snorting and throwing back their heads. The drayman shouted at her for interfering with his driving. Thrilled to find the two so easily, she ignored him. She reached down with both hands and helped the children up. They crowded around her feet. The children were ragged, very thin, tanned by the sun and had tangled dark hair and solemn eyes.

She turned to the burly, whiskered driver and beamed. "I apologize and promise to make thee no more trouble."

The driver looked bemused. He shook his head and slapped the reins, starting off again for Number 14

Madison Boulevard. Madison Boulevard proved to be a long avenue with wide lawns and massive houses, which struck Felicity as mansions. Very soon, the wagon pulled up to a very large, three-story white house on a wide piece of land with oak and fir trees and bushes. Looking through the porte cochere on the side of the house, she glimpsed a carriage house at the back of the estate. The grounds were well tended but the house looked uninhabited with its shades and lace curtains drawn.

"Is this your house?" the little girl asked, sounding impressed and scared at the same time.

Felicity was experiencing the same reaction. She had known that Mildred Barney was a well-to-do woman, but Mildred had always come east for the abolition meetings and work. "Yes, my new house." Felicity tried not to feel intimidated by the home's quiet grandeur. This did not strike her as a neighborhood which would welcome an orphanage. *Indeed I have my work cut out for me.* "I've just come for the first time. Thee may get down now, children."

Within minutes, the silent driver had unloaded her trunk and valise and had carried both up to the front door. She paid him and tipped him generously for his trouble.

He looked down at his palm. "Unlock the door," he ordered gruffly, "and I'll carry that trunk upstairs for you."

As Felicity turned the large key in the keyhole, she hid her smile. She stepped inside, drawing the children after her. "Please just leave it here in the entryway. I don't know which room I will take as yet."

The drayman did as asked, pulled the brim of his hat politely and left.

Felicity stood a moment, turning on the spot, drinking in the graceful staircase, the gleaming dark oak woodwork, the obviously expensive wallpaper with its lavish design of pink cabbage roses and greenery. Her parents' parlor could have fit into this foyer. In this grand setting, she felt smaller, somehow overwhelmed and humbled. When God blessed one, He didn't stint.

"Miss?" The little girl tugged her skirt. "You said you'd give us food and a place to sleep tonight."

"I did indeed. Come let us find the kitchen." Felicity picked up the covered oak basket that she'd carried on her arm since leaving Gettysburg. In it were the last remnants of her provisions for the trip. She hoped it would be enough for the children.

"Hello," a woman hailed them from the shadowy end of the hall that must lead to the kitchen in the rear. "Who are you, please?"

When the woman came into the light, her appearance reduced Felicity to gawking. She was a tall, slender woman in a blue calico dress with a full white apron and red kerchief tied over her hair. Neat as a brand-new pin. She looked to be in her late twenties and had skin the color of coffee with much cream. Her smooth oval face reminded Felicity of drawings she'd seen of Egyptian queens. And her thick, black eyelashes were perfection. Felicity had been told that a housekeeper would stay until she came. But was this the housekeeper? She'd never seen a beautiful housekeeper before.

Felicity held out her hand, hoping the woman hadn't noticed her momentary preoccupation. "I am Felicity Gabriel. I've inherited this house."

The woman shook Felicity's hand, firm and quick. "I been expecting you, miss. Mrs. Barney's lawyer told me you would be coming any time now. I been keeping things ready for you. I'm the housekeeper, Vista."

Felicity listened to the woman's low musical voice with pleasure. Beautiful to both the eye and ear.

"Miss?" the little girl prompted, tugging on Felicity's skirt again.

"Vista, we have company for lunch." How would this very neatly starched and pressed woman deal with unkempt, ragged children in this elegant house? This was something she must be able to handle or there would have to be a change. Would she understand how to handle this situation?

The woman considered the children, tapping one finger to her cheek. "Why don't I bring lunch out onto the back porch? There be a shaded table there. Mrs. Barney liked to eat outside in the summer. And it's such a lovely September day." Then Vista nodded toward the door behind Felicity.

Felicity got the message. She was to take the children outside and around to the back porch. And so she did.

Vista met them in the back and greeted them beside the pump. "I don't allow anyone with dirty hands or a dirty face to eat at my table." Vista pointed to a white bar of soap and a white flour-sack towel, sitting on an overturned wooden box nearby. Then she began to pump water.

As the water splashed, Felicity slipped off her bonnet and gloves and tossed them onto the nearby back-porch steps. Setting an example, she lathered her hands with the soap, then handed the bar to the little girl. "Be sure to keep your eyes shut so the soap doesn't sting them," Felicity cautioned. After scrubbing her face and hands, she rinsed off in the cold water Vista was still pumping. And then, since she'd taken her own advice and shut her eyes, Vista put the towel into her hands.

When Felicity opened her eyes, she looked over to find that the girl was teaching the boy how to lather his hands and face. When they were done, she passed the towel to the children, who left dirty prints on it. The girl said, "I 'member washing up. He doesn't."

"Does thee?" Felicity resonated with the impact of that simple but telling sentence.

The girl nodded. "Can we eat now?"

Felicity wondered how she could persuade these waifs to stay. She sensed a deep caution in the girl, wise for her years. *Father, guide me.*

"Right now, chil'run." Vista led them to the small

round table on the trellised porch, shaded by lavish, bright purple clematis. She went into the kitchen and returned with a cup of coffee, a plate piled high with slices of buttered bread and cheese and two glasses of milk on a tray. The minute she set the plate on the table, the little boy grabbed two slices of bread and shoved one into his mouth as deep as he could.

"Donnie, that's not good manners," the girl scolded. "Sorry, miss, but he don't 'member eating at a table."

Felicity choked down her reaction. Was eating at a table another privilege she took for granted? "That's all right. I'm sure he will get used to it. What are thy names?"

"I'm Katy and he's Donnie."

Felicity gave them a smile. "Happy to meet thee, Katy. Now I will thank God for this food." She bowed her head. "Thank Thee, God, for food and friends."

After that, Vista was kept busy bringing out more bread and cheese. Finally, she murmured to Felicity that she didn't want the children to eat themselves sick.

After her last swallow of milk, Katy stood up. "Thanks for the eats, miss. We'll be back later to sleep."

"Where is thee going?" Felicity asked, rising to stop them.

"We got to go beg. Donnie's going to need shoes before the snow." The child glanced down at the little boy's bare, dirty feet.

"Does that mean thee doesn't have a home?" Felicity asked.

"No, miss, but I take care of Donnie." Katy took the boy's hand and began edging away.

"Would thee like a home?" Felicity blurted out.

Katy stopped and eyed her with suspicion. "What's the catch?"

"Catch?" Felicity echoed.

Vista spoke up. "The catch is that you got to be scrubbed clean to come inside. I know you chil'run can't help it, but you have to be scrubbed head to toe before you come in. No vermin allowed in any house I'm living in or cleaning up."

Vista's calm but firm pronouncement slightly embarrassed Felicity. But better to start as one plans to go. Katy glanced at Felicity, who nodded her agreement with Vista.

Katy glanced around and then pointed to the door mat. "What about out here? Could we sleep here on the porch?"

Felicity turned to Vista. After all, she was the one who would be cleaning and she was the one who'd brought up the issue of cleanliness.

"You can," Vista replied, "as long as the weather is warm like this, but if you stay till Donnie needs shoes, you will have to be clean to stay inside."

"You mean we could really stay here?" Katy asked with an appraising expression.

"That's why I've come—"

Vista cut Felicity off. "We got no chil'run and I need help with chores and such. The gardener has been away so the weeds have started getting thick. If I show you how to weed today, would you pull weeds, not my flowers?"

"And we might need errands run," Felicity added, catching on. These children had probably rarely known generosity which asked nothing in return. Better to draw them in slowly, gaining their trust. Vista was already proving to be an asset.

Katy nodded. "We got a deal. Where are them weeds?"

Felicity glanced at Vista and lifted one eyebrow, asking her to proceed.

"Over here. I have a garden patch that is choked with them. And I do not like pulling weeds."

Katy followed Vista down the steps and around the house with Donnie in tow. Relief whispered through Felicity. Vista had displayed a practical kindness and sensitivity that impressed Felicity. And the children were staying—at least for now.

Vista returned and Felicity helped her carry in the dishes. After waving Felicity to a chair at the kitchen table, Vista began to wash them. "I see you are planning to start the orphans' home right quick."

Sitting down after eating caused exhaustion to sweep through Felicity and she closed her eyes. "I want to give children who have no home a place, a safe place to grow up strong and good."

"That's why Mrs. Barney left you this house and all the money?" Vista glanced over her shoulder.

"Yes, she came to Pennsylvania and we worked together coordinating movement on the Underground

Railroad. She was a wonderful woman. And she was certain that many children would be left orphaned by this dreadful war."

"And just generally, too?"

Felicity nodded, blinking her eyes to keep them open. "Will thee stay with me and help?"

Vista gave her a sidelong glance. "I got no plans to leave…yet."

So Vista was sizing her up, too. Felicity stretched her tight neck and sighed.

"I got a room ready for you upstairs, miss. Why don't you go on up and rest?"

Felicity sighed again—a habit she must overcome. "No, first I must walk back into town and speak to Mrs. Barney's lawyer."

Her hands in the wash basin, Vista frowned. "Well, first of all, if you going into town, you're not walking. The groom will hitch up the gig for you. But what do you need to talk to the lawyer about?"

"Why mustn't I walk into town?" Felicity asked, not answering the housekeeper's question.

"Mrs. Barney had a certain standing here. I know she wouldn't want you to walk to town," Vista replied firmly.

Felicity tried to think of a polite answer to this. Yes, Mrs. Barney had been a lady of generous means. But Felicity didn't ride where she could eaily walk. But here and now, she was just too tired to argue.

"And the lawyer, Miss Felicity?" Vista asked again.

Clearly there was no putting anything past this woman. "There's a child who needs my help," Felicity answered. "And I'm going to need a lawyer in order to give it to him."

That evening Ty paced his library, wishing he were deaf. After four years of listening to cannon fire and bombs bursting in air, he should be. Unfortunately, he could still hear well enough to suffer each evening's ordeal. The rocking chair on the floor above him creaked in a steady but rapid rhythm. Every once in a while, Camie cried out as if someone had jabbed her with a needle.

No one should have to rock a five-year-old girl to sleep. But if no one rocked her, Camie would stand by the door in her room and sob till she fell down with exhaustion. Then upon waking in the night as she always did, she would scream as if someone were scalding her.

Ty rubbed his face in time with the rocking chair. The sounds of the rapid rocking and Camie's sudden cries of terror shredded his nerves into quivering strings. He halted by the cold hearth and rested his head on the smooth, cool mantel. When would this nightly torture end? *Dear God, help my little daughter, help us.*

Finally, the rocking above slowed and quieted, then ceased, along with the outcries. Ty's tension eased. He slumped into the wing chair by the fireplace. His mother's light footsteps padded down the stairs. As always, she paused at the doorway to wish him good-night.

Tonight, however, she came in and sat down across from him. His mother, Louise Pierce Hawkins, perched on the tapestry seat, a small canary of a woman with silver strands liberally mixed into her faded blond hair. Her kind face showed her distress.

His heart beat faster. "Did something happen?" *Something worse than usual?*

She gazed at him. "Nothing out of the ordinary, unfortunately." She locked her hands together. "I'm becoming more and more concerned about our Camie."

Ty chewed his upper lip and frowned. He wanted to ask if she thought Camie needed…no, he didn't want to know.

"I don't think she's mentally unbalanced, son," she said, answering his unspoken question. "But nothing I do appears to help her get past her panic. In fact, I don't know why she has such fear or what exactly she is afraid of." She shook her head. "She fights sleep as if it were death itself."

Her face twisted with concern. "Whenever she feels herself slipping into sleep, she cries out to wake herself and hold…something at bay. I wish I knew what it was."

Ty could think of nothing to say, nothing that could end this nightly struggle. Guilt weighed on him. He hadn't been able to tell his mother the part he may have unwittingly played in making his daughter's night terrors worse.

Louise rested her head in her hand. "I confess I'm at my wits' end. God must send us help, an answer, someone who knows what to do."

His mother's strained, defeated tone alarmed him. "I could hire someone to care for her. This is too much for you—"

"No." His mother's tone was firm, implacable. "Camie is a sweet, biddable child all day." She looked to the cold hearth as if seeking warmth, encouragement there. "It's just the falling asleep. She can't face the night."

His mother left out the other worrisome problem, which was that Camie would not look at him. Or suffer him to come near her. He clenched his jaw and then exhaled. "Mother, I appreciate all you do for Camie. Maybe we should do what Mrs. Crandall—"

Louise hissed with disapproval. "Ty, you know my opinion of that woman." She jerked her head as if warning someone away. "I try to be charitable, but I think much of the cause of this worrying behavior lies at her doorstep." She pressed her lips together.

Ty looked out into the night. The question of what to do hung unspoken and unanswered between them.

That evening, Felicity stood at the kitchen window, looking out at the two children huddled together on her back porch like stray puppies. She had been tempted to overrule Vista and let the children come inside without cleaning up first. But Felicity hoped Vista would become a part of her work here, and she didn't want to do anything that might upset the housekeeper.

By staying here and keeping the house safe and cared for after Mrs. Barney's death, Vista had proven herself to be honest and hardworking. It would be hard for a stranger to town like Felicity to replace Vista. Trust took time to forge.

And Vista was right. Basic cleanliness must be established for the benefit of all the children who would come here to live. Cleanliness was healthy. A home with children—Felicity hoped to have many children here in the future—must be a house with firm, sensible rules.

Felicity wiped the perspiration on her forehead with the back of her hand. It was a warm, humid night. Sleeping outside was probably more comfortable than sleeping inside. Still, homeless children sleeping on her porch grieved Felicity, causing a gnawing ache deep within.

Donnie snorted in his sleep and opened one eye. She realized he could see her through the window because he wiggled one of his little fingers as if waving to her. The boy, barely more than a toddler, hadn't spoken a word to anyone all day. Though nearly moved to tears, she grinned and wiggled her little finger back at him. The child closed his eyes and fell back to sleep.

Felicity sighed. And then reminded herself that she must stop this new habit. Sighing sounded lonely and a bit sad, pensive even. She caught herself just before she did it again.

Dear Father, please bring me children, the lost ones, the ones that the evil lion Satan wishes to devour. Give me strength and wisdom to carry out the work Thee has given me. I will depend on Thy promise from Psalm 37. I will trust in Thee and do good.

Felicity turned from the window to go upstairs before she remembered one more request.

And Father, please give me the courage I will need in court tomorrow so that I may right the wrong committed against a child—a wrong that has been committed in my name.

Chapter Two

The next morning after breakfast with Katy and Donnie on the back porch, Felicity stood in the kitchen. The heat and the humidity were already growing uncomfortable. How could the calendar say September when it felt like July?

While the children pulled weeds, Felicity and Vista discussed the grocery list. Underneath these routine concerns lurked apprehension over what she would be facing in town today. Felicity glanced at the kitchen wall clock. She needed to get busy and set off for town. The lawyer had told her to be in court at 9:00 a.m. The coming test tightened her midsection. She was pitting herself against the powers of this world.

"What are you children doing here?" A strident female voice flew through the open window, followed by squeals of pain.

Felicity burst through the back door and sailed over the grass toward the woman, her heart outracing her feet. "Stop! Let them go!"

A tall, slender, very well-dressed woman had Katy and Donnie each by an ear. The sight sent anger rushing through Felicity like a hot spring.

The woman was brought up short and glared at Felicity. "These children can't possibly belong here. This is a respectable neighborhood."

Pulling them from the woman's grasp, Felicity drew the children to her. "Katy and Donnie are my guests." She gasped for air, trying to catch her breath after running in the sultry air.

"Guests?" The woman's eyes narrowed as they took in every detail of Felicity's attire and face. "Who are you?"

"I am Felicity Gabriel. Who is thee, please?" Standing very straight, Felicity offered her hand, which was ignored—a sting that tried Felicity's temper.

"Thee?" the woman snapped, her face crimping up. "Are you some kind of Quaker?"

"There is only one kind of Quaker that I know of." Taking another sip of the humid air, Felicity tried to keep her irritation out of her tone. "And yes, I am a member of the Society of Friends."

"Well, I am a God-fearing Christian and this is a re-spectable neighborhood. We don't want riffraff from the riverfront here."

Felicity could think of nothing Christian to say to

this so she merely looked at the woman. She knew she wasn't to judge others, but…

"Why are these children *here* on Madison Boulevard?" The woman pointed at the ground as though it were sacred ground that Katy and Donnie were not worthy to walk upon.

Felicity gripped her spiraling temper with both hands. "They are here because they had no one to feed them and nowhere to sleep," she replied in an even tone. "They are doing a few jobs for me in return for food and shelter."

"You are not from around here," the woman said, her attractive face reddening like a bull about to charge. "So you don't know that we keep the river rats and their spawn down at the wharf. We don't let them roam through town—"

Felicity gritted her teeth. "I met Katy and Donnie at the wharf and invited them home because they are hungry and homeless orphans. I hope to invite many more to come here." Felicity quoted, "'Pure religion and undefiled before God and the Father is this, To visit the fatherless and widows in their affliction.' So since thee is a God-fearing Christian, I would think thee would be pleased."

The woman leaned forward as if trying to either read Felicity's mind or intimidate her. "Are you telling me that you're starting an orphanage here?"

Felicity's forced smile thinned. Her hold on her temper was slipping, slipping. "I think 'orphans' home' and 'orphanage' are unpleasant titles. They sound so institutional and unkind. This will be the Barney Home for Children. I am going to welcome homeless children into this house and make sure they are kept warm and well fed. So yes, thee can expect to see many more children here in the future."

The woman began making a sound that reminded Felicity of a dog growling at trespassers. "The law won't let you disrupt our quiet neighborhood with an orphanage."

Churning with righteous indignation, Felicity patted the children's backs, trying to reassure them, and felt their spines sticking out, no padding of fat over the knobby vertebrae. This woman saw only their bare feet and ragged clothing, not their need. *Father, help me make her see these children with Thine eyes.*

"Mrs. Barney's lawyer has already checked all the legalities of this charitable work which that good woman requested in her will. She asked me to carry it out in her stead." Felicity took another breath of the sultry air. "I am breaking no laws. I don't know why thee assumes that a small number of orphans will disrupt—"

The woman raised her chin another notch. "We don't want beggars and sneak thieves living among us."

"Neither do I." Felicity gazed at the woman, trying to reach the soul behind all the vainglory. "Thee hasn't introduced thyself. I'd love to talk to thee about my plans—"

"I am Mrs. Thornton Crandall," she interrupted,

"and I am uninterested in your plans to despoil our good neighborhood."

Mrs. Crandall turned, lifted her skirts as if the ground had been defiled by Katy and Donnie and marched off. The kitchen door behind Felicity opened. She glanced over her shoulder toward the sound.

Vista gave her a wry smile. "I see you met Mrs. Crandall, one of the leading ladies in Altoona society."

Stirred as if she'd just fought hand-to-hand in the opening battle of war, Felicity shook her head. She tried to return Vista's smile and failed. How could this woman look at these children and not be moved to pity?

Katy tugged Felicity's skirt. "Miss, was you telling the truth? Are you going to take in children that don't have homes?"

"Yes," Felicity gentled her voice and stooped down. "Katy, would thee and Donnie like to come live here?" With the back of one hand, she touched the little girl's soft cheek.

Katy looked back and forth between Felicity and Vista. "I'll think on it, miss."

"Yes, please do, Katy. We would be so happy to have thee and Donnie with us." Rising, Felicity squeezed her shoulder. "Now I must get into town. Please do whatever Vista tells thee and I'll be back by lunch."

I hope.

Ty walked into the stark, whitewashed courtroom with its polished oak floors as the bailiff declared,

"All rise. Judge Tyrone Hawkins presiding." Ty settled himself on the high platform in the judge's seat and looked out over the sparsely filled courtroom. And there she was.

The woman with blue eyes he'd seen arrive in town the day before whose purse had been stolen was sitting on one of the spectator's benches. A tingle of recognition coursed through him. Hadn't anyone told her that she need not suffer coming to court? He never liked to see ladies in court. It was such a rough setting and often the defendants used coarse language.

No doubt she'd come out of a sense of duty. He tried not to stare in her direction, but she kept drawing his tired, gritty eyes. In this stark setting, she glowed, the only appealing face present.

The first dreary case began and then another, and another. Finally, the boy who'd snatched the newcomer's purse was ready to be heard, making his plea. The boy was marched into the room by Hogan, the arresting officer. Ty wondered if there was any hope for this lawless child. He hated this part of adjudicating the law. He could not believe that children should be treated as adults by the courts. But what was he to do? The law was the law.

One of the prominent lawyers in town, John Remington, with his silver hair and imposing presence, rose and approached the bench. "I am defending young Tucker Stout."

The young, already portly prosecuting attorney

looked back and forth between the defendant and Remington, his mouth open in disbelief. Ty felt himself goggling at Remington. Surprise crashed through him, making him even more aware of his bone-deep fatigue. Months of little sleep was wearing him down, making him vulnerable. "Did I hear you right?"

"Yes, I am defending Tucker Stout." The elder lawyer continued in his distinctive, deep voice, glancing over his shoulder. "Miss Felicity Gabriel has hired me to act as his counsel."

Still unsettled, Ty looked to the woman. She responded with a half smile. Even her subdued smile had the power to dazzle him.

The prosecuting attorney blurted out what Ty was thinking, "But she's the plaintiff. Hers was the purse stolen."

Remington nodded. "She is aware of that. But she is anxious, in light of the defendant's tender age, that his rights be protected." Remington paused and then added as if in explanation of such odd behavior, "She's a Quaker."

Ty sat back and studied the woman, who sat so deceptively prim in his courtroom. A Quaker. Well, that explained the situation somewhat. He'd met a few Quakers. They spoke strangely and didn't fight in war. Peculiar people.

Loose jowled, Hogan snorted where he sat on the prosecution side of the courtroom. Ty drew himself up. He'd lost control at home—he wouldn't also lose control of his courtroom. "Very well. Bailiff, please read the charges against the defendant."

The bailiff did and Ty asked, "How does your client plead, Mr. Remington?"

"We plead not guilty."

"And you realize that I witnessed the purse-snatching myself?" Ty responded dryly. Was this woman trying to play him and the other men in this room for fools?

"Yes, but Miss Gabriel believes that the boy is too young to be held to adult legal standards of behavior."

"What Miss Gabriel believes may be true, but not in the sight of the laws of Illinois," Ty retorted, antagonized at having to defend what he did not believe.

The lady suddenly rose. "God does not hold children accountable for their sins until they reach the age of reason. Are the laws of Illinois higher than God's?"

The question silenced the courtroom. Every eye turned to the woman who looked completely at ease under the intense scrutiny. Ty chewed the inside of his cheek. *Does she expect special treatment because she is a woman?*

"Females," Hogan grunted, breaking the silence.

"Miss," Ty said curtly, "you are not allowed to speak in court without permission. You must let your counsel do the talking."

She nodded and sat down without dispute, giving him an apologetic little smile. He found he had no defenses against her smiles. They beckoned him to sit beside her and be at ease.

"Your Honor," Remington spoke up, "Miss Gabriel has asked me if I might have a word with you in your chamber during a short recess."

"What is this?" the prosecutor asked, rearing up.

"You'll be included, of course." Remington bowed to the man whose face had reddened.

Ty passed a hand over his forehead. After falling asleep last night, Camie had cried out with nightmares twice more, keeping the whole house up. He closed his eyes for just a moment, then opened them. He couldn't let the situation at home interfere with his work. Though the headache was making his right eyelid jump, he forced himself to act with magisterial calm. "Very well. The court stands adjourned while I meet with counsel in my chambers."

He rose and so did everyone else. His black judge's robe swirling out behind him, he strode into his paneled chambers just behind the courtroom and sat behind his oak desk, waiting for the attorneys to knock. The bailiff let them in and the two men sat down facing him. "Remington, what's this all about?" Ty asked without preamble, able at last to release some of his spleen.

"Miss Gabriel is Mildred Barney's heir. She has inherited the Barney house and all the Barneys' considerable estate."

The prosecutor let out a low whistle.

Remington nodded. "Miss Gabriel is also following Mrs. Barney's instructions and turning her house into a private orphanage which the Barney money will support."

Ty lifted his eyebrows. His mother-in-law would love that. He studied Remington, thinking of Miss Gabriel's pretty face. He shook his head, resisting. Pretty or not, he had to judge this case fairly. "The boy is guilty. What can I do but sentence him to jail time?"

"This isn't his first arrest," the prosecutor was quick to add.

"We know that." Remington folded his hands in front of himself. "Miss Gabriel would like you to dismiss charges so that she can take the boy with her to the orphanage."

The prosecutor made a sound of derision. "And how long would he stay there? Till her back's turned and then he'd just go back across the river to St. Louis, picking pockets and snatching more purses. Women are idealistic but we men must be realistic. The kid is from bad blood. He'll never be anything but what he is."

Ty didn't like the sentiment the prosecutor expressed but he suspected that the man was right. If he released the boy, he wouldn't stay at the orphanage. Like a wild horse, Tucker Stout had never been broken to bridle. And at eleven or twelve, it might already be too late to salvage the boy. Weighed down by this unhappy thought, Ty rose. This signaled the end of the conference.

The attorneys left to meet him on the other side of the wall back in the courtroom. By his desk, Ty waited, chewing the inside of his cheek, giving them time to reach their places. Then he strode back into court and took the judgment seat.

Remington waived the boy's right to a jury and the trial was brief, proceeding just as Ty had expected. When they reached the time for sentencing, he looked out at the few people sitting in the benches of the courtroom.

Miss Gabriel's head was bowed as if she were in prayer. Her smile still glowed within him, a tiny ember of warmth. He hated to disappoint her. He opened his mouth to sentence the boy to a month in the county jail.

"I am sentencing Tucker Stout to six months' probation," he said, surprising himself. "The conditions of probation are that he live and work at the new orphans' home under Miss Felicity Gabriel's supervision. If Tucker leaves Miss Gabriel's house and refuses to follow her orders, he will be sent to jail for a year."

The prosecutor gawked at him. Hogan balked with a loud "What?"

Miss Gabriel rose, beaming at him. Her unparalleled smile brightened the whole of the sad room where no one ever found cheer, least of all Ty. The ember she'd sparked flared inside him. "Will you accept this responsibility, Miss Gabriel?"

"Of course!" she beamed.

Ty caught himself just before he returned her brilliant smile.

He struck his gavel once, unusually hard. "Case closed. Bailiff, please announce the next case."

Outside, under the sweltering noonday sun, Felicity gripped the lawyer's hand. "I cannot thank thee enough, John Remington."

The lawyer shook her hand. "Good luck," he said, eyeing Tucker. "The judge was kind to you, young man." He tipped his hat and was gone.

The intriguing face of the judge popped into her mind. So the man she'd seen in town that first day was a judge. A judge who could show mercy as well as justice. And a man who looked worn down by some secret pain.

Felicity shook off her thoughts and turned to Tucker. "We need to get home in time for lunch."

Tucker looked like he wanted to say something rude. But he shrugged and got in step with her. They walked in silence down the busy, noisy street. "Does thee have parents?" she asked.

"Everybody's got parents. Somewhere." The boy didn't even bother to look her way.

"A good point." People kept turning to look at them. Felicity resisted the urge to lift her chin. She hoped in the coming weeks that people would become accustomed to the sight of her walking beside uncared-for children. "Are thy parents living?"

He shrugged again. "Might be. Don't know. Don't care."

Felicity had spoken to souls scarred like this before. At this tender age, Tucker had given up on people. "How old is thee?"

"Old enough."

Felicity gave up questioning him. If this one ever opened up, he would do it in his time and in his way. "I am from Pennsylvania. I am the middle daughter of seven sisters. I grew up on a farm near Gettysburg."

Tucker kicked a stone and ignored her.

Felicity was glad to see home ahead—until she noted that Mrs. Crandall was coming toward them. *Oh, dear.* Could they get into the house before she reached them? "Two children have already come to my home, Katy and Donnie. They are deciding whether or not they want to stay with me."

"Oh, goody."

"But thee will be staying." Felicity walked faster. "Or thee will be in jail."

Tucker snorted. "Been there before. Be there again."

"The question is, does thee want to go there again?"

He gave her a sidelong glance. "I don't have much use for do-gooders."

Felicity knew what he meant. She'd met many do-gooders who lorded their superiority over those they "ministered" to. Many of these, she would gladly have kicked. She knew that wasn't a Christian thought but it was the truth.

As she and Tucker turned up her front walk, Mrs. Crandall bustled up to her. "I see you have brought another undesirable into our neighborhood. If you go forward with this orphanage, no decent person in town will have a thing to do with you."

Felicity's first inclination was to give this woman a talking to about Christian charity. She settled on, "I'm afraid I'm very busy right now, Mrs. Crandall. Could we discuss this later?" *Or when thee has had a change of heart?*

The woman turned and huffed away.

The back of Felicity's neck was unusually tense. She began to lead the boy toward the back door. He surprised her by saying, "That lady's right, you know."

Struggling to quench the aggravation burning inside, Felicity paused and then fixed her gaze on Tucker's face. "I doubt what she said is true. If it is, then I don't think much of the decent people in this town. Now let's get our hands washed and sit down to lunch. I think thee will find that Vista's food is worth the effort to stay and do what is expected of thee."

"I'll let you know."

Felicity hid her smile at his unexpected savoir faire. And then the moment of lightness was gone. What a world this was where boys became cynics before they even began to shave. She led Tucker to the pump and handed him the soap. He made a face of sincere distaste, but began lathering his hands.

For a moment, she lingered on the memory of the judge's sad drooping mouth, troubled dark eyes. It was a strong face with eyes that didn't flinch from meeting hers.

He also had that lean look many veterans had. Too many hardtack meals and days of travel, and then the ordeal of battle after battle. How did a good man put aside his rifle and sword and go back to life, put the war behind him? Her mourning for Gus, a dark chilling wave of loss, welled up and swelled, tightening her stays.

Felicity almost sighed, but stopped herself. *Father,*

*bless Judge Hawkins and keep Tucker here while Thee
works Thy will upon him.* Felicity decided to keep
mum on the topic of Mrs. Thornton Crandall. She was
certain that the Lord had heard quite enough already
about Mrs. Crandall from others.

The next afternoon Felicity tried to slip away and
walk to town, but was caught by Vista and the groom.
The groom drove the half mile into town and helped
her down at the clothing store on Merchants Street.
How could she persuade them that she should walk?

Inside the door of the large well-appointed store, a
man in a crisp dark suit greeted her. "Hello, miss, I am
Robert Baker, the proprietor. May I help you?"

She smiled. "Thank thee, friend. I need clothing for
children and I'm afraid I have never bought much
before."

The man smothered his obvious surprise and
asked, "What are the ages and gender of the children,
please, miss?"

She pulled a list out of her reticule. "I will need an
assortment of clothing for boys and girls of all ages."

The salesman looked confused.

"I should tell thee—"

"Are you here buying clothing for those orphans of
yours?" A lady with a jarring voice bustled up to them.

Felicity didn't appreciate the sound of the question.
Worse, there was only one way this woman could
have heard of Felicity's plans for the Barney house—
by listening to gossip. Disapproval ground inside her.

However, Felicity gagged it down. She smiled hopefully. "Yes, I am. Would thee advise me on clothing for children?"

"No, I would not. I live on Madison Boulevard. I, along with many of your neighbors, don't want an orphanage in our neighborhood."

"Thee doesn't like children?" Felicity asked, her spirit suddenly simmering, bubbling with displeasure.

"We don't need riffraff from the wharf infesting our lovely avenue."

"I am truly sorry thee has that opinion. How does thee know of my work here?"

"Mrs. Thornton Crandall is one of my best friends. She told me all about your despoiling the Barney mansion." The woman brushed past her. "And she is going to do something to stop you!" The woman departed with a slam of the door.

If God be for me, who can be against me? Still prickling with outrage over the gossip being spread, Felicity looked at the proprietor. She calmed herself. "Would thee show me some clothing now?"

The man stood looking back and forth between the woman's retreating form and Felicity with her long list in hand.

Well, Robert Baker, does thee want my business?

Finally, he bowed. "Don't orphanages usually order a large quantity of uniforms—one for boys and one for girls?" The man led her down the aisle.

"I considered that and rejected it. It's like marking the children as odd, different from other children.

Being orphaned is bad enough without being branded. Doesn't thee think?"

He nodded. "But it is less expensive—"

"Funds from Mrs. Barney's estate are more than adequate."

"Follow me, miss. We'll look at my selection for girls first, if you please."

She followed him down the neat aisle of folded shirts for men over to the girls' section. Felicity was relieved to discover that the man was not about to lose her as a customer, just because her children's home had evidently ruffled a few fancy ostrich feathers in town. With any luck, Felicity would be rewarding the man's decision by becoming one of his best customers, ordering more children's clothes than he could possibly keep in stock for the many children she planned to care for.

Felicity's eyes opened wide. By the scant moonlight, she distinguished the gray outlines of the furniture in her room. What had wakened her? She listened. The house was quiet. Still, something had roused her. She rose and donned her blue-sprigged wrapper and slippers. She slipped down the hall and peeked into the room where a very clean Katy and Donnie should have been sleeping in the high four-poster bed. Except that they were sleeping on the rag rug *beside* the bed. The forlorn sight wrenched her heart.

She nearly stepped into the room to lift them onto the bed. Then she halted. They would adjust eventually. She would never forget the image of the two of them with tightly shut eyes and agonized expressions sitting in the heaping soap-suds, neck-high tub of water on the back porch. Vista, singing under her breath, had ruthlessly scrubbed them with a soft brush. Such beautiful children.

Felicity turned away to the room across the hall and found the bed where Tucker should have been sleeping— it was empty. Her heart tumbled down. If the boy had run away—a year in jail. She hurried down the stairs and out the front door, looking up and down the dark street. Just turning the corner ahead was Tucker. No! She kicked off her slippers and picked up her skirts and ran.

Within seconds, she was at the corner and around it. The boy didn't hear her. He was walking, head down and hands in his pockets. She put on speed. Just before she reached him, he turned. She clamped a hand on his shoulder.

"Tucker," she said, her heart beating wildly, her breath coming fast. "Why are thee out here?"

His expression showed his shock. Before he could say a word, a man came around the corner ahead of them. Felicity's heart began doing strange antics. It sank to her knees and then leaped into her throat. The fact that she was outside barefoot and in her night clothing hit her like a wet mop in the face. This could spawn gossip for years to come.

The man walked toward them, head down and hands in his pockets just like Tucker. She saw it was the judge. She wished she could become invisible.

"Turn around and start walking normal," Tucker whispered and did what he'd just told her to do.

Felicity hurried to follow his example. The two of them walked, her hand on the boy's shoulder. Every moment she expected to hear the judge call for her to stop. And since she couldn't lie, what possible explanation could she give to explain why they were out in the night?

Tucker and she came to their house at last. When they came to her abandoned slippers, they paused as she slipped her feet into them. Then they walked up the flagstone path and through the front door. Felicity had never been so grateful to hear her door close behind her. Either the judge had not seen them or he had chosen to be merciful again and behave as if he had not seen them. And she must make certain that Tucker's night wandering ended now.

Tucker tried to go on, but she squeezed his shoulder and led him down the hall to the moonlit kitchen. "Sit down at the table." When he made no move to obey, she added, "Please."

The boy sank into the chair. She sat down across from him. He would not meet her gaze. "Tucker…" What could she say? He knew he should be upstairs in bed. So she just sat, letting her tight, serrated worry flow out. She prayed, waiting for the Inner Light to lead her.

"Are we going to sit here all night?" the boy finally snapped.

She stared into his eyes. "That's up to thee."

"What's that supposed to mean?" The boy's tone showed plainly that he didn't hold her in any respect, probably held no adult in respect. The defiant eyes that returned her gaze told her much more than she wanted to deal with tonight.

It grieved her. "Tucker Stout, I don't understand what took thee out of thy comfortable bed in a comfortable home—"

"I like being on my own. I don't like people interfering with me, see?" His brows drew together.

"I must on the whole agree with thee." Peace began trickling through her, soothing her rasped nerves. "I also like being on my own. And I don't like interference of any kind either. So we have that in common. What interference are thee expecting from me?"

The boy snorted. "You'll be telling me to wash my hands and do this and do that and say grace at the table and don't pick my nose—"

The last forced a chuckle from her. Her good humor surged back. "Does thee do that often?"

Rebellious, Tucker made as if to rise. She pressed a hand over his and said, "Sit, please."

He stared and then capitulated, scowling.

"May I ask thee a question?" She waited for his permission.

Finally, he realized that she wasn't going to speak until he granted her the opportunity. "Okay, ask me."

"If thee runs away and is caught and sent to jail, won't they tell thee to wash thy hands, and do this and don't do that?"

He stared at her.

"I would think that Vista and I would be preferable to jail guards." She folded her hands in front of her on the table and waited. Would he accept this simple truth?

He lifted one shoulder and demanded, "So what do you want me to say, lady?"

"Nothing, really. I will ask for no promise from thee. And I am not going to tie thee to thy bed. Or bolt thy door and window shut. And this is the last time I will come after thee. Thee must decide for thyself which to choose—this home or jail."

Tucker looked at her as if she were speaking in ancient Greek.

Felicity rose. "I will bid thee good-night. Will thee turn the lock on the back door, please? Thank thee." She walked up the stairs without a backward glance. *Oh, Father above, heal this wounded heart. Only Thee can. I cannot.*

In her room again, she took off her robe and slippers and sank onto the side of her bed, still praying. Forcing herself to have faith, she lay down again, trying not to listen for Tucker's footsteps on the stair. Her final thought was not about Tucker but about Judge Hawkins. What was he doing out well after midnight? And had he seen her with Tucker? And if he had, what would he do?

Chapter Three

After a too-short, two-block walk, Felicity strode up the Hawkins' front stone pathway. Her every step tightened her anxiety. She mounted the steps. And before she could turn tail, she sounded the brass knocker on the door twice politely. The judge's troubled eyes had haunted her for several days, etching her heart with sympathy. What beset the judge? Did God have work of mercy for her to do at this home?

Even if the answer had been no, she couldn't have stayed away. She'd stewed for hours till she'd come up with a reasonable excuse to visit him at his home, where she might glimpse a hint of what tortured his eyes. So here she was with deep apprehension—deep, gnawing apprehension.

While she waited, golden twilight wrapped around her with its heavy humidity. She took out a handkerchief and blotted the perspiration from her face. Why did women have to smother themselves with gloves, high shoes and hats even in summer?

Drawing in the hot, moist air, she resisted the urge to pluck the bonnet from her head and tear off her gloves. She needed all her "armor" to meet Tyrone Hawkins face to face without a courtroom of people looking on. Her hand again tingled with his remembered touch that first day at the wharf…

The door opened, revealing a dainty older woman with silvered blond hair.

Felicity smiled, uneasiness over the unsolicited visit skating up her spine. "Is Tyrone Hawkins at home, please?"

The woman looked her over thoroughly. "Yes, my son is home. Won't you step in?"

This gave Felicity another jolt. The judge's mother had answered the door herself? The judge lived on Madison Boulevard in a home nearly as large as the house she had inherited. These types of estates needed staff to maintain. Wondering at this discrepancy, Felicity crossed the threshold. She followed the woman through a long hallway out onto the shaded back porch. "Ty, we have company."

He was already rising from his wicker chair. "Miss…"

Though her heart was fluttering against her breastbone, she said, "I am Felicity Gabriel." She offered him her hand, a fresh wave of awareness of his deep sadness flowing through her. "We met yesterday in court?"

"I remembered your name," he said, taking her fingers, not her full hand, as if holding himself at a distance. "However, I didn't expect to see you here this evening." He bowed formally. His words and expression warned her away as if he'd thrown up an arm to fend her off.

Grateful for the excuse to turn from his intense, unwelcoming gaze, Felicity offered her hand to his mother.

"My mother, Louise Hawkins."

"Louise Hawkins, I am pleased to meet thee," Felicity greeted her. His mother's eyebrows rose at her Plain Speech but Felicity was used to this and made no comment.

"Won't you sit down, Miss Gabriel?" Louise invited. The woman watched Felicity as if she were an exhibit in a sideshow. Had Louise Hawkins heard gossip about her, too?

Looking anywhere but at the tall, brooding man and the rudely inquisitive woman, Felicity noted a little girl with long dark braids, sitting far from the adults, rocking in a child's rocker. She held a rag doll and was sucking her thumb.

Felicity sat down in the white wicker chair that her hostess had indicated, which put her opposite Tyrone and beside Louise. Why hadn't he introduced the little girl?

"What can I do for you, Miss Gabriel?" Ty Hawkins's brusque voice snapped Felicity back to the fabricated purpose for this visit.

"I have come to thank thee for letting me take Tucker Stout to my home."

"No need to thank me. Prison isn't the place for children." He didn't look her in the eye, but focused on a point over her shoulder.

"Indeed." She resisted the temptation to lower her eyes. *I have nothing to be ashamed of.*

Her disobedient eyes went over his face again, noting the dark gray puddles beneath his eyes and the vertical lines in his face were so pinched and somber. She sealed her lips to keep from asking him plainly what was wrong.

From the corner of her eye, Felicity noted that the little girl had stopped rocking and was listening to the conversation. Her intense brown eyes studied Felicity with an unnatural solemnity in one so very young. Felicity smiled bravely, trying to shove off the oppressive gloom of these three. "Still, I wished to thank thee."

He made a dismissive gesture. "No doubt some, many of my colleagues, would not agree with my giving a miscreant into another person's hands as in Tucker's case."

Felicity nodded, drawing up her strength. She glanced sideways at the little girl and saw so much pain in the little girl's face—unmistakable unhappiness. The child's misery thumped Felicity in her midsection. She tore her gaze back to the judge. "I wonder if thee has followed the career of Mary Carpenter."

Ty raised an eyebrow. "I'm sorry, I'm not acquainted with the lady."

"Just fifteen years ago in England, she wrote *Reformatory Schools for the Children of the Perishing and Dangerous Classes, and for Juvenile Offenders*. Mary Carpenter said good free day schools and reformatory schools were urgently needed."

As she spoke, Felicity realized the child had her chair turned away so she couldn't see her father. The child looked only to her. Felicity's unmanageable heart contracted.

"We have good free day schools here in Altoona," Louise said with a touch of irritation in her tone.

Felicity turned and smiled though she could sense that they wanted her to leave. The little girl was still watching Felicity with an unnerving intentness. For a child with a family and a home to look so forlorn, so lost, was unnatural. Felicity wanted to gather the child into her arms and hold her, comfort her. "Louise Hawkins, I'm sure Altoona has excellent day schools. But what of a reformatory school for young ones like Tucker Stout who have no parents and who fall afoul of the law?"

"I thought you were just here to start an orphanage—" Tyrone began, sounding unaccountably frustrated.

"I prefer to call it a children's home," Felicity interrupted, yet smiled to soften her words. "A place where children will be loved and cared for."

"You got a home for children?" the little girl asked. Both her father and grandmother jerked and swung around to look at the child.

Felicity smiled. "Yes, I do. Hello, I'm Felicity Gabriel. What is thy name?"

The little girl tilted her head to one side. "My name's Camie."

"Hello, Camie." Impulsively, Felicity offered the child her hand.

Looking uncertain, Camie rose, still clutching the doll and sucking her thumb.

Felicity kept her hand out, open palm up as if offering it to a cautious stray. Camie edged closer and closer to her, keeping as far away from Tyrone as possible. *Oh, dear. A troubled child. A troubled man. And a gulf between them.* Felicity sensed the father and grandmother tensing. Were they afraid that the child would do something abnormal? Camie finally reached Felicity and took her hand. "Do you like little girls, too?"

"Little girls and boys. I want them to be well cared for, loved and happy like I was when I was a child." Felicity leaned forward and smoothed the moist tendrils around the child's face.

Camie tilted her head again like a little sparrow and then lifted her arms in silent appeal. Felicity gathered the little girl onto her lap and kissed the top of her head.

Camie nestled against her, hiding her face against Felicity's gray bodice. Though the added body heat was unpleasant, Felicity smoothed her palm over Camie's back, trying to soothe the tense child.

When Felicity looked up, she was shocked to see

tears in Tyrone's eyes. Louise was dabbing her eyes with a handkerchief. Why was this a matter for tears?

Something was very wrong here—something had happened to this family and something needed to be done to help them. Felicity did not want to ask for an explanation in front of the child, or pry.

The four of them sat in silence for many minutes. The child's stiffness didn't leave completely, but the little girl did rest against her. Stroking Camie and crooning whispered words, Felicity watched Tyrone master himself, bury his reaction. She longed to smooth his worried forehead and speak comforting words to him also.

Finally, Louise broke their silence as oppressive as the summerlike heat. "I think setting up an orphan— I mean a children's home—is admirable." Louise's voice had softened. "I had heard that Mildred had left her estate to someone in the east."

Felicity nodded. "Perhaps thee would like to help the work she wanted me to carry out."

The softly spoken suggestion appeared to surprise Louise. Tyrone sat forward, staring at Felicity, hawk-like.

Felicity continued stroking Camie's back and said, "I have a housekeeper and a groom. I will of course hire staff as necessary, but I would like to have men and women from the community volunteer to help out. So often in children's homes, the children are kept clean, fed and schooled. But who is there to rock them and read them stories? Teach them how to play games? Would thee be interested in such work?" She included Tyrone in her glance.

"I never thought of that," Louise said.

"My mother helps me with my daughter." Tyrone's face had frozen into harsh, forbidding lines that didn't seem to fit him. "Camie's mother passed away while I was at war." His anguish came through his words. And yet she sensed immediately that this wasn't just the grief over losing his wife. Something had been added to that grief.

"I'm very sorry to hear of your loss." She squeezed Camie, reiterating her sympathy. "Perhaps Camie would like to visit and play with our first little girl, Katy, some afternoon?"

Tyrone looked away.

"Perhaps," Louise replied, looking at her son with uncertainty.

Felicity hoped that this lady didn't deem her grand-daughter too good to play with Katy. Her welcome here had been cordial enough, yet the sense that she was treading on just a skim of ice kept her cautious. "I think it's time I left." Felicity stroked Camie's cheek and looked into her eyes. "I have to go now. I have a little boy and girl at home to put to bed."

Camie sat up. The sudden look of alarm on the little girl's face was startling. Felicity almost asked what was the matter but checked herself. *At this point, these people are just acquaintances. I must not pry or meddle.*

The kind of do-gooders that Tucker mistrusted were

people who thought their good intentions allowed them to stick their long pointy noses into other people's private lives, to trample the feelings of those who needed help, wielding their "good" deeds like weapons. Felicity did not want to be like that. Ever.

She urged Camie, who was trying to cling to her, to slip down and then she rose. "I will see thee again, Camie."

"I'll walk you to the front," Tyrone said gruffly.

Felicity accepted this with a nod. "Good night, Louise, Camie." She couldn't stop herself from cupping the little girl's cheek. "I hope to see thee again soon." Tyrone followed her down the steps of the back porch and around to the front walk. There, Felicity turned and offered him her hand. A mistake. When he took it, in spite of her sheer summer glove, her awareness of him multiplied.

"I saw you out with Tucker Stout the other night," he said in a harsh tone. His unexpected, unwelcome words rolled up her sensitivity to him like a window shade, snapping it shut. Recalling that she had been in nightdress at the time, Felicity felt herself blush.

"Maybe I should come over and impress on him why he shouldn't run away."

Looking at him sideways, she glimpsed his face, which had turned a dull red. Perhaps he was regretting causing her embarrassment.

Felicity pulled together her composure. "I thank thee but I think that he has decided to stay with me for the duration."

"I hope so."

"I do, too." Felicity withdrew her hand. "Thank thee, Tyrone Hawkins. I am glad I met thy mother and thy sweet daughter. Thee has been blessed."

His face contorted with some unspoken pain, then he bowed. "Good evening."

Felicity started off toward home, feeling his gaze on her back. Behind her, Camie cried out with shrill panic from an open window in the judge's house. Felicity halted in midstep, her heart fluttering wildly. She forced herself to go forward. She had come here suspecting that there was a need, but she'd had no idea how deep, how grave a need. *Heavenly Father, what is amiss in that house?*

Ty walked back into the house. Dread settled over him again like a shroud. The Quaker's visit had been equally beneficial and upsetting. It had done Camie good yet highlighted how cruelly broken his family remained. His mother must have taken Camie upstairs to get ready for bed. The nightly ordeal had begun. Now Camie's cries were most likely heard all down the block. The Quaker had heard them—as she walked away. He'd noted her stiffening. What did the neighbors think? Did they think that he was abusing his little girl?

He stopped beside the stairs in the foyer and clutched the finial on the bottom railing. His emotions churned, threatening to spill over. He pressed his mouth to his fist. He'd go up if that would help, but his presence only made it worse.

He recalled his amazement when watching Camie go to Felicity and ask to sit in her lap. What did this Quaker have that drew hurt children to her?

Drew him to her?

He shook off this thought. *Nonsense.*

Now he regretted letting Felicity know that he had seen her outside in nightdress, no doubt chasing Tucker Stout. She was quite an unusual woman, willing to be caught in dishabille in order to help a child. And she was able to draw Camie in a way no other person had in his memory. Maybe it would do Camie good to pay a visit to the little girl at Miss Gabriel's children's home. Camie screamed again, a serrated blade through his soul. Something had to be done. The situation had become unbearable—for all of them.

After putting Katy and Donnie to bed with a story and a prayer for the night, Felicity walked out to the back porch. She couldn't go to sleep with her nerves tangled and snared by unanswered questions about all she had observed and felt at the Hawkins' home. In any event, she couldn't stay within walls in the heavy summery heat. Barefoot, gloveless and hatless at last, she enjoyed the feel of the smooth hardwood under her soles and the air on her skin. She found Vista watching the sun, a molten ball of gold, lowering behind the maple trees along the alley. Vista sat fanning herself and holding a locket that hung around her neck.

Felicity hadn't noticed the locket before. She hesitated to intrude on Vista's privacy. Finally, she murmured, "May I speak with thee?"

Vista looked up, startled, and slipped the locket back out of sight. She studied Felicity and then nodded.

Felicity sat down on the wooden loveseat, leaning forward with her hands planted just behind her. She stared out at the sunset and wondered about the locket Vista felt the need to hide.

Felicity took herself fully in hand. "Of all things, I abhor gossip. But sometimes information is necessary. I would not want to say or do anything out of ignorance that might cause hurt or harm. Will thee give me some information?"

Vista made no response. Felicity waited, images of the sad little girl niggling her. Finally, Vista said, "Go ahead."

"This evening I went to thank Tyrone Hawkins—"

"You mean Judge Hawkins?"

"Yes, the judge. Friends don't use titles. We think they separate people and feed pride."

"More than titles separate people around here."

Felicity thought this over, Mrs. Thornton Crandall's anger-twisted face coming to mind. "I was disturbed by my visit at the judge's home." *More than disturbed.* She pursed her lips. "Something is very wrong there. The little girl…"

Felicity couldn't go on, couldn't divulge the distress she'd witnessed. Her throat dammed up. Cicadas and a carriage going down the street alone broke the silence of evening.

"There is trouble in that house." Vista's voice was solemn. "That stuck-up Mrs. Crandall is Camie's grandmother. Camie lost her mother and Mrs. Crandall took care of that child till the judge came home from war."

Felicity waited for more, but none came. "I thank thee." She certainly would not have to worry about Vista gossiping about matters at the children's home.

Felicity rose and went into the house. Poor Camie had fallen into the hands of Mrs. Crandall. And had Camie's mother taken after her own mother? *Poor Camie. Lord, show me if Thee wants me to help this child and show me how. Please.*

In midmorning two days later, even though her feet itched to walk off her lingering restlessness, Felicity ventured into town in the old carriage. In an act of faith, she had purchased new clothing for more orphans. Now she set out to find more children to wear those clothes. Flashes of memory—Camie's wan face, her alarming outcries, the judge's grim expression—circled in her mind like a train on a track.

With his drooping gray mustache and matching eyes, the groom let her down near the hectic wharf. "Miss Gabriel, you shouldn't be down here by yourself. I should stay with you."

This restriction of her freedom of movement chafed Felicity. Still, she smiled up at the man's lined face. "I will not be alone. I always try to tread as close as I can to the Lord. Thee need not come back. I will walk home—"

"No, you won't," the man said, huffing. "Mrs. Barney wouldn't like that at all, miss. Not at all. In an hour, I will drive back into town and wait for you by the post office over yonder."

Felicity shook her head. "Very well, Abel Yawkey. I will do as thee wishes." *For now.* "At the post office in an hour." She consulted the watch pendant that was pinned to her collar.

She turned and headed down the less than clean streets near the wharf. The Mississippi River was the major trade route, transporting goods from the center of the nation down to the Gulf and thence to the world. She threaded her way through the steady stream of people going to and from the barges, but the loud voices and sounds of river traffic did nothing to cheer her. Camie's cries for help echoed in her mind.

And the judge's pain-lined face would not leave her.

Felicity walked and walked but did not see any children like the ones she had already taken home. Wondering if she should have come in the afternoon, she halted near where she had met Katy and Donnie on her first day in town.

"You in trouble, miss?" a deep voice asked.

She turned her head and looked into an older black man's deeply lined face, lifted in a kind smile. "I am looking for needy children."

"I'm Jack Toomey, Miss Gabriel. I saw you arrive in town a few days ago."

"And thee already knows my name?" Felicity offered him her hand. She wasn't pleased to hear that gossip had spread this far. But that wasn't this man's fault.

Shaking her hand, Jack matched her grin and raised it a few notches. "Yes, miss. This town isn't as little as it was when I was a boy. But it's still small enough that information spreads pretty quick."

Felicity drew in a deep breath. "And what do the people of Altoona say of me?" From the corner of her eye, she glimpsed the policeman who had nabbed Tucker watching her talk to Jack Toomey. What was his name?

Jack rubbed his clean-shaven chin and ignored her question. His gaze was assessing. "You be a Quaker, right?"

"Yes, I am a member of the Society of Friends." Hogan, that was the man's name.

"The Quakers were friends to black people who were in bondage for a long time."

"Yes, we voted against slavery in our Pennsylvania Friend's Assembly in 1758." Hogan was watching her closely. Did he resent her actions to help Tucker?

"Did you know that Altoona was a stop on the Underground Railroad?"

"Yes, in fact, the house I inherited from Mildred Barney was one of those stops. There is a concealed room in the attic."

Jack laughed. "No doubt Sister Vista told you about that. She made use of it herself."

Felicity nodded. She filed away that bit of Vista's history and returned to her object for the day. She gazed at the foot and horse traffic.

"You be looking for more children for that orphans' home of yours?"

"Yes, I am. So far I have only three. Does thee know of any children who need a home?"

"You willing to take in black children?" he asked.

"Of course."

Jack smiled broadly. "I think there are a few children our church has been feeding and trying to find permanent homes for."

"Excellent. Would thee please bring them to Mildred Barney's house?"

"I surely will." Jack bobbed his head. "And if you go along the wharf, you might find a few more homeless children. I saw some begging this morning at the back of the bakery for stale bread."

"Thank thee, Jack Toomey. I will look forward to receiving those children." Felicity waved and walked along the quay. Men with bulging muscles wrestled large sacks and wooden crates onto and off barges. Passengers from a riverboat were filing down a walkway onto shore. Then two little boys ran from a side street and began begging there. A shabby older man followed them out of the alley and looked around in what struck Felicity as a furtive manner.

She paused and observed him until he blended into the jostling crowd. Then she focused on the two boys. Both towheaded blonds, they looked to be around eight to ten years. It was hard to estimate age accurately since lack of proper food always slowed or stunted growth not only of the body but also of the mind. After the passengers had all passed by, Felicity approached them. "Good day, children."

They both looked up, their blue eyes alert and wary, without the innocence of childhood. Then they looked around as if fearing someone. The boys' faces were grimy and their clothing tattered. The sight twisted her heart. How could people just pass them by? But then times were hard after the war. And in any season some people had little pity to spare for others.

"My name is Felicity Gabriel and I have a home for children who don't have a family. Would thee like to visit my home and see if thee would like to stay?"

They stared at her, no comprehension in their eyes, only suspicion.

She smiled. "I have three children who have decided to stay with me, a little girl and her brother and another older lad. Would thee—"

"What do we got to do for you?" the older of the two asked, casting a nervous glance over his shoulder.

Their distrust grieved Felicity but no doubt it had been learned the hard way. She looked in the direction of the boy's glance but saw nothing worrying. "Thee must only follow the house rules. I am a Quaker and this is the kind of work we do. We are honor-bound to help others."

"Would a visit include lunch?" the older one asked, scrutinizing her.

"Yes, indeed it would. If thee will come with me—" she paused to look at her pendant watch "—my carriage is waiting near the post office." She turned and walked away without looking back, letting the two decide whether to come along or not.

When she reached Abel Yawkey, he got down and helped her into the carriage. The two boys climbed in after her, still looking guarded and edgy.

Felicity was delighted but hid it. She must present a calm presence before the distrustful children. But her spirit lifted, which she desperately needed after being haunted by the tormented eyes of little Camie Hawkins—and of her father.

Felicity and the children ate on the back porch. Vista had enforced her clean-hands-and-face rule, and then served a delicious lunch of Welsh rarebit. The new boys, Butch and Willie, had eaten three helpings and helped finish off a dozen large oatmeal cookies.

Felicity had introduced the new children to Katy, Donnie and Tucker. For just a moment, she had the notion that the boys knew Tucker. But Tucker had shown no evidence of this. At first, there was only silence at the table. But after the new children had eaten their first helping, they started eyeing the others already in her care. Would these two stay for more than just lunch?

Vista came out and put down another dish of melted cheddar cheese on toast and said, "Miss Felicity, will you come into the kitchen a moment?"

"If you will excuse me, children." Felicity left her napkin beside her plate. Inside, she looked to Vista questioningly.

"I called you in to give the new chil'run a chance to talk to Katy and Tucker. They will trust what they say more than what you or me say."

Felicity beamed at Vista. "How wise thee are."

Vista shrugged. "I don't know if I'm wise, I just know how it feels…"

Felicity looked into Vista's eyes, waiting. But the lovely housekeeper left the rest of her sentence unsaid, making Felicity wonder again about the locket. She perceived its outline under Vista's demure collar but still did not ask. After a few minutes, the two women carried out more milk to the children.

"Well," Felicity said as brightly as she could, "are thee two staying or returning to the wharf?"

The boys looked to each other and then to Tucker.

Felicity was glad she was watching closely or she might have missed what came next. Tucker gave the slightest nod.

Butch and Willie turned their gazes up to her. "We'll give it a try, lady."

"You supposed to call her Miss Felicity," Katy prompted. Vista had insisted that the children follow her example.

"Miss Felicity," the two said in unison, and Tucker nodded in approval.

Felicity's awareness zoomed. It was clear that Tucker and these children knew each other. How? Just because they had all lived on the streets? Felicity decided not to let herself be caught napping. She must be as gentle as a dove but wise as a serpent.

Later, Felicity looked out the window at the two new boys who—in between digging in the dirt for fun—were weeding the side garden. Then she looked back down at her sketch of needed alterations to Mrs. Barney's house to make it into a home for many children.

Turning her mind to the issue at hand, Felicity smiled at the builder. The man said, "I'd have to see if any of the interior walls are load-bearing before I start taking them down."

"Yes, I don't want to bring the roof down on our heads." Felicity grinned, trying to lighten the exchange. The builder seemed to be brooding on something. "I also want thee to make an outside staircase on each side of the house in case of fire. I need the children to be able to get out safely."

"Outside staircases?" He looked at her sketch and grimaced. "That will give a very odd appearance to this house."

"With so many more children than in a usual family home, we must take extra precautions. And I want to add a small room off the kitchen where the children will bathe. I'd like an indoor pump and stove in that room."

He looked dubious. "This is a lot of work. And I have other jobs—"

Whether due to his hesitance to work for a woman or something else, she would have none of it. *My children can't wait just because thee doesn't want to bother getting the work done.* "I suggest that thee hire more help."

He rubbed the side of his nose. "These projects change the whole appearance of this house. I hate to take such a lovely dwelling and—"

Oh, that's what this is about. More consequences of Mrs. Crandall's gossip. "A house filled with healthy, joyful children is what I think is beautiful. Now if thee cannot take on this work immediately, I will contact another builder."

The door knocker sounded.

"I need the work." The builder added cryptically, "And I don't care what anybody says. Your money spends just like everyone else's."

Felicity flushed with annoyance over the implied criticism. A person would think she had proposed to establish a house of ill repute on Madison Boulevard. She heard muted voices in the foyer and rose.

He rose, too, rotating his hat brim in both hands. "I'll go up and take measurements."

Felicity offered him her hand, hearing Vista greeting someone at the door. "I think thee will do an excellent job."

As he started up the steps, Felicity moved toward the open door. Louise Hawkins and Camie stood at her threshold. Vista slipped away to the kitchen.

Felicity's breath caught in her throat. She hadn't

expected them so soon. Again, it struck her how slight Camie was. She spoke like a child who should be in school but looked barely five years of age. Instantly, Felicity was on her guard. This was a fragile child. *Father, make me sensitive.* "Louise Hawkins and Camie, I'm delighted to see thee."

"We thought we would take you up on your invitation and come and visit," Louise said, her nervous gaze roving here and there as if fearing this was a trap.

"Hello," Camie said, looking up at Felicity.

Felicity stooped down, frantically trying to think what to do with this brittle child. "If thee will follow me, we will go to the kitchen. Vista is there and two of our children are helping her bake cookies." Not giving them time to refuse, Felicity led the way through the hall to the kitchen.

Katy was draped with a white kitchen cloth around her neck as a full apron. Standing on the chair, she had both hands in a small bowl of cookie dough. Donnie was sitting in the chair beside her and rolling dough on the table with cheery good humor. The sight melted Felicity's heart like butter on toast. Just days ago, these had been waifs. Both children stopped and gawked at the newcomers.

"Katy and Donnie, a new friend, Camie Hawkins, has come to visit," Felicity announced with a smile, hoping that the children would be welcoming. "And Camie has brought her grandmother with her." Felicity leaned over, looking into Camie's eyes. "Would thee like to help bake cookies?"

Her thumb in her mouth, Camie turned to look up at her grandmother.

"Would you like to help, Camie?" Louise asked with a slight tremor in her voice.

Camie looked to Donnie and Katy and shook her head, gazing down and pressing against her grandmother's skirts.

Felicity tried to think of what to say. Maybe trying to put Camie with other children had been a mistake. Outside, someone was shouting. Felicity tried to identify whom.

"It's not hard," Katy piped up. "You'd prob'bly be good at it. You got hair ribbons."

Felicity did not understand this connection, but caught the hint of longing in Katy's voice. She promised herself she'd buy ribbons on her next trip to town. She had been raised without ribbons but immediately saw their allure for Katy. As she was pondering where to purchase them, Felicity thought she heard shouting outside.

"If you don't want to help, you could sit and watch," Vista invited. "I'm baking in the outside oven. It's too hot to cook inside on a scorcher like this."

Louise raised one eyebrow, no doubt over Vista's forwardness in speaking up. However, she nodded in agreement. "Camie, would you like to sit down and watch the cookie making?"

Camie pressed herself into her grandmother's skirt. "You sit," she muttered.

"I think I'll sit down and help, too," the grandmother announced. She took off her gray bonnet and black lace gloves and put them on the bench by the back door. "Show me what I can do, Vista. And Miss Gabriel, why don't you show Camie where she can sit to watch this? I hope we're going to get to sample the cookies when they are done."

Heartened by the grandmother's attempt at sounding merry, Felicity led Camie by the hand to a free chair. "Here, Camie, thee may sit here."

"You." Camie pushed Felicity toward the chair.

Though the shouting outdoors was becoming much louder, Felicity didn't hesitate; she sat down. Camie climbed up on her lap. Felicity caught the flicker of some strong emotion on Louise's face and wondered again about this little girl and her family. The demeanor of both the judge and his mother made it clear that they viewed Camie's attraction to Felicity with surprise and uncertainty. Felicity rejoiced silently for Camie's taking to her.

She asked for some dough and began rolling it into small balls, hoping Camie would venture to help. Then the front door brass knocker was hit in an angry tattoo, making them all jump.

Oh, dear, what now?

Chapter Four

The insistent and irksome sound plucked Felicity from her chair. Camie clung to her, so she swung the child into her arms. As the pounding became frantic, Felicity rushed down the hall and threw wide the door.

"You! Are you that Quaker?" demanded a fashionably dressed young woman of about thirty, not wearing either a coming-to-visit hat or gloves.

"I am a member of the Society—"

"What do you mean, letting children behave like that?" The woman's voice rose shrilly.

Felicity stared at the young woman. "What children? Behaving how?"

The pretty, dark-haired woman grabbed Felicity's elbow, dragged her down the steps and ran, pulling her around to the side of the house. There the two new boys, Butch and Willie, were throwing clods of dirt from the side garden toward a peculiarly dressed little boy on the line between the two yards.

"Look at that!" The woman's face was red. "Your little ruffians are attacking my son, Percy!"

The outfit Percy was wearing appalled Felicity. Topped by a wide-brimmed straw hat, Percy wore a white ruffled shirt with a large round collar, blue knickers, white knee stockings and shined shoes that were fastened by straps, not laces. Why would anyone dress a boy in ruffles—and *white* ruffles to boot? Felicity gawked at the poor boy.

"He started it!" Butch declared as he lobbed another mud ball at Percy. It streaked the boy's cheek and knocked his hat cockeyed.

Tucker came charging out of the carriage house, looking angry and ready to fight.

"We don't want your kind in our neighborhood!" Percy yelled. He aimed and threw a small rock, hitting Butch on the forehead.

Felicity rushed forward and interposed herself between her boys and Percy. Then Tucker placed himself between Felicity and Percy. His unexpected protectiveness caught Felicity around the heart. Abel, limping with arthritis, was also coming to her aid.

But she kept to her main concern. "Butch, is thee all right?" Camie still on her hip, Felicity bent down and took the boy's chin in her hand. She examined him, turning his face back and forth. "Thee will come in and I'll take care of that before a bump starts."

"You keep away, pretty boy," Tucker jeered. "Or you'll have a fight—"

The woman shrieked and began shouting, "We don't want your riffraff here starting trouble—"

At the word *riffraff* Felicity turned on the woman, her anger shooting out like bright lights of fireworks. "*Thee* started this trouble! Thee has poisoned thy son—thy innocent child—against defenseless orphans! No child would say, 'We don't want your kind' on his own. How dare thee put the blame for this on my boys! If thy son cannot play peaceably with others, I suggest thee take him inside." Felicity stretched out her hand. "Come, Butch, I must see to thy injury."

Garbled words issued from the woman's mouth, "Effrontery…gall…undisciplined." Then she marched to her son, grabbed his hand and headed into their house next door, Percy squawking all the way.

With Willie at her heels, Felicity took Butch's hand and hurried him to the back porch, her anger still pounding within. Tucker followed them. Looking disgruntled, Abel met them on the way in.

Vista was there with a silver knife. "This will take care of that bump before it gets bigger." She pressed the knife against the spot where an angry red bump was rising.

Felicity wondered at this home remedy which was completely new to her, but said nothing. Butch was not fighting Vista so it must not be hurting him.

"I see," Vista said, "that you met our neighbor Mrs. Eldon Partridge."

Felicity glanced at Mrs. Partridge's house and tried to extinguish the molten lava bubbling in her stomach.

"You best calm down. Pretty soon," Vista remarked, "you're going to start letting off steam like an engine."

Felicity couldn't help herself—she laughed.

Louise Hawkins stood in the doorway between the kitchen and the back porch. "Camie?" she asked in a strained voice.

Felicity had momentarily forgotten that Camie was still on her hip. She looked down into Camie's face, hoping that the scene had not frightened the child. "Is thee all right, Camie?"

"I don't like Percy." Camie smiled. "And you didn't let Percy hurt the boy." She snuggled her face into Felicity's blouse.

"Don't worry, Braids," Tucker said, tugging one of Camie's long dark braids. "We know how to fight."

This brought a smile to Felicity. "Thank thee, Tucker."

"No thanks needed. I'm the oldest, see?"

"Yeah," Willie said. "Tucker watches out for the littler kids." Butch nodded. This comment gave Felicity another hint. Filing this away for future use, Felicity looked over Camie's head to the grandmother, who was wiping her eyes yet trying to reassure Felicity with an approving smile. Felicity tucked the child closer. *Dear Father, help me help this troubled family.*

After Butch's bump had settled down to more of a red welt, Butch and Willie asked to go back outside.

"I will let thee go outside but thee must not throw mud, stones or anything else, or call anyone names, please."

"That fancy boy started it all," Willie insisted with a dark, stubborn look.

"I do not doubt that to be true," Felicity said. "However, I always try to get along with my neighbors. And I expect thee to do the same. If anyone else comes to stir up trouble, I want thee to promise to run to me or to Vista or Abel Yawkey in the carriage house. Will thee do that? Please?"

"Butch and me ain't sissies," Willie said with his lower lip stuck out. "We ain't gonna run from a fight."

Felicity didn't know quite how to deal with this. She'd grown up among sisters and the peculiarities of the male gender had always puzzled her. However, experience with her childhood friend Gus had taught her this attitude was the prevailing one with males. "Would thee call out to one of us before thee defends thyself?"

Butch and Willie considered this. "We'll try," Butch answered.

"I thank thee. Thee may go outside and finish thy weeding."

The boys didn't look delighted by this prospect, but went out. Felicity suddenly felt very tired. She sighed and instantly, silently scolded herself. *No more sighing. Especially not in front of the children.* Children, even children who were being raised by their own good families, were a handful. She would have to pray for enough energy to keep up with these new boys and Tucker.

The memory of that little signal that had passed between Butch and Willie and Tucker niggled at her. Also the way Tucker had come to their defense against

Percy. How, exactly, did the boys know each other? And how would that affect her success in helping them? And, perhaps most important of all, would other town children be poisoned by their parents' prejudices against her orphans?

That evening, Ty walked up the steps to his house. Despite the continued heat, he was in a gray wintry mood and so tired he could have fallen asleep standing up. Years of soldiering had given him the ability to plod on even when his whole body wanted only to collapse, unconscious. Yet the thought of suffering through another night hearing his daughter scream had the power to make him halt on the top step. *My little girl is suffering. I can't help her. And she hates the sight of me.*

If there were anywhere else he could go, he'd be sorely tempted to turn tail and flee.

His mother opened the door. "Come in, son."

Her tone and expression weren't easy to read. Still, he recognized something was different about her face. He studied her, not moving. "What's wrong?" *Not more bad news. Please.*

"Nothing is wrong, son. I just hope you won't be upset." Stepping out onto the porch, she knotted her hands together.

"Upset?" he repeated, apprehension chugging through his veins.

"Yes, well—" Louise took a deep breath "—I left Camie with Miss Felicity at her children's home."

Shock shot through him icy cold. "You what?"

"This morning Camie kept asking to go visit Miss Felicity, so I finally gave in by afternoon. She has never asked to visit anyone else. We walked over and were invited inside to help make cookies." His mother seemed to run out of words and just stood looking at him.

"And?" What dreadful scene had Camie enacted there?

His mother drew in more air. "After a while, Felicity said it was time for Katy and Donnie to take their naps. Somehow, Camie managed to go up the stairs with Miss Felicity as she was helping the children to lie down. When the Quaker came back, she said that Camie insisted on taking a nap with the two orphans."

Ty just stared at his mother, waiting for the worst to come.

"I didn't think you'd like it so I went up to get Camie. And…she was already asleep beside Katy." Louise looked into his eyes. "You know she never gets enough sleep. She fell asleep *without fussing* at all. At all. Not a peep." Louise smiled suddenly, wiping a tear from her eye with the heel of her hand.

Ty could not think of a single word to say to this unbelievable news. He sank onto the top step. Lack of sleep must be dulling his mind.

His mother came farther out onto the porch and sat beside him, gazing into his face. "Miss Felicity didn't seem to see anything out of order and asked me to feel free to leave Camie for her nap."

Ty tried to fit all this news into his numb mind. "Isn't it past naptime now?"

"She suggested I leave Camie to nap and then play with Katy—"

"Katy? Who is this Katy?" Ty hated how he sounded cranky, like an old man with rheumatism.

"Katy is an orphan girl who has a little brother, Donnie. Camie took a liking to her. Anyway, Ty, Miss Felicity invited us to supper tonight."

Camie had taken a liking to another child?

"Supper?" he asked.

"Yes. I accepted. We're expected—" she looked back into the house "—in fifteen minutes." She clasped her hands together even tighter and looked at him in unmistakable appeal.

He dragged himself upright. "Then we better start now or we'll be late."

Eyeing him, Louise rose, got her hat and gloves from the foyer. They covered the two blocks in silence. Ty repeatedly went over his mother's report about Camie with the Quaker and Katy. He walked up to the front door and sounded the knocker. A little boy opened the door. "Who are you?" he asked.

"Hello, Willie," Louise said, "this is my son, Judge Hawkins. Ty, this is Willie." The boy gawked at him, looking ready to run. It stung Ty. Why did children always behave as if he were about to harm them? His hand started to cover his scar but he lowered it.

Miss Gabriel walked up the hallway, smiling radiantly. "Please, let's walk around to the rear of the house.

It's so warm this evening that we will eat our meal on the back porch. We'll be finished before the mosquitoes come out in force."

"How is our Camie?" his mother asked.

"I hope she behaved," Ty added as he doffed his hat, trying not to be snared by the woman's infectious smile.

"Oh, Camie is a delight. After the nap, she played with Katy and Donnie, and helped set the table."

A delight? His daughter had taken a nap and played? Yes, but all this had taken place in the daylight. Night was different. Dreadfully different. How was he going to get her home tonight without a scene? As soon as it started getting dark, Camie sank into her fear. At the thought of trying to carry home a screaming Camie, Ty's stomach roiled with nausea.

As they walked past the side bow window, Felicity glanced at him. "Did thee think thee should be concerned about Camie? She's quite safe with us."

Neither he nor his mother replied. He racked his brain for a reasonable reply. Finally, he came up with the completely inadequate, "Camie is shy."

"Really?" The Quaker paused and gave him a quizzical look. "In that case, I'm happy that she took to Katy. They have been chattering and playing with Camie's doll as happy as can be."

As happy as can be? They had reached the back porch. She led them up the steps to the long white-clothed table there. The handsome housekeeper rang a bell. The sound of footsteps heralded the haste of children all through the house.

The boy who had opened the door for them veered around Ty and went to the chair that Felicity was indicating. Then came a little girl leading both a toddler and his Camie by the hand. This must be Katy. She led them to their seats, eyeing him all the while.

His daughter glanced up once and then lowered her gaze. Of course, not even here would she look at him. Her continued rejection of him carved another notch in his mangled heart.

Finally, Tucker, the lad he'd sentenced to serve probation here, climbed the steps, also staring and giving him a wide berth. Ty kept a tight lid on his reactions to this assembly and its varied reactions to him. He was definitely getting tired of being viewed by children as a leper, a dangerous one to boot, especially by his own blood.

Soon they were all seated and Miss Gabriel had said grace. The housekeeper passed around broiled beefsteaks, tomato-and-lettuce salad and light biscuits. Ty began to eat, watching the children tuck into their food.

"Katy," the Quaker said, after introducing Vista to him, "will thee tuck Donnie's napkin into his shirt neck?"

Katy did as she was asked. Then she pointed to Ty. "What happened to your face?"

Ty kept his irritation to himself. The child meant no harm.

Felicity frowned. "Katy, thee should not make comments about a person's appearance. It causes the person to feel uncomfortable. Camie's father was in the war. Isn't that where thee got the mark on thy cheek, Tyrone?"

"Yes. I know it's not pretty but there's not much I can do about it." He watched Camie for any reaction. But as usual, she would not look his way. He fought the urge to cover the scar with his hand.

"It will not be so noticeable with time," the Quaker said. "Time heals all wounds."

Ty wished that were so. He began eating, trying to appear unconcerned while his stomach knotted and re-knotted itself. In contrast, the children all were eating quickly and heartily.

"Children, remember what I told thee," Felicity said in a gentle tone. "Thee don't have to rush thy eating. Chew thy food and thy stomach will thank thee. And thee may have seconds, even thirds of everything. But please chew the first helping. Will thee?"

All the heads bobbed. Ty noted that even Tucker slowed up. Ty looked at Felicity and she smiled at him, momentarily transfixing him once more. He turned his gaze to his plate, hoping her marked effect on him had passed unnoticed.

"Did thee have a productive day, Tyrone Hawkins?" Felicity asked.

He didn't look at her. "I suppose so. Just the usual." He chewed the food, trying to enjoy it. Yet he was sick with dread over the scene his daughter would most certainly create when they tried to go home to put her to bed.

"We were so happy that Camie came to visit us, weren't we, children?" Miss Felicity asked.

Katy nodded so hard her braids jumped. "I like Camie. Does she belong to you, mister?"

"Yes, she is my daughter." He glanced at the thin girl.

"She's nice. And she talks polite and pretty. She let me play with her dolly."

"I'm glad that she met with your approval," Ty said.

Felicity beamed at him. "Louise, I hope thee will visit us again soon with Camie. I am hoping that my children will make friends with the other children in town."

Ty thought this was probably unlikely to happen. As it was, he was sure that he and his mother would hear a lot of negative comments about letting his daughter associate with "riffraff."

Tucker snorted, giving a similar opinion to Ty's.

The image of Felicity, barefoot in nightdress, walking beside Tucker in the moonlight flashed through Ty's mind. He hadn't decided yet whether or not the fact that this woman was prepared to go to any length to help Tucker—even public embarrassment—was good or not. An idealist with this kind of fervor wouldn't let well enough alone. That much he did realize. He tried to take a deep breath; his chest was tight with apprehension.

"What church does thee attend, Louise?" Felicity asked.

"We've always attended the Altoona Bible Church on Church Street," Louise replied, slicing another bit of beef.

"I asked Vista and she said there is no Friends Meetinghouse here. So I think we'll all visit thy church this Sunday."

"Church?" Tucker's head snapped up. "I ain't goin' to no church."

Tense, Ty barked, "You'll do as you are—"

"Tucker," Felicity interrupted, "while thee is with me, thee will go to church on Sunday and also school when it begins again. Thee children will receive food, clothing, shelter and love from me, Vista and Abel, but thee must do what we say. That is how a family works. The guardians or parents provide what the children need. The guardians in turn are obeyed because they are older and know what is best for the children. That is how I was raised. Wasn't thee, Tyrone?"

"Yes, I was." He wondered at the way she took time to explain this to a child who probably had never been provided for by his family.

"You mean you're going to be like our ma?" Katy asked.

"Yes, unless some other good family would like to adopt thee as their daughter—"

"I ain't leavin' Donnie," Katy said, standing up, nearly upsetting her chair.

Felicity held out a hand. "Katy, I would never separate thee and thy little brother. Never. I give thee my solemn promise. Come here and I will give it to thee."

Ty watched, uncertain of what Felicity was up to.

Katy came around the table and stood face to face with the sitting Felicity.

"Now, when a person makes a promise she will never break, this is the way it's done. First, spit into thy hand like this." She demonstrated. "And then press it to mine." The little girl followed the Quaker's example. The two pressed palms.

Ty recalled doing this type of childish ritual with his boyhood friends. It wasn't something he thought girls did. Again it revealed how different this woman was from the usual, different from Virginia. He shoved the thought away.

"Now I have given thee my promise. I will never separate thee and Donnie—"

"Except when he gets too big to sleep with the girls. Then he's got to sleep with the boys," Vista said as she brought in another platter of beef.

Katy looked uncertain about this. But then Donnie spoke for the first time. "I a boy." He pointed to himself and began chewing again.

"Yes," Felicity said, clapping her hands together, "thee is a boy and a boy who can speak."

Camie smiled at Donnie and then looked to Tucker. "And Tucker is the biggest and he doesn't let anyone hurt us."

"That's right, Braids. You don't need to be afraid here."

Ty felt tears smart in his eyes. He couldn't ever recall seeing Camie smile. The thought sliced his heart in two. And how had she decided to trust a boy he'd almost sent to prison? The dinner went on. The children tucked away a considerable amount of food. The little girl and his daughter were the only children who spoke, usually answering some question from Felicity. The boys just ate, each keeping a distrustful eye on him. What did they expect that he would do? Grab one of them and drag him off to jail? In any event, his traitorous eyes would not obey him; they continually drifted to Felicity's reddish-blond hair and expressive face.

After dinner, the adults sat on the back porch, fanning themselves and watching the children trying to catch fireflies. Ty found himself captivated by Felicity's lively mind. They discussed the recent amendments to the Constitution, the state of the still-rebellious South and the latest news. Was there any topic she couldn't converse about intelligently? Diverted, he couldn't recall ever having such a conversation with Virginia, or any other woman.

Finally the mosquitoes drove them inside. Fine but heavy cloth with weighted hems hung over every open window. The pleasant interlude must come to an end. Ty nodded toward his mother, signaling that it was time for them to leave. His whole body stiffened. How would Camie react?

Louise turned to Felicity. "Thank you for entertaining Camie today. And for a lovely supper." Then she turned to Camie. "Come now. It's time we got you home to bed."

His daughter's face shouted her panic. She turned, raced down the hall and pounded up the stairs. He ran after her, his heart thumping. "Camie! Camie!"

Felicity came up right behind him. His heart thudding, he paused at the top of the stairs, not knowing where his daughter had run. His worst fear had come true. There would be a scene here tonight.

"Let's try Katy's room." Felicity passed him.

He followed her to a closed door. She tapped on it. "Camie, dear, it's Felicity. May I come in please?"

No answer.

Ty held on to his frustration, unwilling to let this stranger know how bad things might become.

"Camie, dear, thee can come and visit Katy tomorrow. Tyrone, thee will let Camie come visit tomorrow, won't thee?"

"Yes," he snapped, "of course, Camie can come if you invite her." In the war, he had seen men so distraught that they had torn out their hair. He felt himself nearing this disaster point.

"Camie, dear, I'm opening the door now. Thee will always be welcome here. And thee knows that I like children and I protect them. Thee saw that today." Felicity entered slowly, peering around the door. "Camie," she called in a soft sweet voice. "Camie."

Ty waited in the hall, powerless to act and burning with embarrassment and frustration.

Felicity kept calling his daughter. Finally, she came out to him. "She's not in this room. I think perhaps it might be best if thee went down and kept thy mother company and let me look for Camie."

He couldn't stop himself from making a sound of irritation.

She touched his sleeve. "Camie is a good little girl, but remember, she was born into a war just like most of these other children. It affects us and them in unusual ways."

His heart throbbed with the agony only a father of a child with "problems" could know. What could he say to this woman who was offering him understanding? Nothing. He nodded brusquely and went back downstairs, his chin nearly touching his chest.

Many minutes later, Felicity walked quietly down the steps. Camie was hidden within the folds of her gray skirt. Ty met them at the bottom of the stairs near the front door. His mother waited behind him, uneasy.

"I told Camie I would ask thee if thee would let her spend the night with Katy." Felicity looked him in the eye, appealing to him to allow this.

He couldn't. He couldn't subject this household—this kind woman—to the ordeal of getting Camie to sleep. "I'm sorry, but Camie must come with me. It's time to go home."

Camie clung to Felicity. Ty was forced to pry her fingers from Felicity's skirt. He swung her up into his arms. Camie began fighting him and screaming, "No! No!"

He tried to thank his hostess but was forced to carry his hysterical child outside. He ran the two blocks home. His child's screaming ripped him apart. Humiliated, he glimpsed people peering out their windows at the disturbance.

When he reached home, his taut nerves ruptured, flying apart. He climbed the stairs two at a time, set Camie in her room and slammed the door. He slid down to the floor and put his head in his hands.

Memories from the war flooded his mind—brutal bloodshed, staggering grief, crushing fear. Images too ghastly for a human to believe flickered in his mind. Bodies mutilated, faces unrecognizable. He tried to force the memories out. But cannons exploded in his ears. Black smoke billowed from rifles. Men fell around him.

Joining the mayhem of their outcries, Camie's hysterical screams stabbed him over and over. She began kicking the door, pummeling his body. His mother hovered at the top of the stairs. He wanted to say something to her, reassure her, but he couldn't. Would the horror never end? Would he never have peace?

I can't take any more. I can't. Oh, God, please, help.

He didn't know how long he'd stayed there like that, sitting on the floor, drenched in despair, unable to speak or move. Finally, his mother came to him and handed him a cup. "It's a chamomile tea with a few drops of laudanum. Drink it. Don't argue."

He looked up at her and realized that the house was quiet and very dark. His daughter must have finally given in to exhaustion. How could he have become senseless to Camie's screaming? Fearing for his state of mind, he sipped the bitter tea which would bring sleep. Finally, he managed to rise. He again longed to reassure his mother but he was empty, as empty as the cup he handed his mother.

"Go to sleep now, son. We will talk in the morning. We will pray tonight and tomorrow come up with some way to help our little Camie."

Without hope, he nodded and trudged the few steps to his door. Inside, he sat on the edge of his bed. Then without undressing, he collapsed and slept.

Moonlight glowed faint at the window. Ty realized that he was on his bed and still in his clothes. Then it all came rushing back—his daughter's hysteria at leaving Felicity's home. But he couldn't have left Camie there and put the kind woman through Camie's night terrors. He sat up. His guilt prodded him to go and reassure himself that his child was sleeping peacefully at last.

He crept out of his room and opened the door stealthily, fraction by fraction. He tiptoed into the room and looked down, expecting her to be crumpled on the floor right inside the door. She wasn't. She wasn't in her bed, under her bed, in her dressing room.

Thin and flat with fatigue, he felt his heart begin to pound. The sensation nearly nauseated him. He had experienced this reaction before when pushed past endurance.

He forced himself to go over the room once more. Then he searched the entire house, all the way to the basement. Finally he hurried outside to the yard. He didn't find her.

Camie had run away.

Pressing the heel of his hand to his pounding right temple, he considered what he should do. The only place he could think that she had gone was to the Barney house. She had wanted to stay there and must have gone back. If she wasn't there…

He walked down the moonlit street, trying to keep his footsteps as quiet as possible. When unable to sleep, he had taken to walking at night and had mastered how to move without disturbing anyone in the quiet dark houses with their windows open to let in any faint breeze.

He reached the Barney house and stood on the porch. Now that he was here, he didn't quite know how to proceed. Waking a maiden lady in the middle of the night was not appropriate. Then he recalled Felicity pursuing Tucker Stout in her wrapper, barefoot. She wasn't like other ladies. He knocked softly and waited. He was about to knock again when the door opened.

There she stood in her wrapper and slippers. The very light blue cotton caught the low light, gleaming.

And he sensed the same beckoning quality as always from her. Somehow she drew him as a fire on a cold night.

"Tyrone, I've been dozing by the door, waiting for you." She let him in and motioned toward a rocking chair that had been stationed at the base of the staircase, barely visible. Her voice was low and so gentle.

"Is Camie here?" The words cost him. His eyes burned. His head ached. His body cried out for undisturbed sleep. He wanted to lay his head on this woman's shoulder and find ease and peace, just as his daughter had.

"Yes, I didn't hear her come in, but I always get up at least once a night to check on the children. I found her at the foot of the bed with Katy and Donnie. She must have crawled in through one of the open windows in the parlor." She paused. He thought she must be looking at him, but the foyer was so dark he doubted she could actually see his face. The two of them were only shadows here.

His knees weakened with sudden relief. He stumbled over to the stairs and sat down, needing to put space between them. Weakened as he was, the urge to reach for her was nearly overwhelming.

"Has thee come to take her home?"

Something in her voice alerted him. "You don't think I should?"

"No, I don't. Please let us talk."

He heard her sit and the rocker begin to creak. "I'm

just so tired," he said at last with his elbows on his knees, his hands hanging down limp.

"I said earlier that the war has left its mark on these little children. We do not know what they have suffered through, even if it was only to be separated from a parent. And thy wife died while thee were away, I would guess."

"Yes." The word was so low it scoured his throat.

"For some reason thee or I do not understand, Camie feels safe here. I do not think for a moment that she has anything to fear in thy home. I cannot believe that thee would hurt thy daughter in any way."

It was odd to sit here in almost total darkness speaking to a woman he barely knew about something he had not discussed with anyone but his mother. But her gentle words soothed the knot that was his heart.

"Perhaps if thy daughter is allowed to stay here, she will be able to get past her fears. Of course, if thee wants thy child home with thee, I would do nothing to prevent thee from carrying her home this night."

The darkness shielded him, freed him to speak plain truth. "I'm too tired to think."

"Why doesn't thee ask thy mother to come over during the day tomorrow and visit Camie? Let us see how Camie feels after being allowed to stay here for the night."

He knew he should go get Camie and carry her home. What would people say when they heard that he had left his only child at an orphans' home?

He didn't care.

He recalled how happy Camie had been at dinner. "I should have left her here instead of carrying her home. She…she hates the night."

"Ah." Felicity sounded as if this explained much to her.

"My mother and I try to be kind and loving and patient with her, but she fights sleep every night…and screams if she feels herself falling asleep." He passed a hand over his forehead, trying to rub away the strain.

"I see."

"We've tried letting her cry herself to sleep. That doesn't work so my mother rocks her to sleep every night and Camie screams…" Tears were barreling up through him, ready to spout past his self-control. He clamped his mouth shut, damming up his words and tears.

A hand came through the darkness and rested on his arm. "Thee has been carrying a heavy burden, friend."

Her touch comforted him. But what if Camie never wanted him? He folded a hand over his mouth to hold back words that had collected in his throat. All those years so far away, he'd imagined his little girl on his lap. He'd planned to read her fairy tales by the fire and in summer, push her in a swing in the backyard. Those thoughts of home and a little girl had sustained him through the unimaginable chaos and slaughter.

"I will pray that the God who loves us will show us the way to help thy little one. She is so dear. Such a lovely, sweet child. A blessing to thee surely. I always have taken God at His word. He says to trust

Him and do good. We cannot heal Camie, but God and our love can."

Her kind, uncondemning words spoken in the dark soothed him like no others. He rose, his exhausted body aching, but with hope and peace flickering like a candle flame inside him. "I will go home now. My mother will come tomorrow. Thank you for your understanding."

"My understanding is limited, friend. But our God is not. Do not despair. Jesus said, 'Suffer the little children to come unto me and forbid them not, for of such is the kingdom of heaven.' We must trust God and do good. He will not fail us."

He forced himself to walk away from her comforting presence. He had often heard the scriptures she quoted, but for the first time they meant something real. Felt true. Somehow this young woman, this Miss Felicity Gabriel, was different than any other woman he'd met. Her smile dazzled him. Love flowed from her. Why should it surprise him that Camie had been drawn to her? She had drawn him, too.

What would tomorrow bring for them all? Would his sweet little girl ever run to him, asking him to swing her up into his arms?

Or would she remain lost to him—alienated— forever?

Chapter Five

Felicity and the children were still at breakfast at the long table on the back porch when Louise Hawkins ventured up the sidewalk.

"No!" Camie cried out and jumped from her chair. "I won't go home!" Camie tried to flee inside but was intercepted by Vista at the kitchen door.

Felicity leapt up and hurried to Camie, who was struggling with Vista. She lifted the girl in her arms. "Camie, thee is not being polite. Thy grandmother has just dropped by for a cup of coffee and to bid thee good morning." Felicity turned to Louise, who had paused on the first step. "Isn't that so, Louise Hawkins?"

"Yes, why, yes. I just stopped to chat with you and see how Camie is enjoying her visit with Katy."

Felicity nodded at the grandmother, who wore a bright smile that contrasted with her tired, worried eyes.

Louise came to the table and pulled out an empty

chair. "Vista, I recall what excellent coffee you always make."

"I'll get you a cup right quick, ma'am." Vista nodded and turned back to the kitchen.

Camie still didn't let go of Felicity. This told Felicity that some adult had treated her unfairly or capriciously in the past. Children who were lied to or cheated found it hard to trust. What kind of person had Camie's mother been? Felicity sat back down with Camie on her lap. Felicity hoped that Alice Crandall's daughter had been nothing like her.

And then she glimpsed something next door that ignited worry in her stomach. The pretty, dark-haired woman was standing in her backyard. Why was her neighbor staring at them?

"You act like a baby," Butch said to Camie with obvious disgust.

"Leave the little kid alone," Tucker said.

Felicity frowned at Butch, but Tucker's protection of Camie raised her spirits. Yet Camie was acting like a baby. What had happened when she was actually a baby? What had given her night terrors? Could Felicity hit upon a polite way of finding the answer to this question from Camie's grandmother?

"Camie's just a little girl," Tucker said. "Braids, don't worry. You're safe here. You heard Miss Felicity stand up for Butch yesterday." Felicity let this pass. Tucker's protective impulse intrigued her. What did it stem from? She thought of the boys she'd grown up with. Who had acted like Tucker and why? A possible answer glimmered in her mind. But she would wait for the right time to test her theory.

Vista delivered a cup of coffee to Louise. The somber lady smiled her thanks and sat quietly sipping.

Felicity tried to give no outward reaction to her neighbor, who was now pacing outside her back door and glaring at Felicity.

"What do I got to do today?" Tucker asked in a sour tone.

"I think that Abel wants thee in the barn and carriage house again today, Tucker. Thee appears to have a gift of working with horses."

Tucker shrugged.

"We don't got to weed some more today, do we?" Willie asked in the same tone as Tucker.

"I'm afraid so. Vista wants thee to pull the weeds and grass in between the cobblestones in the path around the house." She added brightly, "But soon all of thee won't have as many chores to do. School began weeks ago. In a few days, thee will all be attending school, and only doing chores when thee comes home. After supper, thee will do thy homework and then go to bed."

Willie and Butch and Tucker all exchanged glances loaded with disbelief, resentment and rebellion. Felicity found herself sighing again. She had always loved school, but then she had never lived on the streets. She patted Camie and pulled the little girl's plate and fork to her, nudging Camie to start eating scrambled eggs again.

"Do I get to go to school, too?" Katy asked, looking pleased rather than irritated.

"How old is thee?" Felicity asked, watching the woman next door prop her hands on her hips and behave as if she were about to storm over. *Oh, dear.*

"I'm seven years old, Miss Felicity. Donnie's four."

A seven-year-old forced to care and provide for a four-year-old. For a moment, Felicity could not speak. Even though she had known this already, hearing their tender ages struck her deeply. Her heart hurt. She pressed a hand over it.

"Katy, I believe that you will be able to attend school then." Louise was carrying on the conversation for Felicity. "But Donnie will have to stay home and help Vista and Abel."

Katy fired up. "But—"

"Don't sass," Tucker barked. "No kid four years old can go to school. Any sap knows that." Then Tucker halted, looking shocked at his own outburst.

"I here," Donnie announced. "Here." And he pointed to the floor. "Katy school." He pointed at his big sister.

Felicity smiled. Donnie had already adapted to having a home. No doubt the younger the child, the easier that would be accomplished. She looked at Tucker. Had he ever gone to school? Should she keep him home and tutor him? She didn't know the answer to that. But she knew enough not to ask here and now.

She looked next door again, and was relieved to see her neighbor storm into her house and slam her back door. What was the fuss all about? Felicity's stomach jiggled with unsettled nerves.

"I've never been to school but I could go with you, Katy," Camie said from her place on Felicity's lap. "I'm seven, too."

"You could?" Katy's troubled face cleared. "That would be nice. We could go together."

Camie nodded vigorously and grinned at Katy.

Felicity called down the blessings from heaven on Katy, this sweet little girl who was somehow reaching Camie's troubled heart. Felicity sipped her hot coffee, hiding her joy though her mouth quivered with the desire to grin. *Thank thee, Father of the fatherless.*

But why hadn't Camie been sent to school this year and last year?

Soon the children finished eating. Hands, as usual, in his pockets, Tucker headed toward the carriage house. Willie and Butch grumbled their way to the sidewalk to pull weeds. Katy and Camie helped Vista gather the dishes and then followed like chicks behind a mother hen into the kitchen to help dry them.

Felicity told Donnie that he could get his box of blocks and play. Abel had bought them from a cabinet maker in town who made children's blocks from odd remnants of wood. Donnie beamed at her and hurried to his box at the other end of the porch.

Her family had encouraged her as well as her sisters to let the Light lead them to their life's work. And for a woman who had never meant to marry and have children, Felicity felt she wasn't doing too badly at starting to understand how to keep children busy.

She turned to Louise. "Camie spent the night and we had no trouble with her except once."

The grandmother pressed her lips together. "Did she cry out?"

"Just once. I went and talked to her a few minutes. Then she settled back down and fell asleep again."

"She fell asleep again?" Louise echoed softly as if not quite believing this. "What a miracle. Miss Gabriel, you don't know how this has worried my son and me. Made our lives miserable. I can't even keep any live-in help. No one can bear the nightly—" the woman shuddered "—ruckus. I just have a woman who comes in to clean every day."

That explained why Louise had opened the door when Felicity visited. "I don't want to pry but why hasn't Camie been to school?"

Louise shook her head. "My son stayed in the army for almost a year after the war. There was so much that still needed to be done. I wasn't able to take charge of Camie till he came home. Mrs. Crandall insisted Camie stay in her care."

"Mrs. Crandall didn't send her to school?"

Louise looked pained. "She said that Camie would be tutored at home when the time was right. And that education for a girl wasn't that important."

Felicity reached a hand toward Louise's but before she could say another word of comfort, an angry voice assailed her from behind. She turned and swallowed a barely suppressed groan.

"What is my granddaughter doing in this…" Mrs. Crandall seemed to be unable to say the words.

"Children's home," Felicity offered.

She ignored this. "Louise Hawkins, what do you mean to be sitting here with this, this…interloper? Who wants to spoil our lovely boulevard with baseborn children no one wants—"

Baseborn children? Felicity reared up. "No one is going to slander innocent children, poor orphans with no one to protect—"

Mrs. Crandall turned her back on Felicity. "Louise—"

Louise rose, stiff with obvious disapproval. "Alice, I will not let you barge in here and tell me what to do with Camie. You've done enough harm to that poor child."

Felicity was worried that Camie might hear this exchange. She was just about to go to Camie and take her farther into the house when Vista slammed both kitchen windows shut.

Felicity turned back to the two women who were now quarreling in loud voices, nearly shouting.

Alice Crandall accused, "Your son never treated my Virginia right—"

"Your daughter was a conniving, spoiled little girl!" Louise snapped back. "There was a war on! How was my son supposed to stay here and cater to her every wish?"

"He didn't need to enlist when my daughter was expecting their first child! He could have waited—"

"Waited to be drafted?" Louise actually shook her fist. "My son would never do such a cowardly thing! His country needed every able-bodied man and he volunteered!"

"He was needed here." Alice leaned forward, red-faced. "My poor, sweet Virginia needed him! My daughter died and your son lives! And he made the last years of Virginia's young life a misery!"

Felicity couldn't believe the harsh words that were being used like swords between these two well-dressed, genteel ladies.

"I will not speak ill of the dead," Louise said, standing with hands fisted. "But why did your daughter think that a whole nation of wives could do without their husbands as long as *she* had hers at home under her dainty thumb?"

Alice Crandall looked as if she had swallowed the wrong way. She turned an alarming bright scarlet.

Felicity was just about to call Vista for help when a familiar voice spoke up. "Miss Gabriel, sorry to bust in on things here, but I got those children we talked about the other day."

Felicity looked past the two women and there was Jack who shined shoes down near the wharf. She popped up from her seat, grateful for his arrival. "Jack! Welcome to the Barney Home for Children! Who has thee brought for me?"

Four children, two girls and two boys, ranging in

age from around three to eight, clustered around Jack. Felicity grinned. None of these children would fail Vista's test for cleanliness. They were all scrubbed and dressed in faded but ironed and starched clothing. Their eyes were big and they stared at the two older women who had been shouting. A young woman probably around fourteen stood just behind Jack, glancing at the women and then away.

"Our church wouldn't be bringing them to you but times are hard. We're barely able to feed our children," Jack apologized, his hat in his hand.

"I am delighted that thee has brought them." Felicity went down the steps and stooped down to be at eye level with the newcomers. "Children, I'm so happy that thee have come. We have been waiting for thee to arrive. Now tell me thy names." She looked at the eldest child.

Jack nudged the child's shoulder. "Speak right up. This lady likes children."

"I am Eugene, ma'am."

"Welcome, Eugene." Felicity shook his small hand.

Each of the other children said their names bashfully: Dee Dee, Violet and Johnny.

"Do you," Alice Crandall demanded in a fire-and-brimstone pulpit voice, "plan to mix black and white children?"

Felicity should have been able to predict how this woman would react. "Orphans come in all colors, Alice Crandall."

The woman responded with a loud huffing sound.

"I will not tolerate this. I am going directly to my lawyer. I will not allow my only grandchild to be dropped off at an orphanage. If her father no longer wants her—"

This was the final pebble that released the avalanche. Outrage shot through Felicity like flames. From the little she'd seen of this woman, she imagined that Alice Crandall was responsible for much of Camie's fear.

"Thee is wrong," Felicity declared, facing the woman, "Tyrone Hawkins is just allowing Camie to visit the other children here. I don't know why that should upset thee."

Sniffing loudly, Alice Crandall marched down the steps and off toward the street.

As Felicity turned back to Jack, she realized that once again, her neighbor next door was peering out. Felicity guessed that her neighbor was responsible for this horrible scene. She must have been the one who had gone to Alice to tell her that she'd seen Camie at breakfast here. Felicity sighed and then scolded herself for it.

"Miss Gabriel, I thought that I would bring my granddaughter Midge along," Jack said, gesturing toward the young woman with the children. "She has been seeking work and is very good with children."

"Wonderful! Can she start now?"

Jack looked to Midge, who stepped forward and replied, "Yes, ma'am. Thank you, ma'am." The very pretty girl beamed and curtsied.

Felicity smiled in return. "Thee may call me—"

"You will call her Miss Felicity," Vista interrupted from the kitchen doorway, "even if she is a Quaker and doesn't want us to use *miss*."

Felicity shook her head. "And thee will call Vista miss, also. And the children and I will call thee Miss Midge. If one of us must be miss, then all of us will be miss."

Grinning, Midge bobbed another curtsey. Vista chuckled, shaking her head.

"Also, Jack, though the children will all have chores, we will need a day maid and two laundresses. Will thee send women thee recommend to do the work?"

Agreeing to this, Jack told the children to be good, shook Felicity's hand, and left to go to work.

Felicity sent the youngest boy to play with Donnie. She let Vista take Midge into the kitchen with the other children to get them set with chores for the day.

When it was just the two of them again, Felicity turned to Louise. "Thee may stay as long as thee wishes today. I hope that Tyrone will come this evening and we can discuss Camie and what is best for her."

Louise nodded and sighed long.

Felicity resisted the urge to join her. Alice Crandall was a problem, all right. And Felicity's spying neighbor, too. Felicity had expected some difficulty starting an orphan home. Evil always tried to stop good work. But could this unfriendly situation be changed for the better?

* * *

The shadows of twilight were about to be swallowed by night when Ty walked up to the Barney house. A visit at the end of the day from his mother-in-law's lawyer necessitated he discuss his daughter with Felicity. Alice Crandall was the most troublesome woman he had ever known. Why hadn't he seen that before he'd married Virginia? *She hid her true face because she wanted me to marry her daughter.* This thought was a boulder on his heart and lungs.

Then he thought of Felicity. To be honest with himself, Ty was drawn here just as his daughter had been. In a harsh world, Miss Gabriel seemed to beckon all the brokenhearted to her peaceful oasis. But would he disturb his daughter by coming here? He didn't want to upset the small progress they'd made.

Passing by the side bow window, he found that he'd guessed right about where Miss Gabriel would be. She and her housekeeper were sitting on the back porch, fanning themselves. Ty resisted the urge to tug at his stiff white collar. When would the cooling west winds of autumn finally arrive?

"Tyrone Hawkins," Felicity said, welcoming him with one of her irresistible smiles, "I was hoping thee would stop by this evening. Would thee like to go up and look in on Camie?"

"Is she…is she asleep?" He almost didn't want to ask. In fact, despite what his mother had reported to him over supper, he had been surprised to walk up Madison Boulevard and not hear Camie's screams.

"Of course. The children had a busy day. They weeded, dried dishes, played tag, jumped rope." Felicity smiled. "They nearly fell asleep in their baths."

"Baths?"

"Yes, we set up the large tub here on the porch and pull down the canvas shades. The girls go in first because for some reason," Felicity wrinkled her nose and gave him one of her teasing smiles, "they don't seem to get as dirty as the boys do. I find that freshly bathed children settle down more easily to sleep in warm weather."

"And it keeps the sheets cleaner longer," Vista commented.

Felicity chuckled.

The sound loosed something inside him. The back of his neck relaxed a degree and it didn't hurt to draw breath. How could this woman affect him the way she did? Her smiles and laughter released his somber mood like uncapping a bottle of warm sarsaparilla. A smile tugged at one corner of his mouth.

Felicity rose. "Let's take a walk." She came to him. He automatically offered her his arm. She refused it with a smile, but nodded toward the alley.

A wise choice. The two of them could speak more privately walking down the tree-lined alley. He thought of what nasty gossip would spread if she had accepted his gallantry and he'd been seen walking with this woman on his arm. Again, he found he didn't care very much.

He tried to tame his rampant thoughts about Camie,

about this woman's marked effect on her—on him—to begin a coherent discussion. He gave up and said what he really didn't want to say. "You really didn't have any trouble getting Camie to sleep?"

She glanced up at him. "No, she followed Katy right to bed. I spoke with thy mother this morning. She was quite candid about Camie's night terrors. I have seen other children like Camie at an orphanage in Pennsylvania. I often helped the matrons get the orphans to bed at night. Some of them fought sleep or had nightmares that woke them up and frightened them."

Other children? "What did you do for these children?" He found himself walking closer and closer to her. Was it true? Was his Camie not alone in these disturbing fears?

"The head matron had worked with children for years. She said that calm, consistent care helped the most. And when the children wished, letting them talk about their nightmares and fear. And being sympathetic and reassuring."

"That worked?" he asked, gazing at her slender, graceful neck.

"It did for the children that I was caring for."

Her calm tone and reassurance nearly unmanned him to tears. He swallowed a sob threatening to break forth. For months and months, he and his mother had tried to help Camie get past her fear of sleep. Now for the first time, he had hope that Camie would come through this and in time be just a normal little girl. Was that possible?

Felicity paused and glanced up at him. "May I ask thee a few questions? Personal questions?"

He tensed. *No, I don't want to answer any questions.* He had hit bottom last night and they knew it. Still, answering her questions was the least he could do for the woman who had given him so much. "Yes," he said, mustering his nerve.

"When her mother died, how old was Camie?" The deep concern for his daughter radiated with each word. This woman's essence, her spirit, seemed always to be reaching out, offering help where needed.

"Around five years old." Thoughts of Virginia made him see the difference between the two women. Felicity had the honesty and compassion that Virginia lacked.

"Do you think that Camie was a witness to her death?" Felicity asked.

Their footsteps crunched on the cinder-paved alley. Ty wanted to hide from shame. He was the father. He should have protected his child. He made himself reply. "Yes, her grandmother insisted she be at her mother's bedside."

Felicity nodded. "I'm sure that thy mother told thee about Alice Crandall's visit—"

"My mother-in-law's lawyer visited me today." This admission ignited the acid in his stomach.

Felicity halted and gazed up at him. "What did her lawyer say?" Her pale skin glowed in the dim light.

"If I leave her in your care, Mrs. Crandall will try to gain custody of my daughter." His voice shook, exposing his turbulent outrage.

Worry moved over Felicity's pretty face and then disappeared. "I doubt that her suit will succeed."

"Why?" The sky had turned nearly charcoal. Daylight was slipping away but he could still see her radiance—it drew him, soothed him, stirred him.

"It is very hard, isn't it, to sever a parent's right to a child? No doubt thy mother-in-law merely wants to make as much trouble for thee and me as she is able."

"Experience has taught me that is her usual goal," he muttered, old insults stirring inside. "In everything." Yet overshadowing his anger, he sensed a fine thread of trust forming between Felicity and him.

"It is sad but true. Some people delight in causing strife and stirring up contention. Since our first meeting, I have been praying for Alice. But I sense that the walls around her heart are thick and towering." Felicity shook her head in obvious sadness. An invisible warmth flowed from her to him.

How did this woman care so much? This world was so filled with grief, pain and cruelty. He sucked in air, keeping his unruly emotions under strict control.

She looked up at him. "Do you mean to leave Camie with me until she is better, recovered from these night terrors?"

In the near darkness, he gazed down into her glistening blue eyes. Inside, he heard a preview of all the squawking and criticism he would get for doing what she proposed.

"People will think it odd that thee have given thy daughter into my care," Felicity spelled out for him as if he might not know what she was really saying.

"I know they will." Unable to stop himself, he took her hand. "But I must do what is best for Camie." *I must make up for the harm I may have done her.* He longed to tell this woman all about it, about his disastrous marriage to Virginia, the war and how badly he'd handled coming home to Camie.

Felicity squeezed his hand. "I hope that I can help her and thee has my promise that I will do whatever lies within my power to put these night terrors behind her and return home to thee."

Help had come at last. Ty drew her hand to his lips and kissed it. As soon as he did this, shock went through him in waves.

Felicity looked startled and gently pulled her hand from his. She turned and began walking again.

He could have kicked himself around the block a few times. Many eligible widows in town had already cast lures toward him. He had deftly kept himself from giving any woman any reason to hope that he would marry again. After his marriage, he wasn't interested in starting a romantic relationship with anyone. And certainly this fine woman was only interested in his daughter and her orphans. What had come over him? "I beg your pardon."

"I have been wondering," she said. "Does thee play baseball?"

The question took him so by surprise that it forced a chuckle from him. "What?"

She paused and looked up at him, so earnest in the pale last glimmer of day. "I know that soldiers played baseball during their days of waiting between marches and battles. I think it is an excellent game. Would thee believe that I have swung a bat a few times?"

He chuckled again, the sensation releasing his pent-up tension. What an unusual woman. "About you, Miss Gabriel, I would believe anything."

She grinned. "I was quite a tomboy as a girl."

He grinned in return, his mood suddenly lighter still. "Yes, miss, I have played baseball. Why do you ask?"

"I think it would be beneficial if the town children and my children played together and got to know each other. And I think baseball would be a good game to start with. What does thee think?"

What did he think? He thought most parents wouldn't want their children associating with orphans. Hating to disappoint her, he clasped his hands behind him and said in a repressive tone, "There is a deep stigma attached to being an orphan."

"I know. It is hard to believe that people somehow hold a child accountable for being orphaned. I do not understand such illogical thinking."

"It's hard," he agreed, suddenly sorry he had no chance of changing this for her.

"My mother told me she thought it was somehow related to people's fears of dying and leaving their own children orphaned. She said orphans remind them that the same thing could happen to their dear children."

He gave a sound of reluctant recognition. "That sounds logically illogical." The woman beside him unconsciously beckoned him to come closer.

"And people tend to think that people are poor because of laziness when that often isn't true." Felicity sighed. "Thy mother-in-law called my children base-born, a wicked thing to say of any child. How is a child responsible for having been born out of wedlock?"

He'd had these same thoughts over the years. He wished there was some way to shield her from the realities of this world. But what could one man or woman do against such irrational prejudices?

"Will thee come and help the boys and girls learn to play baseball? And will thee invite children of thy friends to join in our games? I will prepare the lawn near the alley with bases and I've already bought several bats and balls." She looked up into his face expectantly.

In spite of his honest intention to the contrary, they had drawn closer as the darkness had grown. For once, she wasn't wearing her plain bonnet. Now moonlight illuminated her lovely face surrounded by strawberry curls that refused to stay pulled back into her severe bun. His fingers tingled with the imagined feeling of those vibrant, reddish-golden curls. Her blue eyes revealed her open soul of kindness and charity. How did she manage the bravery it took to confront and try to change the ways of their miserable, often cruel world?

"I don't seem to be able to refuse you," he murmured, his hands straying up to those tempting curls. He let his fingers comb through them, which caused him to brush her soft cheek. He sprang to life inside as if he'd just connected with sunlight. He was suddenly awake, so very awake. The short inches between them crackled with awareness. He lowered his face toward her mouth.

She took a step back and turned away. "I'm so happy to hear thee say that. Thee will do such good for these children." She turned quickly around, heading back toward the Barney house.

He would have thought his touch had not affected her, but her voice quavered just enough to tell him she had not remained unmoved.

He took a deep, steady breath. He had nearly kissed her, and out in the common view. The shock of this vibrated through him. He would have to be very careful, very. Tonight he'd been drawn against all logic toward her. This woman was obviously devoting her life to the care of others. And he still cringed at the thought of remarriage. His course was clear. No more weakening to her innocent allure.

"Look." She pointed toward her neighbor's house. "That little boy tugs at my heart. He looks so lonely."

Ty followed her direction and glimpsed Percy Partridge standing in his window, looking out. The child's form was backlit by candlelight. Ty watched as the child was pulled from the window and the light went out.

"Poor boy," Felicity murmured. "He never gets to have any fun. He just stares out the windows at our boys playing."

Just then, an outrageous idea burst into Ty's mind. An idea that would allow him to help Felicity in her mission, and give back a small measure of what she'd given him. It was outrageous, yes—but why not?

Felicity waited until the next evening to carry out her plan. She had asked Tucker to help her set up the baseball field. All the other children were doing chores or playing on the back porch under the watchful eyes of Vista and Midge.

Felicity's memory tried to take her back to her walk with Ty. No doubt Ty was merely being appreciative of her help. But the sensations she'd experienced walking beside him, was still experiencing… She clamped down on the memory and turned her mind back to the matter at hand. She had been doing a lot of thinking about how to approach Tucker, how to get at the truth. She had finally decided just to talk to him alone.

"Here is the piece of paper that will be our guide to carving out bases in the grass," Felicity said, showing him, "and we will need to dig shallow base lines for the runners to follow to each base."

"I don't know what you're talking about," Tucker said with irritation. He held two hoes in hand.

"Look." With the point of one hoe, she traced in the

dirt a rough diamond. "Here is the baseball diamond with its four bases." She gestured to each of the four points of the diamond. "The pitcher throws the ball from here to home plate. The batter tries to hit the ball. If he succeeds, he tries to make it to first base before he's tagged with the ball. How long has thee known Butch and Willie?"

"A couple of years—" Tucker stopped and his head reared up. "I don't know what you mean. I never seen them before you brought them home."

She had taken him by surprise as she'd planned. Still, she kept her voice and expression neutral. "Lying is quite unnecessary, Tucker. I guessed that thee three knew each other the first time I saw thee together. How does thee know Willie and Butch?"

"I told you. I just met them here when you walked them into the yard." He propped his hands on his hips and glared at her.

"Very well." She would have to try to get more of the truth from Tucker on a different topic. "Let's begin digging up the sod for the bases. I'll have to ask Ty Hawkins about what to use for bases. It seems to me that wood might be slippery."

Tucker eyed her, but took the hoe and began disturbing the sod for home plate. Felicity walked to what would be second base and began cutting through the thick green sod, too. Tucker's fondness toward Camie must have a root. What could it be? She worked in silence for a time, then went over to comment on Tucker's progress. "Very good. How much younger was thy sister?"

This time the ploy of the unexpected question did not work. Tucker merely glared at her and turned away. Nonetheless, she glimpsed a flicker of something in his eyes, something like pain. This added weight to her belief that Tucker had had a little sister. No doubt a little sister he had lost.

Felicity ached for him, for all the children this world judged sullied, tainted by death and poverty and irresponsible parents.

"Hey!" a voice hailed her. "Hey! Is this the orphanage?"

Felicity turned toward the boulevard and saw a man climbing down from a farm wagon. Waiting on the buckboard seat, a crushed-looking woman in a threadbare dress and bonnet looked after the man.

"What can I do for thee?"

"I just drove into town to do business and somebody told me there was an orphanage here now. I'm looking for a couple of boys—strong ones." The man eyed Tucker. "This boy looks about right. I need someone who knows how to work. Boy, get any stuff you got. We'll take you, and lady, you got another one just about like him?"

Felicity was flabbergasted. Tucker just stared at the man who spit tobacco out the side of his mouth.

"Well, get moving, boy. I don't give orders twice. You'll mind or you'll be sorry."

"I'm afraid that thee misunderstands what Barney Home for Children is. We take in children—".

"Lady, I don't have time for a lot of folderol. Now

I'm ready to take this boy off your hands. What's the problem?"

Felicity drew herself up and looked the unpleasant man in the eye. "There is no problem. Tucker is not going with thee."

"What?" The man took a step toward her menacingly.

She didn't flinch. "Nor any other child here. I will only allow orphans to be adopted by loving families who want children, not unpaid workers. In case thee hasn't heard, slavery has been outlawed."

The man glowered at her, but Tucker moved the hoe so that it became a weapon. "You better clear out, mister," Tucker said. "Miss Felicity isn't a woman to mess with."

The man cursed, turned and stormed back to his wagon. He drove away without a backward glance.

The man's curses set her teeth on sharp edge. "Thank thee, Tucker."

"I can't stand bullies," he said. "But that's what got me into trouble in the first place."

Still seething over the man's effrontery. Felicity contemplated asking him what he meant by those cryptic words. But decided to let it pass. For now.

They both turned back to their work. Shock and outrage at the man's attitude consumed her for a time, giving way to misgivings about Tucker, Butch and Willie.

She couldn't think of why she should be filled with such uncertainty. Why shouldn't the three homeless boys know each other from life down on the wharf? But why would Tucker lie about it? She shook her head, unable to put a name to her fear.

Bright and early on an October Saturday morning, Tyrone Hawkins showed up at her back porch, dressed in a casual shirt and trousers for the first baseball practice. It was the first time Felicity had seen him without a formal suit or judge's robes. But the biggest change in him was due to his cheerful expression. The sight had quickened her pulse.

She stuttered her good morning and introduced the children to Ty. Camie came to her and buried her face in Felicity's skirts. She decided it best not to comment on this.

The main reason for baseball was to bring together the town children and her orphans. Yet Tyrone had come alone. She murmured a question to Tyrone about the possibility of other children coming. He merely shrugged, but a smile lingered in his eyes. What did that mean? And why was she suddenly breathless?

Soon she had all the children outside, and Tyrone was showing Tucker how to hold a bat. Then movement caught Felicity's eye. She turned to see a man walking from her neighbor's yard to hers, clasping hands with a little boy on each side of him.

"Partridge!" Tyrone greeted him. "I see you brought Ernest as well as Percy."

Felicity goggled at the sight. Percy in her yard? And he looking decidedly different. No ruffles or knickers. He was dressed in plain pants and a dark shirt, as was the other child.

"Miss Gabriel, may I introduce you to my old friend, Eldon Partridge, his son Percy and his nephew Ernest Brown."

Felicity greeted them, still not quite believing her eyes. And then from the alley came another friend of Tyrone's and his son and daughter. Felicity was introduced to them and then the batting practice started.

Thrilled by success, she moved away and sat in the shade of an oak tree with Donnie and Camie. The rest of the children were lined up, waiting for their turn at bat and calling encouragement to the other children as they tried to master how to hold the bat. Donnie was watching raptly. Every once in a while, Camie would chance a glance at her father. Felicity fought the urge to do the same. She sat with her back against the broad trunk and praised God for Tyrone Hawkins.

After a while she looked up and noticed that Percy's mother was standing at the line of bushes that partially separated the two yards. Concern tempered Felicity's elation. She pondered for a few minutes and then rose. *Lord, make me a peacemaker.*

Chapter Six

Felicity ventured toward Mrs. Partridge. Camie trailed after her, hurrying to catch her hand. Donnie didn't move; he was concentrating on the baseball lesson.

"Mrs. Partridge," Felicity said, using the title *Mrs.* because she didn't know the woman's first name. "I am happy to see that thy son is going to learn baseball—"

"You're happy, are you?" Mrs. Partridge snapped. "You are a meddlesome intruder in our town. You've caused trouble from the day you arrived."

Felicity stared at the woman, disbelieving her ears.

"Don't you say mean things about Miss Felicity," Camie declared, stepping away from the shelter of Felicity's skirt. "She loves children and protects them. Percy is a bad boy—"

Felicity stooped down and drew Camie to her.

"Thank thee, Camie, but thee must not scold an adult. It is not polite."

"See!" Mrs. Partridge said as if to an audience. "You have alienated this child from her own home and are teaching her to be impudent."

Felicity rose and faced the woman. "Camie is visiting here for a while. Pray, what business is that of thine?"

The woman stepped forward. "Meddler! Old maid!"

Felicity looked into the woman's eyes and saw tears. Her anger dissolved like sugar in warm water. She chose to ignore the other impolite epithet. Why was it rude to call a woman unmarried? Bachelor was an honorable title. "I am very sorry that thee is so upset, but what have I done to meddle in thy affairs?"

"My Percy is a delicate child." The woman began wiping away tears. "He can't play with other boys. He'll get hurt." The woman glared fiercely. "And what's wrong with how I dress Percy? That's how Queen Victoria dresses her sons!" With this parting shot, Mrs. Partridge whirled away and ran, weeping, into her home.

Stunned, Felicity watched her go. She stopped herself from following. Her father had always told her not to try to reason with unreasonable people. Had someone, perhaps Ty, said something about Percy's clothing? She turned, drawing Camie back with her to Donnie. They sat down again on the dry grass and watched Katy come up for her lesson in batting. Felicity felt drained. Who might appear next? Did Alice Crandall hate baseball?

"You can hit the ball, Katy!" Camie called to her friend.

Felicity stroked Camie's hair and then kissed the top of Donnie's head. In only a few weeks, she had gained ten children, children who were now getting enough food, clothing and love. This was worth any unpleasantness from her neighbors. God would have to take care of the rest of the town. And what they thought of her and her work.

"Miss Gabriel," the builder called to her from the back porch, "I've come with the plans for you to approve!"

She'd known she wouldn't be left in peace. Suppressing a sigh, she rose. "Camie, will you stay here and keep Donnie safe while I go in with the builder?"

Camie nodded and moved closer to the little boy, her eyes not straying from the batting practice. Felicity felt herself smiling broadly. This was the first time that Camie had not clung to her at a parting. Felicity hurried to the builder, eager for the renovations. Mildred Barney would have been so happy today.

Dalton stood down the alley concealed by a grouping of fir trees. He'd come to see the Quaker's orphan home for himself. As he watched the judge teaching the kids some game with a ball and stick, anger rose in him like steam in a kettle. Not only had she nabbed Tucker, but Willie and Butch, too, three of his best boys. He'd have to put a stop to this. Then he recalled something he'd heard from his crony on this side of the river. The Quaker had taken in the judge's daughter. His anger turned to glee. He knew just what to do to ruin this Quaker and get her run out of town.

A week later, Ty timed his visit after what he thought would be bedtime at the Barney house. His mother had told him that Felicity wanted to discuss some matter with him, so here he was. Against his better judgment. Miss Felicity Gabriel threatened his ability to show a bland face to the world. That had been very important once. But Miss Gabriel demanded honesty. She demanded action. What would she want from him this time?

Vista let him inside. "Miss Felicity is upstairs putting your child to bed with Katy and Donnie."

He would have liked to watch his child go to sleep but kept this to himself. If Camie was able to lie down and go to sleep without any distress, he didn't want to do anything that would upset that. "I'll wait, then. Miss Gabriel said she had something she wanted to discuss with me."

"You come and sit out on the porch. This cool north wind has tamed the mosquitoes. They aren't busy tonight." Vista led him through the hall. "I'll go let Miss Felicity know that you're here."

He considered cautioning her not to let his daughter know. Vista must have guessed this. "Don't worry," she said, walking away. "I won't upset your little girl."

Choking down the humiliation of others knowing he was unwanted by his own blood, he sat on the wooden loveseat. He leaned forward, his hands hanging between his knees. The sound of crickets heralded the first touch of fall. Of course, there would be many more hot days when Indian summer came, but autumn was whispering its coming tonight. He tried to swallow down the bitterness on his tongue, bitterness which had come with the destruction of all his hopes about what life could be after the war.

"Tyrone Hawkins," Felicity greeted him as she walked onto the porch, "I'm so happy thee has come."

He rose and lost himself in her bright eager eyes. "I wish you'd call me Ty. I've always hated Tyrone." The words were out of his mouth before he knew it.

"As thee wishes. Please sit." She sat on a chair across from him. "The cooler temperature is lovely, isn't it?"

He did not want to discuss the weather. "Why aren't you married?" He was shocked by his rude, personal question. What had gotten into him?

She chuckled. "I am not interested in marriage. I know that makes me odd, a spinster by choice. But I want to devote my life to bettering the lives of children. That is my calling from God. And that brings me to something I wish to discuss with thee…if I may?"

"That's why I came. What's on your mind?" He took himself firmly in hand. Why was it that this woman provoked words and actions from him that no one else did or ever had?

"When we first met," she began eagerly, "we discussed the fact that Illinois law makes no distinction between lawbreakers over the age of reason and those younger."

He nodded.

"I think the laws must be changed."

He stared at her. *Just like that?* "Change the laws?"

She nodded decidedly. "Yes, how does one go about changing a law in Illinois?"

He sat back and studied her. How did she muster such pluck? And what did she want him to do in order to change these laws? He quelled the childish urge to fidget. "I suppose the first step would be to write to the state senator and representative for our district in the state legislature."

"I was thinking that might be the way to start. Every state is different and I know nothing of Illinois law. You do and I was hoping…" She paused and caught her lower lip with her teeth like a girl.

"Yes?" he asked, charmed by her sudden shyness.

"I was hoping that *thee* would write the letter."

His eyes widened. "Me?"

"Yes, I will of course write one. But men in government rarely pay attention to women, unfortunately. If thee, a judge, would write the letter, it would have to be taken seriously. Doesn't thee think so?"

He couldn't argue with her logic. Her letter would be dismissed as mere feminine sentiment. His would be read and considered seriously. He nodded. But was that all?

"And perhaps thee could encourage the county

prosecutor and thy other law friends and acquaintances to send letters, too?"

He grinned. Did this woman ever stop? "Aren't you
busy enough with the children here? Too busy to set
in motion a task like this?"

Her brows rose quizzically. "I have an interest in all
children. And I don't think that treating children as
adults in court makes good sense. What does a child
sent to prison learn except how to improve his criminal
skills? In 1813 in England, Elizabeth Fry visited
Newgate Prison and found three hundred women and
children living in appalling conditions."

Ty sat back, watching her light up like the dawn.
This woman was nothing like his wife, who had never
cared about anything except the latest *Godey's Lady*'s
fashion plates.

"That was the beginning of prison reform in
England," she said, her voice gaining intensity. "And
our own Dorothea Dix has worked most of her life to
improve living conditions for the mentally ill here and
abroad, not to mention her work during the war for our
wounded at President Lincoln's request."

He held up both hands in surrender, trying not to
chuckle like a pleased lad. Trying not to reach out and
brush her soft, tempting cheek. He pushed down these
odd reactions. "I will write the letter and I will see if
I can persuade my colleagues to do likewise." After the
way she'd taken Camie in, how could he refuse her
anything? "Anything else? Do you want me to run for
governor or senator?"

She laughed. "I thank thee. Truly. And also I owe thee thanks for thy batting lessons on Saturday. The children were thrilled. They keep asking me when thee will come. They are so eager for this Saturday." In spite of her cheery words, her face took on a somber cast.

Her change of mood deflated his momentary happiness. "What's wrong?"

She looked up, her expression arrested. "I was happy to see thee did not come alone. I was so grateful for thy persuading four fathers to bring their children here last Saturday. But I fear Mrs. Partridge was very vexed. I hope I didn't sow seeds of discord between a husband and wife."

"I don't think you sparked Mrs. Partridge's dislike of your work. My mother-in-law did that. Partridge is an old friend. He and I served together in the war. He feels his absence in his son's early life keenly. He has been upset with his wife and how she refuses to let Percy be a boy. He just couldn't figure out how to change things."

"I see." She remained still, head down, probably deep in thought. Probably wondering how to help Martha Partridge, who would like to box Felicity's ears if she could and still look the lady. He shook his head, admiring Felicity.

"How…how is Camie doing?" he forced himself to ask, his throat swelling, constricting his airway.

Felicity looked up. "She is doing better, sleeping and eating well. She is very attached to Katy and to me. I try to encourage her to spend most of her time with Katy. But she will be playing with Katy and stop and come to find me. I think she needs to know that I am here for her, and I won't leave her. I hope that soon she will begin to feel safe." She gazed at him as though trying to read his heart.

Regret dragged like a rough, heavy sack over his raw, ragged soul. He must let her know some of what had caused Camie's problems. "When she…when Camie was born," he began, "I wasn't here. And I was only able to visit twice on furlough. Both times she was still a baby." He drew in air, fighting his feeling of failure. He had not been able to be the father he had wanted to be. The war, the terrible war. His hand itched to cover his scar which he felt certain must be part of the reason he frightened his child. "You said the other day that the war had affected these children."

"Yes, it is a dreadful weight they all carry. Katy's father was killed in the war and her mother died about a year ago. The two of them had no family. A woman took them in for a while, but mistreated Donnie so Katy took him and ran away. Can thee imagine a seven-year-old trying to provide for herself and her little brother? The thought hurts my heart." She pressed her fist over her breastbone as if she were indeed in pain.

He felt a sympathetic pain with her. "Do you think that Camie will ever be able to come home?" he spoke, rushing his words, almost panting as if he'd been sprinting.

She smiled. "Yes, I do think she will want to come back to thee and Louise. We must give her time to heal. I hope that thee and thy mother will visit here every day. I think that will help Camie begin to see thee as friends of mine and of all the children here. The other children let your daughter know how much they enjoyed thy coming and teaching them baseball. Actions like these will begin to build a bridge between thee and thy daughter. I hope."

He nearly shouted at her to stop, stop giving him hope. This pushed him to his feet. Suddenly he wanted to run down the street, to escape. He didn't want to hope. That way lay the possibility of being hurt more. If he had chosen a wife wisely and not just based on how pretty she was, this all might have been avoided.

He turned his back to Felicity who'd become his guide, his hopeful link to his daughter, and said, "I will trust you. Do you think she's asleep? I'd like to look in on her." He put distance between himself and this disquieting woman.

"Come." She motioned to him. "We'll go up together. We'll peek in on her." She led him inside and up the steps to the second floor. She held her index finger in front of her lips and then opened the door to one of the bedrooms. Ty noted that the deconstruction of walls had begun farther down the hall.

Felicity turned and waved him in.

He stepped silently into the room. On a high bed, his daughter slept on one side of Katy with Donnie on the other side. Instantly, he saw how much more comforting sleeping with two other children would be to a frightened little girl. He tiptoed over to Camie and gazed down at her. Love for his only child poured from him. Suddenly he was able to draw an easy breath. She was happy at last. She was sharing a bed in an orphans' home, but she was happy.

He glanced toward Felicity, who stood at the foot of the bed. Her head was bowed and he was certain she was praying for him and Camie. He tried not to notice what a lovely picture she made in prayer. She was a woman dedicated to children, not a woman who wanted a husband. And evidently God listened to this woman. *Thank God for Felicity Gabriel.*

Felicity couldn't get last night's conversation with Ty out of her mind. In a starched white apron, she stood in the warm, clean kitchen, kneading bread dough beside Vista, who baked eight loaves twice a week. Felicity rolled and folded the soft, pliant dough. The dread issue of registering the children for school had become the next hurdle. Today, Felicity was discovering if any of the children knew their letters or numbers so she would be able to discuss the learning level of each child with the town teachers. She hoped they would welcome her children.

"Miss Felicity," Camie said, "see? I made a flower." The children, sitting around the table had been given dough to form into whatever shapes they wanted.

Felicity looked over her shoulder. "Is it a daisy? A pretty one?"

"Yes." Camie glowed.

Felicity gazed at the child. Ty had asked her why she wasn't married. Why?

"Snake," Donnie said, pointing at his long curve of dough. "Snake."

"And a very fine snake, too," Felicity said, enjoying the yeasty scent of the dough. Images from her conversation with Ty the night before kept coming to mind. He'd grinned when she'd suggested he persuade his colleagues to write letters, too.

"Katy, it's your turn," Felicity prompted. "How high can you count?"

"To twenty." Katy did so, holding up fingers one by one for each number.

Camie knew how to count to ten but nothing else. Felicity wondered again about Alice Crandall and her daughter. A child of seven in a good home should know her letters and numbers by sight and Camie did not. "Very good, Katy."

Last night had meant so much to her. Being able to discuss weighty matters with a man had been a treat. Most men thought women unable to discuss politics, But Ty Hawkins had taken it in stride.

Vista spoke up briskly. "Now, children, the bread is ready for its first rising. You leave your dough and I'll cover it with a moist cloth. You all go out and wash your hands and play in the backyard."

Felicity took off her apron, hung it on a peg and

headed outside, too. She ambled toward the carriage house. It was a perfect day—bright sunshine, blue sky, white puffy clouds.

Still, she felt the burden of concern. When Ty had gazed at his sleeping child, he had worn such a look of defeat and pain. She inhaled, filling her lungs, trying to temper the weight of her concern for them. She must focus on today's chore. She still needed to find out if Tucker knew his letters and numbers. And she would broach the subject of school with him. She wanted him to get an education but doubted he would agree. Praying, she approached him where he sat talking to Abel. Both of them rose.

"Abel, I'd like to walk with Tucker for a bit."

Abel bobbed his head. "He's been doing good work."

Felicity smiled. "I have no doubt." She motioned and Tucker followed her into the alley.

This was where Ty had walked beside her not long ago—where he had kissed her hand. The spot his lips had touched still tingled at the memory. She covered it with her other hand. She cleared her throat. "I will get right to it. Tucker, does thee know thy letters?"

"You mean the alphabet?"

"Yes."

"Yeah, I know them when I see them."

She paused at the sandy edge of the alleyway. This near the river, sand was generously mixed in the soil. "Will thee trace an *A* for me in the sand?"

Tucker gave her a disgusted look and stooped and traced an *A* in the dirt.

"Now a *Q*, please."

Tucker traced a *Q*.

"Can thee read words?" She started walking again.

She heard Katy and Camie's voices. Suddenly she heard again Ty's words: *I will trust you.* For some reason, her spirits lifted every time she thought of her conversation with Ty last night.

"Some." Tucker walked alongside her, his hands stuffed in his pockets.

"Numbers?" she asked. Overhead, geese honked, flying south. She shaded her eyes and looked up. The seasons were changing. How long would Camie stay with her? How could she reunite her with her family?

"I can count to a hundred and I know what numbers look like." Tucker also gazed up at the migrating flock.

"Good." She paused again. "Does thee want to go to school, Tucker?"

"No."

She recalled that this was the exact place where she was certain Ty had almost taken her in his arms. Turning away, she blushed warmly. "Very well." She headed toward the house, away from these dangerous memories. After a few steps, she glanced back and noticed Tucker had not moved. "Tucker?"

"That's it? I say no and you say okay?" He sounded almost miffed with her.

She faced him, suppressing a smile. This boy never liked it when she didn't react as he expected. But then he had often surprised her, too, as with his protectiveness of the younger children, especially Camie.

"Tucker, I want very much for thee to get an education. But I think it will be best if I tutor thee at home this year. Thee will need to catch up."

"So you think you'll make me go to school next year?" His tone was belligerent.

She chuckled. "No, I think I will *allow* thee to go to school next year, if that is what thee wants."

He stared at her, obviously disbelieving. "I can't figure you out. What's your game?"

There it was again, his distrust. Would she ever be able to shatter his hard shell of suspicion? "My game is helping children who need help. That is my only game." She waved for him to go back to Abel. He turned and went back to the horses he loved. She hoped that she had planted seeds that might bloom in the future.

Ty's face came to mind again. She hoped she was planting seeds of reconciliation for this good man and his child. Her honesty also scolded her. Was she starting to have more than friendly feelings for Ty? She pursed her lips. That would not do. She must cultivate only camaraderie with Ty, nothing more. Of course that was the right plan. Still, she couldn't forget the way he looked at her sometimes—as if she were a beautiful woman. No man, not even Gus, had ever looked at her quite that way.

Dalton stood, looking out the grimy window in the warehouse loft. Murky dawn was leaking out from darkness. His head hurt from imbibing too much last night. He rubbed his throbbing temples. That reminded him of his other headache. He'd been too busy to take care of matters with that interfering Quaker across the river. He'd worked it all out and his plan would work.

He walked over to one of the lumps on the floor and kicked it. The girl of about twelve got up, rubbing her side and glaring.

"Make the morning gruel, girl, and get the rest of the brats up. Time's a-wasting." *Time's almost up for you, Quaker.*

On the next Monday morning, Felicity walked up to the white clapboard primary schoolhouse only three blocks from home to enroll the children. Would Alice Crandall's vile gossip make this a difficult day? *Father, I don't want these children hurt. Protect their hearts today.*

Behind her, like a parade, all the children except for Donnie and Tucker walked in a double row. Camie and Katy were holding hands. Felicity's nerves were taut. And she had the strange feeling that someone was following her. But every time she looked around, she saw no one. Just nerves, no doubt. And, of course, the repeated experience of having Alice Crandall coming out of nowhere to scold and accuse her caused her an unsettled stomach.

On the school grounds, children were calling to each other, playing on the swings and jumping rope. Several large burr oaks, whose ruffled leaves were turning bronze, surrounded the school yard. Her children eyed the town children and vice versa. The town children started whispering and pointing. Felicity moved quickly to set the right tone.

This school, for children from first grade through fourth, had two rooms and two teachers. The women, wearing severe black dresses and dour expressions, were standing outside the school door, one on each side. Felicity marched up to the one who looked older. "Good day, I am Felicity Gabriel. I've come to register my children for school."

The woman with gray at her temples looked at her and then the children. No doubt the mix of children of different colors was what made her raise one eyebrow.

The teacher with a disapproving twist to her mouth asked, "Are you that Quaker who has started an orphans' home?"

"I prefer to call it a children's home." Felicity beamed at her, ready to object to any prejudice with the invincible cheerfulness she'd learned from her mother. "Who can help me register the children?"

The two grim teachers scowled back and forth. "This school is for the children of residents of this town," the older one said.

Felicity replied, "Yes, and these children are residents of this town."

"But they don't have parents," the younger teacher pointed out, her lower lip dipping down farther in more disapproval.

"No, but now they have me," Felicity said with a

touch of steel in her tone. "I am here to register these children for school. Which of thee will handle this?"

The two teachers exchanged glances and then the older one said, "Follow me, please."

Shrugging off the insistent feelings of someone watching her, Felicity waved the children to follow her inside the schoolhouse. In a few minutes, the children's names had been registered and they had been divided between the two teachers. When Katy and Camie were assigned to the same class, Felicity was relieved and grateful. The children were curtly dismissed to the school yard to play.

Just as Felicity started to leave, the older teacher said sourly, "You know, in this school we don't spare the rod and spoil the child."

Felicity raised her chin. "All my children are very well behaved. So I must let thee know that I will not allow my children to be mistreated in any way just because they have suffered the misfortune of losing their parents."

At the door, the younger teacher, her thin face sinking into critical lines, commented, "I see that it's true. Judge Hawkins has abandoned his own daughter."

Felicity stared at the uncharitable woman and had to fight her natural heated reaction to this provocative statement. She gave a tight smile. "Camie is visiting with me. The war affected all the children in this town. And indeed, in this nation, in one way or another. Ty Hawkins is a fine man and is doing the best he can for his daughter. I hope none of thee will make the mistake of trying to cause Camie to feel unwelcome here. Or to make her feel that her father does not have the right to do whatever he thinks best for his child. Ty Hawkins would not appreciate it."

Without another word but with a cheery wave to the children, she marched away. A block from school, she glanced over her shoulder but still saw no one. She heard the school bell ringing and said a prayer. The two unwelcoming teachers had not given her any confidence in their ability to nurture her children as well as teach them. And she couldn't shake the feeling that someone was very curious about her and her movements. She headed for home, resisting the urge to look over her shoulder again.

Felicity woke suddenly in the dark.

"Help! Help!"

She bolted from her bed.

She heard the sound of someone falling downstairs, loud bumping and grunts and groans.

"Stop!" a voice yelled. And then a yelp of pain. A little girl screamed. A crash and glass breaking.

Hand trembling, Felicity lit a candle and ran barefoot into the dark hall. Now she recognized the shouting. It was Tucker's voice. She ran down the stairs toward the sounds.

"What's happening?" she called out.

"Miss Felicity! Help!" Camie shrieked.

Felicity raced into the dining room. A man, his face covered with a cloth bag, was swinging a chair at the cracked bow window. Tucker gripped the back of the man's jacket. The intruder swung around and hit Tucker in the head with the chair. The boy fell.

Felicity screamed.

The man swung the chair at her, hitting her on the side of the head, knocking the candle from her hand. She bumped against the walnut buffet. And then fell hard onto the oak floor.

More glass breaking. The candle rolled against the long sheers at the bow window. They burst into flame, lighting the room suddenly. The intruder scrambled out the shattered bow window.

Tucker jumped up. At the window, he yelled, "Abel! Get your gun! Abel!"

Felicity rolled to her feet. Dazed, she looked around for something to fight the fire with. She ran into the hall, picked up the needlepoint rug and raced to the burning wall. She began beating the flames with the rug.

"The children! Tucker! Go get the children and Midge out of their beds!" she ordered. "Get them outside! Fire!" she shrieked out the window. "Fire!"

A gun discharged. A man cursed. Another gunshot.

Felicity beat at the fire. The wallpaper burst into red-orange flames. Sparks and ash flew around her head. Then Vista was there beside her beating the flames, too. Outside, people began appearing at the bow window. The cry of "Fire! Fire!" burst out from everywhere, echoing, echoing.

Felicity began coughing with the smoke. Then Vista

turned and struck her back with a rug. Felicity dropped to the floor, coughing, coughing. The front door burst open. Felicity could feel the pounding of feet through the floor. She tried to speak, but only coughed violently, retching.

"Get Miss Felicity outside!" Vista shouted. "She's been burned!" Then Vista began coughing, too, staggering forward.

Light-headed, Felicity felt herself being dragged by her wrists. She wanted to get up, but the hands dragging her were stronger than she. When the hands dropped her, she lay on the chill dew-dampened grass. By the light of the fire, she saw that a man was working the pump in the backyard. A bucket brigade had been formed. She lay gasping for air.

"Are you all right?"

Felicity looked up and recognized Mrs. Partridge. "Chil…dren! Children?" She tried to get up.

Mrs. Partridge pushed her down. "The children and their nurse all got out safely. I counted them. See?" The woman pointed toward the sidewalk, where the children stood huddled around Midge and Vista. "The big boy got them all down the stairs. He carried the littlest one."

"Thank God," Felicity breathed and then went into another coughing fit.

Mrs. Partridge helped Felicity rest her head in her lap. Lying on her side, Felicity gazed at the men who were putting out the fire.

Then a man loomed over her. It was Ty Hawkins.

"Felicity, are you all right?" he asked, concern etched all over his face.

"She needs the doctor," Vista said. "She got burned."

At these words, Felicity suddenly felt searing pain on her shoulders.

"Here. This will help." Someone poured several buckets of cold water over her back, drenching her. She began shivering uncontrollably.

"We should get her inside," Mrs. Partridge said. "She will catch her death of cold out here soaked and lying on this damp ground."

Ty Hawkins lifted her into his arms. She knew she should protest that she was able to walk. But was she? Chilled to her marrow, she began shuddering, unable to stop. Ty carried her up to her room. "The house?" she managed to stutter.

"Looks like just the dining room was damaged. Now don't worry." He laid her on her bed and was gone. Vista and Mrs. Partridge came in. Together they stripped off her drenched gown and helped her into a dry one. When the cloth touched her shoulders, Felicity nearly cried out.

She began weeping. She didn't want to, yet she couldn't stem the tears. The door opened and Camie ran in. "I want Miss Felicity!"

Felicity opened her arms and the little girl nearly knocked her backward. She felt as if Camie were trying to bore her way into Felicity for shelter.

"He tried to take me," Camie said, crying. "The bad man tried to take me away."

Felicity looked up and found her shock reflected in the faces of the other two women. "The man with the sack over his head?"

"Yes!" Camie's voice rose shrilly. "Tucker came. He fought the bad man."

Stunned, Felicity looked to Vista. "Please get the judge."

Ty paused at the door. Looking wilted, Felicity was sitting on the side of her bed with Camie in her lap. Her fresh gown was tucked modestly around her. The doctor was carefully applying ointment to her slender red and blistered shoulders. Still, her pale skin glowed in the candlelight. Her frailty struck him. She was such a forceful woman that one forgot how delicate she was. Anger stirred in him. Who had done this?

He cleared his throat. "Vista said that someone tried to *take* Camie?"

Felicity looked so tired, crushed. He fought the urge to gather her into his arms. "Bring in Tucker, please. He knows."

Ty turned and found Tucker at the head of the stairs. Ty motioned to him. The boy showed evidence of a violent struggle. One eye was swollen shut. His lower lip was swollen and bleeding, and he limped. Just inside the bedroom door, Ty rested a hand on the boy's shoulder. "Tell Miss Gabriel and me what happened, please."

The doctor was packing his black bag, frowning and listening, too. Vista was securing Felicity's gown in place.

"I heard a sound. It woke me up. I run down the stairs to this floor where the girls and Miss Felicity sleep. Seen that man was carrying Camie away. I had to stop him any way I could. I ran and bumped into him. He fell down the last two steps to the front door. Camie screamed then. I think she was still asleep when he got her at first. But falling woke her."

Ty tried to keep back the anger but couldn't. He slammed his open hand against the door. "What man?"

Tucker jumped at the sound. Felicity began to shiver again. Camie whimpered.

"I'm sorry. I just can't believe that someone would come here and try to kidnap my daughter," Ty protested.

"I suppose I just made it all up!" Tucker glared at him.

"I saw the man—" Felicity began.

"I know." Ty fought for control. "I know. I believe that what took place happened just as you told me, Tucker. It's just that this kind of thing doesn't happen on this side of the river. St. Louis maybe, but Altoona?"

"It seems unusual," Felicity murmured.

"You got any enemies?" Tucker shot him a strange look.

Ty rubbed his taut forehead, unable to think.

"I mean, you're a judge," Tucker continued. "Did

you make somebody mad at you? Somebody that ain't scared to break the law?"

Ty held up both hands as if surrendering. "I can't make sense of this." From the corner of his eye, he saw Felicity begin to slide off the bed toward the floor. He ran to her and lifted her onto the bed. "Vista," he called softly, "come help me, please."

Vista hurried over and helped him lay the lady down on her side, pulling up the covers. Camie clung to Felicity and Vista said to leave the child. The three of them walked out into the hall with the doctor who said he'd be back after breakfast. Ty hung back, not wanting to leave Felicity or his daughter.

"The doctor give her something for the pain," Vista explained to Ty. "That's why she just let go like that. And it was a good idea, too." She looked up at Ty. "Some men helped Abel nail up wood over the broken window. I think you two best come down with me and check to see if everybody's gone home."

Ty nodded and so did Tucker. Abel stood at the bottom of the stairs with a shotgun in his arms. "I shot twice but I missed him. How's our lady doin'?"

"The doctor treated her burns and gave her something to put her to sleep," Vista answered. The stunned-looking children all sat on the floor in the foyer. The housekeeper looked to him. "I'd feel better if you and Abel spent the night in the house."

"Already thought of that," Abel said. "I'm going to settle myself right here on the floor. Nobody else is getting in here tonight."

"Where's Miss Felicity?" Katy asked.

"She's asleep upstairs." Vista held out her hand. "You and Donnie come spend the rest of tonight with me. Camie is sleeping with Miss Felicity." The little girl and her brother followed Vista toward the back of the house.

The boys looked up at him. Tucker spoke up, "The boys and me sleep on the third floor. You should come up there, probably. There's a chair you can sit on. I wish you had a gun."

"I do." Ty patted his belt where a pistol was concealed under his jacket.

"Good," Tucker said and led them up the stairs to the third floor. There Ty saw that the boys were sleeping on pallets on the floor.

"Miss Felicity is getting us beds," Tucker said as if Ty had disparaged the pallets. "They just ain't got here yet."

Ty nodded. "Go to sleep, boys. I will sit in the rocker by the door with my gun. No one will get into this house again tonight. Now settle down."

As Tucker moved away, Ty reached out and grabbed his shoulder again. "Well done, Tucker. Well done."

Tucker shrugged and went to a pile of blankets. The other boys got between their covers, too. A couple of them whispered for a time and then fell asleep.

Wide-awake, Ty sat in the rocker, his loaded pistol on his lap. A loaded pistol in his heart, primed and ready to protect or avenge. His mind buzzed with thoughts and feelings. Why had someone tried to steal his child? And who was the culprit?

Ty burned with outrage and fury. Someone had tried to take his daughter. Why? Then the image of Felicity fighting the fire and then lying on the grass limp and injured sliced his hot anger like iced razors. *I will find out who's responsible and he will suffer the consequences.*

Chapter Seven

Felicity woke and moaned. For a few seconds, she was disoriented. Why was she in such pain? Then a whirring string of images from the night before spun through her mind. She groaned and tried to move. Tears formed in her eyes. *Dear Father, why did this happen? And what will happen now?*

The skin of her shoulders and upper back still burned and felt as if it had shrunk at least one size. She moved inch by inch and finally sat up on the side of the bed. Suddenly she recalled that Camie had slept with her. She looked around for the little girl, but she was alone.

Someone tapped on her door.

"Come in," she said, her voice lower than usual. She found she couldn't breathe easily, as if she were fighting for air. She coughed.

Ty Hawkins peered around the door. "You're awake then?"

She nodded. She wanted to greet him but couldn't catch her breath. The pull to go to him worked on her powerfully.

"I'm going home now. I have to get dressed and get to court," he said, sounding apologetic.

Felicity gazed at him, recalling how he had lifted her last night and carried her here, holding her within his strong arms. Such comfort. In spite of her not being dressed for male company, she wished he would come in. Such comfort. She grappled with persistent tremors, no doubt an aftereffect of last night's violence. "How is Camie?"

The mention of his daughter appeared to strike him with unusual force. His whole face tightened into grim lines. "She's fine and is down in the kitchen finishing oatmeal for breakfast. Your housekeeper asked me to tell you that you don't have to come down. As soon as she gets the children off to school, she'll come up and help you dress."

"I should be able to get up by—" She paused, realizing she did not want to move. Searing pain held her captive.

She tried to take a deep breath and coughed painfully instead. Finally she was able to speak. "Does thee have any idea what happened last night? Why would someone try to take away thy daughter?" Her heart pounded, making her weaker. But she wouldn't let herself sink onto the sheets again.

"No, I don't know why this has happened. I must go. I'm due in court in an hour. I will return this evening. Abel is going to take the children to school and bring them home. They won't be allowed to go anywhere without someone with them. You stay here and rest." Ty looked as if he wanted to say more. But he only shook his head and left.

Though Felicity tried to ignore it, his leaving chilled her. She cautiously eased herself to her feet. She had been worried that she wouldn't be able to stand without the dizziness of last night. But except for her painful shoulders, she felt fine. Well, maybe not fine, but as close to normal as possible after all that had taken place last night. Her weakness and helplessness chafed her.

She drew her light blue wrapper from a peg near the door. The thought that she had run downstairs in only her nightgown and been carried outside like that gave her pause. But in the midst of all the drama and commotion, probably no one had taken much notice.

As she tried to slide the wrapper onto her shoulders, her body rebelled at this usually easy but now intricate set of movements. She found she really couldn't tolerate any added weight, not even a layer of light cotton, on her blistered skin.

Vista knocked once and walked inside with a cup of coffee. "The judge said you were awake. You can't put that on." Vista took the wrapper and hung it back on the peg. "Now you need to rest." She shooed Felicity back to bed and gave her the cup.

Sitting down on the bedside, Felicity tried to take a deep breath and failed, coughing again. She pressed a hand to her neckline. "Thank thee for the coffee. I don't want to be shut up in this room all day. But what can I wear? My shoulders are most painful."

"I been thinking." Vista looked around the room. "I know where Mrs. Barney's niece's party dresses are packed away. I'm going to find one and let you wear that."

"A party dress?"

"Her party dresses were cut low and didn't have much sleeves."

"Oh!" Felicity put her hand to her mouth in surprise. In the past, when in the city, she had glimpsed these kinds of dresses. In the evening, ladies had turned out in low-cut silk and satin gowns. "Oh, no. I couldn't wear anything like that."

Vista just shook her head and left, saying over her shoulder, "I'll be right back."

Setting down the hot coffee, Felicity went to the dressing room and drew out her simple everyday gray dress. She found, however, that even contemplating trying to lift this on bested her. Every movement tormented her tight, burning shoulders. Her already low spirits sank to the cellar.

Vista came in with several dresses over her arm. "Now don't argue. Everyone will know why you're wearing this. And if I know anything, that brass knocker is going to be busy today. You want everyone to see you in that nightgown?"

Felicity gaped at Vista. But before she knew it, Vista had helped her freshen up, even brushing her hair and pinning it up for the day. Then in the face of Felicity's misgivings, Vista helped her don the least embellished dress, a gown of light blue silk with cap sleeves that gathered into a thin soft band around her upper arms.

Feeling nearly naked, Felicity was glad that she'd had the mirror in the room taken down and put at the end of the hall. *I will not look at myself.* "I want to see how bad the damage is downstairs."

Vista helped her down the hall and steps. Felicity halted as she viewed the smoke-blackened ceiling and walls in the hall and dining room. She kept telling herself that it could have been so much worse. Yet it was bad enough. She blinked away tears. "Did the smoke penetrate the rest of the house?"

"Except for the dining room, the downstairs only suffered a little ash and smoke. We can be thankful that it wasn't worse, and be thankful that today is warm and we can open the windows to get rid of the foul burned odor."

Felicity nodded. Vista led her to the kitchen, where she poured Felicity another cup of coffee. Soon, sitting very still, Felicity was nibbling buttery scrambled eggs and golden toast with red raspberry jam for her breakfast. She had held it at bay, but now her main concern crashed over her. "How were the children this morning?" *How was Camie?*

"They were upset, of course. But Tucker told them not to worry, that he and Abel would make sure that no one got in here again." Vista looked her in the eye.

"The judge's little girl was quiet but she seemed to believe Tucker. I mean, he saved her last night, didn't he?"

The confusion and terror of last night slashed ice shards through Felicity again. Fighting to keep rising panic at bay, she sipped her reviving coffee. She leaned her head into her hand. "I can't believe it. I saw it with my own eyes and I still can't believe it. Why would—"

The front door knocker sounded, sharp and loud, twice. Vista took off her apron. "I told you how it would be. I'll make your excuses to whoever it is."

Felicity closed her eyes. She didn't want to see anyone today and was glad that Vista was here to keep her from curious eyes. She made herself finish her eggs and toast. She savored the last few swallows of Vista's good coffee.

The doctor followed Vista into the kitchen. "I am here to check on your burns, Miss Gabriel."

Felicity smiled and offered her hand to the doctor. She was surprised to find that even that simple movement caused her scorched skin to pull and hurt. Vista came inside with a basin of water, a bar of soap and a towel.

"Thank you. Vista knows I like to treat my patients with clean hands. Now let me see if I can't make you more comfortable." He looked at her burns. "Very little evidence of infection. Excellent. Now I'll apply another treatment of this herbal ointment."

As he applied the ointment, Felicity drew in air bit

by bit. But when she thanked him, it was genuine. The ointment made the skin easier to move and soothed the burn.

"I may not be able to come back until tomorrow. If there is a turn for the worse—redness and sign of infection—send for me. Otherwise, I made up a quantity of this ointment and will leave it with your good housekeeper." He turned to Vista. "Apply the ointment every four hours and before bedtime."

"I will, Doctor. I'll make sure she takes care of herself and doesn't try to do too much today." Vista fixed Felicity with a stern look that would have made her laugh if she weren't sick with worry over the safety over her children—and Ty Hawkins's daughter.

After leaving Felicity, Ty strode the few blocks to town to go about his job. He couldn't shake the anger that had consumed him since last night. How was he going to protect Camie and Felicity? And who had tried to take his child? It made no sense.

He jogged up the steps into the courthouse, heading for his chamber. He was hailed by Lyman Kidwell, the chief of police. "Judge Hawkins!"

Ty paused, turning to face the man who was commandingly tall and silver-haired, with a gruff voice that announced that he stood for no nonsense. "I need to talk to you, Judge."

Ty stared at him, his jaw tight. "I was going to come see you over the midday break. What have you found out?"

"Let's go to your chamber. I'll let you know how the investigation is going."

They hurried to Ty's office. Ty unlocked the door, led Kidwell in, and settled behind his desk.

Kidwell sat, facing him. "Now I have my officer's notes from when he interviewed witnesses after the fire last night. I want to hear what you make of this."

Ty couldn't sit, but paced behind his desk. "I am astounded that something like this has happened in our town. And I can't imagine why someone tried to kidnap my daughter. If it weren't for—"

"Kidnap your daughter?" Kidwell snapped. "No one mentioned that to me."

Ty's dour expression settled into harder lines. "Yes, I couldn't believe it at first myself. But my daughter told me that a man was carrying her away and that Tucker Stout knocked him down the steps."

Kidwell's frown consumed his whole face. "My patrolman was told that some thief broke into the house and attacked Miss Gabriel and a fire started."

"That's probably how it appeared to everyone. But I talked to my daughter, Miss Gabriel and Tucker. They all said the business started with a man trying to carry off my daughter."

"Why didn't you tell the patrol officer that?" Kidwell asked.

"He didn't talk to me. I was busy trying to soothe my hysterical daughter. And I carried Miss Gabriel up to her room. She suffered burns, you know."

"Why would anyone try to steal your daughter?"

Ty gave Kidwell a sour look, worry and anger twisting and tangling around his lungs. "I wish I knew."

Kidwell studied him. "Are you sure the intruder didn't just take your daughter because she was the first one he came to?"

"No, Camie was in a room with a little girl and her brother. The intruder could have just as easily taken them. He targeted my daughter."

"It's hard to believe someone would bother a house full of orphans in any case." Kidwell stared at Ty. "Can you think of anyone who has it in for you?"

"You mean besides all the men I've sentenced to prison?" Ty said in an arch tone. "Tucker Stout asked me that last night."

The police chief's eyebrows peaked. "That boy you sentenced to probation at the orphans' home?"

"Yes, and evidently he's the boy who prevented the kidnapper from getting away with my daughter."

Kidwell again scrutinized him for a few silent moments. "I need to ask you. Why is your daughter living there?"

"My daughter suffers what Miss Gabriel calls 'night terrors.' She says it's common among children who have lost one or both parents. My daughter, for whatever reason, feels safe at Miss Gabriel's."

"Even after last night's attempted kidnapping and fire?" Kidwell's tone became harsh.

"After the ordeal last night, she turned to Miss Gabriel and wouldn't be parted from her." The image of his daughter clutching Felicity both comforted him and ripped up his peace.

"You say the Quaker calls what ails your girl 'night terrors?'"

Ty forced himself to speak with measured tones as he revealed facts he wanted no one to know. "Miss Gabriel has worked with other orphans and says this is not uncommon. I am grateful to her for the loving kindness and understanding she has showed to my child. And I won't rest until whoever broke in last night is behind bars." He realized he was clenching his teeth.

Kidwell rose. "I'm with you on that one hundred percent. I'll give this information to my patrol officers and my captain. They'll comb the town and talk to everyone. Someone must have some information. I understand that the intruder wore a sack over his head?"

"That's what I'm told," Ty said.

Kidwell looked sour. "We'll do our best."

"I know you will." Ty rose and the two shook hands. Kidwell left, muttering under his breath.

In the chief of police's wake, Ty's law clerk entered. The serious young man handed Ty the court agenda for the day. Ty sank back into his chair, ignoring the piece of paper in front of him. Just when he'd thought he'd been given a way to help his daughter heal, *this* had to happen.

Propping his elbows on his desk, he folded his hands in front of his mouth. Who wanted to kidnap his daughter? Would his mother-in-law go to such lengths? Was there a criminal whom he'd sentenced who was now free and coming after him and his family for revenge? He scrubbed both hands over his tired face.

The law clerk knocked. It was time for court. He rose, donned his black robe and headed down the hall to the courtroom. He heard case after case as exhaustion threatened to overwhelm him. At the end of the day, as he was trying to focus on the petty thief in front of him, Felicity Gabriel's face, blackened by soot, and her charred night dress and red, blistered shoulders haunted him. How could he keep Camie, Miss Gabriel and her household safe?

He stared at the man, mentally putting a sack over his head as the man made his excuses.

"I seen the error of my ways, Your Honor," the defendant said. "I won't never touch nobody's property again."

Ty wished he could believe the man but this was just another offense in a long list of his thefts. Yet the defendant wasn't violent—

Hogan strode into court and headed right for Ty. "Your Honor," he said, handing him a folded piece of paper. Ty read the note, stiffened, and nodded to Hogan, hiding the sudden increase in his breathing. "The defendant is found guilty and will serve the maximum sentence. I hope this time is the last time I see the defendant in my court. Court is adjourned for the day." Ty sounded his gavel and rose.

In his chamber, he flung off his robe. Outside, Hogan waited for him and the two of them headed to the police station.

Ty's heart thudded, pounded. "What have you found out?"

Kidwell rose. "We got lucky. One of the street vendors, an older widow who sells notions to riverboat passengers, remembered a black man who was asking about where the Barney house was not long ago. She was able to give us a good description. We found him loading grain onto a barge."

"Is he in custody?"

Nodding, Kidwell rose and grabbed a large brass key off a peg on the wall. Ty hurried after him to the two-cell jail that had been erected less than a decade ago. One cell had two men Ty recognized as men he'd sentenced. The other cell held a tall black man who looked like he could lift the jail with one hand. His eyes were wary.

"Judge, have you ever seen this man before?" Kidwell asked.

"No." Ty shook his head.

"One of my officers has gone to get Miss Gabriel to see if she can identify him," Kidwell said with Hogan hovering at his elbow.

Ty swung around and glared at Kidwell. "You know she was burned last night. And I don't think a lady should have to come to a place like this, especially when she's indisposed."

"I'm sorry," Kidwell said, "but she must tell us if this is the man. Hogan, go and see if Miss Gabriel's carriage is outside."

"I'll go, too," Ty said. "I want to make sure that she's

fit enough to come into the jail." Ty didn't wait for the police chief to reply.

Outside, he saw the old black carriage that had been Mildred Barney's approaching the jail. He waved to Abel and the man drove up to him. The blinds on the carriage windows were pulled so no one could see inside.

"Did Miss Gabriel come?" Ty asked Abel.

"Yes," Abel replied, "but I told her I won't let her step foot out of this carriage. Vista had to dress her in an evening gown because she couldn't bear cloth on her shoulders—"

"Ty Hawkins, is that thee?" Felicity's voice from the interior of the carriage interrupted.

"Miss Gabriel," Ty said, stepping to the carriage door. He glimpsed her pale face as she parted the shade. Her woebegone expression tugged at his heart.

"Ty, I don't think I can identify the man from last night." Her voice quavered.

Ty reached inside and grasped her ungloved hand. "I'll go in and talk to the chief of police."

It didn't take long for Ty to convince Kidwell to bring the prisoner in chains outside. Ty hovered near the carriage window. "Here's the suspect, Miss Gabriel."

From the barely parted curtains, Felicity gazed at the large man whose hands and feet were manacled. Four policemen hovered around him. Why had they insisted she come here? She knew she wouldn't be able to identify the man who had invaded her house and who had tried to make off with Camie.

One of the policemen forced the suspect to look toward where she sat at the carriage window. She was immediately struck by the prisoner's large, dark eyes. Fear, pain, humiliation and sorrow flashed from him to her like sharp darts of suffering. But she saw no guilt or defiance.

If she said, "This cannot be the man. He is sad, not guilty," the policemen would pay little attention to her. They would dismiss her view as woman's intuition or sentimentality. Indeed, men usually dismissed what women said in serious situations such as this. So she would not reveal what she had read in the man's eyes. But dissatisfaction with this made her restless.

She looked to Ty. "I'm sorry, but I can't identify this man as the intruder from last night. It was dark. The man had a sack over his head and everything happened so fast."

"Well," the police chief asked, "is this man about the right size?"

"This man appears larger than the intruder, but I cannot be certain. Perhaps Tucker would be able to give thee more of a description."

"Were the man's hands white or black?" Hogan asked.

She shook her head. "I didn't pay any attention to his hands. My focus was trying to get Camie from him. And then he hit me. I fell and the fire started." These few words brought it all back, the horror, the terror of last night. She looked away, shaken.

Ty moved closer to her window as if shielding her. "Miss Gabriel must go home now. I can see that this is upsetting her and she's been through enough."

The police chief thanked her. The men shoved and dragged the prisoner back into the jail. It grieved Felicity to see him handled so roughly. As if he heard her thought, the prisoner turned for one more glance toward her. She read his appeal as if it had been printed on the air. The spirit within her stirred. Was the Inner Light leading her? Telling her she was right about his innocence?

"Miss Gabriel, are you going directly home?" Ty asked her.

"Yes, would thee like to ride with me?" she asked in turn. "Camie will be home from school. Vista and Tucker went to walk them home. I left thy dear mother in the house, expecting the children."

"Much obliged." He opened the carriage door and climbed inside. As he took his seat opposite her, the carriage swayed. Abel called to the team and the carriage moved forward. "I'm sorry you were subjected to that. But the police chief had to ask you. It's routine."

Felicity nodded, holding her lower lip with her teeth to keep from saying what she was thinking. Then she felt herself blush at the thought of how much her low-cut dress was revealing to this man. "I'm not attired as I would like. I've never worn such a revealing dress."

Until now, he hadn't noticed anything but her pained expression and red, blistered shoulders. But now he realized she was wearing a blue dress that made her eyes look otherworldly. He caught himself and tried to speak calmly. "Your costume is attractive. How are your shoulders?"

She shuddered. "Painful, but it could have been so much worse. I'm grateful that only the dining room was damaged and Camie wasn't taken." Then she looked at him, hesitating. "Thee is not intending to take Camie home, is thee?"

"No. But neither can I sleep at your house like I did last night. I have been trying to think of a way to protect you—the children, as well as my daughter."

Ty realized he was staring at the gold-red curls that clustered around her face. He quickly looked away. He was looking at her far too much and with far too much interest. It had to stop.

Ty helped Felicity down from the carriage and insisted she take his arm. Out in the daylight, the sight of her red and blistered shoulders added more fuel to his anger. Whoever had done this would be caught and punished. He considered the black man the chief had in custody. Could anyone actually identify the man with a sack over his head, seen in a dark and chaotic situation? Ty shook his head.

"Miss Felicity!" Camie came running out the door and down the porch steps. Her grandmother was right behind her. "Miss Felicity, thee wasn't here when I got home!"

Felicity stooped to greet Camie, looking pained.

Ty interposed himself between them and caught Camie. She struggled against him. "I want Miss Felicity!"

"You must touch her carefully. She was burned last night, remember? You don't want to hurt her, do you?" Ty set her down.

"That's right, dear," Louise said. "We need to take care of Miss Felicity until she is all better."

Camie edged over and offered her hand. "Come, Miss Felicity, I'll walk thee inside. That's a pretty dress you—I mean thee—has on."

Ty was struck by Camie's new use of Felicity's Quaker words. Was this a good sign or a bad one?

"Thank thee, Camie. How was school today?"

Camie began to skip, drawing Felicity along, Ty and his mother in their wake. "We are learning to spell. I spelled cat *c-a-t,* rat *r-a-t,* sat *s-a-t,* mat—"

A familiar yet unwelcome voice cut in. "It's about time you were home!" His mother-in-law was marching toward them from the street. "And you're here, Tyrone. Excellent. I wanted to speak to you. After last night, neither of you can possibly keep little Camille here. It isn't safe—"

Vista interrupted from the front steps. "Miss Felicity, you got company. It's the mayor."

Felicity looked up, her eyes and mouth wide with surprise. "What? Why?"

Ty stifled a grin. Why, indeed? The mayor always wanted to be in on everything. And he could talk a man's leg off and then start on his arms.

Vista didn't bother to answer her. "Come along. The quicker you listen to his condolences, the quicker he'll leave."

His mother-in-law snapped something about undisciplined servants. And was ignored.

Vista urged Felicity inside to the parlor opposite the wrecked dining room. Ty let his mother-in-law precede him. Of course, as usual Alice Crandall wouldn't leave till she gave each of them an excessive headache. His mother stayed by his side. He noted that his daughter clung to Felicity's hand and regarded her maternal grandmother with fearful distrust and caution. He simmered with irritation and injustice. Alice Crandall would never take responsibility for what she'd done to contribute to Camie's night terrors. Never.

The mayor hadn't stayed in the parlor. He was looking over the fire-damaged dining room and making a tsk-tsk sound and shaking his head. He turned and took both of Felicity's hands in his. "My dear young woman, I am so grieved that this has happened to Mildred Barney's house. I'm Mayor Wallace Law. I have come to offer my sympathy at this calamity and to promise you that nothing like this will happen again. No, indeed. Nothing like this has ever happened on Madison Boulevard."

Mrs. Crandall snapped, "Not till this Quaker moved here and brought riffraff—"

Ty raised his voice, speaking over his mother-in-law's diatribe. "Miss Gabriel needs to sit down. As you can see, Mayor, she has suffered injury." Ty gently took Felicity's arm and led her to a chair near the hearth.

His mother-in-law snapped her fingers as if calling a dog, and demanded that Camie come and give her a kiss in greeting.

Her head down, Camie waited till Felicity was seated and then took her hand again and stood beside her chair. Ty noted that she kept the chair and Miss Gabriel between her and her grandmother. His mother hovered nearby as if backing up Felicity.

Mrs. Crandall snapped her fingers again but was ignored. "Disobedience," she said. "I would not tolerate that in my home."

Ty wanted to snap his fingers in front of his mother-in-law's face and then order her from the room.

Still tsk-tsking, Mayor Law followed them and took the seat across from Felicity. Ty stood on the other side of Felicity's chair, shielding his daughter from Mrs. Crandall.

"I will not stay any longer than necessary," the mayor promised.

Ty hid a sudden smile at this prevarication.

But before the mayor could get rolling, he was interrupted. Another knock on the door and Vista sailed past the doorway to the parlor. She ushered another man in. "Miss Felicity, this is the newspaper editor, Mr. Mac Sharp."

Ty should have expected Sharp to come calling. He moved closer to Felicity, a spark of temper igniting in his stomach.

Felicity stammered a welcome and cast Ty a glance, which he thought meant she wanted him to help her get rid of all these people. He nodded his agreement.

The newsman sat down across from her and scrutinized her.

Felicity blushed. "I'm not dressed as I usually am. My shoulders are too tender…" She trailed off, sounding embarrassed.

Ty's inner bonfire intensified. He glanced at the mantel clock and began tracking the second hand.

Mr. Sharp licked his pencil and asked, "Who do you think started the fire? Do you think it was one of your disgruntled neighbors?"

"Of course not!" Mrs. Crandall announced, glaring at the newspaperman.

Felicity stared at Sharp, openmouthed.

"Why would you say that, Sharp?" the mayor demanded. "No one on Madison Boulevard would commit such a dreadful act."

The editor gave Mayor Law a sharp look. Ty did, too, as he kept an eye on the clock. Soon he would clear this crowded room.

"I'm certain none of my neighbors did anything of the sort," Felicity spoke up. "In fact, the men and women of Madison Boulevard turned out to fight the fire last night."

Vista entered with only one cup of coffee on a silver

tray. "Miss Felicity is right. The neighbors come out with their fire buckets, even before the volunteer fire department arrived."

Felicity accepted the cup of dark coffee. Ty noticed that Vista served no one else, no doubt emphasizing the point that they should all leave sooner rather than later. His mother-in-law was seething at this slight. Ty watched the clock. Time was nearly up.

"Then who do you think started the fire?" Sharp asked as if Felicity knew the answer but was hiding the truth.

Ty spoke up, trying to let Felicity just sip her coffee. "It was more than—"

The brass knocker sounded again. Ty tensed, heat rolling through him. *More* visitors. Vista ushered in Eldon Partridge from next door.

Felicity offered him her hand, appearing harassed.

Sharp ignored Partridge. "I've been hearing all kinds of rumors today. Like one of your neighbors tried to burn you out. Like a band of river rats came to steal you blind."

Felicity covered her eyes with her hands.

Ty could no longer stand to see her in such a state. "Miss Felicity is indisposed. If you gentlemen want to argue, you'll have to leave. She's not well," he said.

"That's right," Vista agreed, bustling into the room. "It's time for her medicine."

Both men apologized but neither looked ready to leave. Sharp glared at Ty. "The free press has a right to get the facts for the people."

Ty snapped, "If you want the facts, talk to Vista. She isn't in pain and she fought the fire, too."

Felicity reached up and squeezed Ty's hand in a wordless appeal. "Mr. Sharp, I will tell thee what I know of last night and then I must ask thee to leave. I must spend time reassuring the children."

After Felicity gave her succinct account, she looked up at Ty. "Will thee see our visitors to the door?"

Gladly. A real pleasure. Ty helped her up.

"Miss Gabriel," Partridge said, "I was going to discuss something with you, but I will consult with Ty, if that's all right with you."

Ty wondered what Partridge wanted.

"Ty Hawkins, I would appreciate it if thee would act for me with my neighbor." Felicity rose and offered her hand to Camie.

"Why hasn't my granddaughter come and greeted her loving grandmamma?" Mrs. Crandall demanded in a false sweet tone as Camie took Felicity's hand. "It's plain to see that living with riffraff—"

Felicity's face flushed red, glaring at the woman.

Ty knew why. His mother-in-law had called her orphans riffraff twice now. And he could see that like a cannon, Felicity had reared back, ready to fire.

"Alice Crandall, if thee were a loving grandmamma, thy granddaughter would have run to thee, not hid from thee. I do not know what thee has done to alienate thy grandchild, but I will not let thee trouble Camie here. If thee would like to try to improve thy relationship with her—"

At this, Mrs. Crandall stormed out of the house, slamming the door behind her. Ty nearly rubbed his hands together in satisfaction.

Sharp raised both eyebrows and the mayor looked stunned. Partridge grinned and tried to hide it.

Sharp narrowed his eyes on Felicity. "How many orphans do you house here?"

"Mr. Sharp," Vista said, "I baked those sugar cookies you like today. I can tell you all about Miss Felicity's orphans and you can meet them in the kitchen. They're having after-school cookies and milk." Vista held out her hand. "Camie, child, you come with me. Katy is missing you. And Miss Felicity got to lie down."

Camie allowed herself to be drawn away with many backward glances. Felicity looked ready to drop. The brass knocker sounded again and she moaned.

Ty took command. "Partridge, answer the door, please. And, Mayor, I think Miss Gabriel must have quiet."

"Of course, of course." Mayor Law headed for the door with Partridge.

Ty led Felicity to the stairs and began helping her to climb them. He tried not to notice how close he wanted to be to her. Given any pretext, he would take her into his arms and carry her up the stairs.

Felicity tried to push him away. "I should be able to go to my room without assistance—"

"No, you just think you should," the doctor said as he followed after them. "I've come to have a look at your burns before I go home."

Disappointed, Ty let the doctor accompany Felicity up to her room. He was about to follow and ask if he could bring her anything when he heard a familiar— and very unexpected—voice at the front door.

Chapter Eight

"Jack," Ty greeted the man, "what brings you here?"

With his hat in his hand, Jack nodded politely. "I come for two things. The first is because of my granddaughter Midge and the four children I brought here to Miss Gabriel. After what happened in this house last night, I am frankly wondering if it's safe to leave them here." He glanced toward the smoke-blackened hallway ceiling.

Ty looked into the familiar face and honest brown eyes. Before he could reply, Partridge broke in, "I came because I'm worried about Miss Gabriel and the children, too."

"Why don't we go into the parlor and talk? It's empty now." Ty led the other two into the tastefully decorated rose-and-ivory room. They sat as if forming a triangle—Jack stiffly on the ornate loveseat, Ty and Eldon on the tapestry wing chairs by the fire.

"What I heard is some man broke in and attacked Miss Gabriel and a fire broke out." Jack looked stern.

Ty took in the lingering odor of acrid smoke. "The police chief and I don't want this generally known, but a man did break in. He tried to carry off my daughter. Tucker Stout heard him and tackled him on the stairs. There was a struggle in the dining room. The candle Miss Gabriel was carrying was knocked from her hand and started the fire."

"He tried to kidnap your daughter? And Miss Gabriel fought with the man?" Partridge asked, sounding aghast.

Rubbing his chin, Jack spoke up. "I know a Quaker's not supposed to fight, but I can see her fighting somebody trying to take your daughter."

"Why would someone want to kidnap your daughter?" Partridge asked.

Shrugging, Ty shook his head. "I'm a judge. I deal with criminals. This might be the fruit of an old grudge." He leaned forward on his elbows, recalling the horror of last night, hearing the fire bell ringing to call the volunteers and neighbors to help. The sight of the flames as he'd run toward the house had taken him back to the war again. The horror shuddered through him.

"My wife told me that Virginia's mother is trying to get custody of your daughter." Partridge looked pained, as if the words he'd said were refuse he didn't want to look at.

"Alice Crandall is a…troublesome woman," Ty

conceded, choosing his words with care. The muted sound of children's voices filtered into the room. "But I don't see her hiring some thug to come and steal Camie from me."

"Yes, sir, that doesn't make sense," Jack agreed. "I mean, where could she hide the child? It would get out that she had her."

Ty assessed Jack in a new light. He'd always just been the affable shoeshine man at the wharf. They'd never sat in a formal parlor together, having a serious discussion.

"Well, then?" Jack looked from Ty to Partridge and back again. "Should I take my granddaughter and the children home?"

"No." Ty was suddenly sure of this. He edged forward on his chair. "We can't let whoever did this get away with destroying Miss Gabriel's work. Mildred Barney was a fine woman and she wanted this house to be used for good after her death."

Partridge agreed, nodding soberly. "That's why I came over. I wanted to know if you wanted me to take a turn guarding the house at night. I know you stayed last night along with Abel, but that will start talk if you do it again."

Ty's face twisted with aggravation. "Yes, there's never a shortage of gossip."

"I'd come and so would some of the men from our congregation," Jack offered. "Some of them are veterans. All of us hunt, so we got guns."

"I can round up the rest of the men in this neighborhood. I'm sure they don't want anything like this happening again," Partridge said.

Ty rubbed his hands together. He wanted to do the protecting here by himself, but that wasn't feasible. He couldn't stay here every night on guard and work at the courts during the day. "I can't do it alone," he admitted, almost surprised to hear the words out loud. "If we could get together another eleven men, we could each take a four- to five-hour sentry duty one night a week."

"That makes sense," Jack said, nodding several times. "I'm sure the men at my church would be more than willing. We take care of our own. Not only are my Midge and Vista living here, but Eugene, Dee Dee, Violet and Johnny have been orphaned or abandoned and we want them kept safe. Black children mean as much to God as white children do."

Ty looked up. "You won't find me disagreeing with you."

"Of course, a child's a child," Partridge said.

"I just wanted that to be clear," Jack said. "Some people don't think our children are as important."

Ty smiled suddenly and sat back more at ease. "Well, I'd warn them not to say that in front of Miss Felicity Gabriel."

The three men chuckled at this.

Partridge rose and so did Jack. "Ty, I'll organize the men in the neighborhood and set the night up into two watches."

Both men shook Ty's hand with extra firmness and turned to leave.

"Wait," Ty said. "Jack, you said you had a second question."

Jack turned back. "Yes, sir, I heard that the police have arrested a black man and he's going to be charged for this crime. Is that right?"

"Yes, I'm afraid it is." Ty pictured the large man who now sat in jail. "Miss Gabriel was unable to identify him as the culprit."

Jack looked down and then up again. "They'll have to release him if they don't have enough evidence to hold him, won't they, sir?"

Ty nodded, but dissatisfaction wrinkled his forehead. "Jack, I may be forced to rule that the man is a material witness and keep him in custody."

Jack soberly met his eyes. "You mean for his own protection?"

Feeling sour, Ty nodded.

"Yes," Partridge said in a harsh tone, "there are a lot of people who don't wait for evidence. We don't want any lynchings here."

Ty looked into Jack's eyes. "Tell the people in your congregation that I won't let *any* man be railroaded in my court. But jail may be the safest place for this man until the case is solved."

"Thank you, Judge." Jack put on his hat again and he and Partridge left.

Ty stood in the empty room, listening to the sounds of the children's voices from the other room. The smell of burned wood hung in the air. Above him, he heard someone moving. Was it Felicity?

His mind went back to the sound of the fire bell and his mother shouting for him to get up. The alarm had ripped through him like barbed wire. He'd run all the way here. When the fire had finally been quenched, he'd been faced with the spectacle of Felicity lying on the grass in her charred nightgown. His hands clenched.

He experienced the phantom memory of her light, soft weight in his arms. He passed a hand over his eyes, trying to banish the memory from his mind.

Then another thought bobbed up in his mind. It had been with him since last night but he hadn't been able to act fully on it. He took a deep breath. He shouldn't put it off any longer.

He walked past the wrecked dining room. Someone had removed the furniture and done a better job of covering the missing window—probably Felicity's builder. He found Vista preparing food in the kitchen. The children were playing a game of tag in the backyard under the watchful eye of Jack's granddaughter.

"Vista, where's Tucker?" he asked.

She glanced up from the huge bowl where she was peeling pounds of potatoes. "Look for him with Abel. Tucker spends most of his time in the carriage house and stable."

"Much obliged." Ty walked out the door and made his way around the children playing in the yard. Hearing his daughter laugh filled him with great joy and great sadness. He still dreamed of picking her up and tickling her into squeals of laughter. But that pleasure had not been permitted him yet. Would it ever?

He approached the carriage house and saw that Abel sat smoking a pipe in an old rocking chair propped against the carriage-house wall. Tucker was perched on a bale of hay, whittling. "Abel." Ty nodded to him and then turned to the boy. "Tucker, I came to thank you for what you did last night. You saved my daughter from being kidnapped." He offered Tucker his hand.

Tucker went on whittling as if he hadn't heard what Ty said.

"Tucker," Abel ordered, "Miss Gabriel wants you children to have good manners. Now stand up and shake the judge's hand. Learn to be a man."

Tucker looked up, flushing at Abel's words and glaring at Ty. But he took Ty's hand and shook it. "I didn't do it for you. I did it for Camie."

"She's a sweet little thing," Abel said. "She brings us a snack sometimes when we're working. Sit a spell, Judge." Abel motioned toward the hay bale. Ty lowered himself next to Tucker, who sat frowning as he whittled.

"I see Jack and Mr. Partridge come by," Abel continued.

Ty explained the night watch that would start tonight. He was aware that the boy was listening even though he didn't act as if he heard a word.

Ty burned with sudden shame around his tight

white collar. He would never have believed that Tucker would do something heroic. And that revealed that he really had deemed Tucker riffraff, just like his mother-in-law. He gave Tucker the same covert attention Tucker was giving him.

"Last night Tuck yelled for me to get my gun," Abel said. "I got off a couple of shots at the man."

"It's an important quality of leadership to be able to keep one's mind clear in a time of trouble," Ty commented.

Tucker shot him a nasty glance. "Think I'm going to be a leader somewheres?"

Abel remonstrated with the boy, telling him not to be disrespectful. "Tucker is already a good leader here with the littler boys," he said to Ty.

Ty was near enough that he caught Tucker whisper to himself in reply, "I tried that once and look what it got me."

Ty nearly asked Tucker what he meant, but stopped himself from commenting. He rolled the boy's words around in his mind. What had Tucker tried to do that had gone badly for him? And where?

Ty wasn't going to make the same mistake twice. He wasn't going to ignore clues and hints about Tucker and the other orphans here. Someone had it in for them. And it was Ty's job to keep them safe.

Ty couldn't blame the boy for being sarcastic in light of what most people believed of him. Again, Ty promised himself not to make the mistake of under-estimating a child merely because he had no family and probably stole to survive. This prejudice against Tucker Stout and the other orphans was a shame to all of Altoona. And Miss Felicity Gabriel was a lesson to them all.

The doctor approached them. "Tucker? Miss Gabriel wants me to ask if you were injured in the fight last night."

"I'm fine." Tucker hunched up his shoulder. "I've had worse."

"You're able to move all your joints then?" the doctor asked.

"I'm fine," Tucker said, sounding nettled.

The doctor took the boy's chin in his hand and looked over his bruised face. "Any ringing in your ears?"

"No."

The doctor released Tucker's chin. "If anything starts bothering you, do Miss Gabriel and me a favor and let us know before it gets so bad you can't hide it. I like to get an occasional full night's rest. I'll be going now. Oh, Tucker, Miss Gabriel wants to see you in her room."

"I need to talk to her, too," Ty said. "I'll come along."

Tucker cast him an irritated glance, shoved his hands in his pockets and started off fast. Ty hurried to keep up.

"Tucker!" Camie called.

Ty watched his daughter run away from a game of tag and head toward the boy. She reached Tucker and walked alongside of him, chattering away. Envy instantly consumed Ty, who fell back so he wouldn't spoil his daughter's happy mood.

Tucker pulled one of her braids. She laughed and ran back toward the game again. And then Tucker turned and sent him an accusing look.

It hit Ty like a gavel in the face. The look told him loud and plain that Tucker thought he must be a cruel parent to have a daughter so frightened of him. Words of self-justification jumbled in his throat and mouth. He held them back.

He had proved the old saying, "Marry in haste, repent at leisure," true. He'd been so afraid that some other lucky young man would snap up Virginia Crandall. He recalled the few words of caution his mother and Mildred Barney, her good friend, had spoken—and which he had ignored. It was only right that he pay for his mistake, but why did his innocent child have to pay, too?

Tucker had preceded him up the stairs to Felicity's bedroom. Ty reached the doorway, but he hung back. Tucker had paused halfway between the door and the bed. The lady lay on her stomach. The silk party gown she had worn had evidently been put away. She now wore a light white gown with only two loose narrow straps to hold it up on her shoulders. Her skin was as red as before but the blisters had all shrunk. He hoped the ointment the doctor had administered was helping with the pain. He reached up and knocked at the door, hesitant to disturb her.

"Is that thee, Tucker?" she asked, sounding as though she had very little energy. "Please come where I can see thee." Tucker moved forward, nearer her face.

Felicity held out a hand. "Tucker, what with my burns and everything else, I haven't been able to express how thankful I am to thee for protecting our little Camie."

"You don't need to thank me, miss." Tucker squeezed her hand and let it go. "I owed you and besides, I wouldn't let *him* take...any kid." Tucker stiffened. "I mean, somebody breaks in, he can't be up to any good, right?"

Felicity studied Tucker's bruised face, as Ty did.

Ty's pulse sped up. It was obvious that the boy had almost said something, revealed something he hadn't wanted them to notice.

She reached for the boy's hand again, but Tucker was looking away. "Tucker, after last night," Felicity said, "thee doesn't have to hang thy head anymore. Thee proved that thee are a fine boy and will become a fine man."

Tucker snorted with derision, looking away.

"Take my hand again, Tucker," Felicity prompted. He finally accepted it, but with a grimace.

"Thee is a good person, Tucker. Never doubt that. Thee heard a sound and acted with great presence of mind. Many others might have given in to panic and hidden. Thee did not."

"I like Camie. She's a good little kid."

The boy's words took Ty by surprise. Ty ached physically, not from the fire last night, but from the emotions and energy he'd expended over the past twenty-four hours. The boy's heartfelt words pierced his unusually vulnerable heart. *My little girl. I could have lost her.*

Felicity smiled. "Yes, Camie is sweet. And thee is a fine boy." Her eyelids tried to drift down. "Thee may go now. I am falling asleep. The good doctor says that I must stay abed and heal."

"The judge is here," Tucker said, nodding toward the door.

"Tyrone Hawkins?" She turned her head slightly.

"Yes, it's me. I'm sorry to bother you in your boudoir. But I have to tell you some important news."

Tucker passed him without a glance on his way out the door.

Ty approached the bed. "I just wanted you to know that Jack Toomey and Eldon Partridge are setting up a night watch on your house, starting tonight."

"Does thee think that is necessary?" Her voice was thin and faint.

Her unusual frailty worried him. "Yes, we all agreed that you and the children need added protection. Now go to sleep. Heal. You have nothing to worry about." He began moving away from her.

"Tucker," she murmured, "I think…Tucker." And she was asleep.

He turned and saw Tucker, whom he'd thought had left, just disappearing from the doorway. What had she been about to tell him about the boy? And why did Ty have the distinct impression that Tucker knew more about last night than he was telling?

Ty took one last glance at Felicity. Even as she lay there in agony, unadorned beauty still radiated from her. He was determined to do everything he could to protect her and the children. And he was becoming more and more convinced that Tucker held the key to Felicity's safety and happiness.

From the bushes in the alley, Dalton watched the judge walk over to the back porch of the house next to the Quaker's place. It pleased him to see the damage that he'd brought to the house, the boarded-up window and the blackened side of the house. But it did not please him to see that Ty and the neighbor were talking with the black shoe-shiner from down at the wharf. All three were glancing over at the burned house. Then Tucker came out of the back door.

I should have wrung his neck last night. *Dalton's hands fisted. If he'd been able to snatch the judge's kid, the Quaker would have been run out of town. And then everything would be back the way it should be.* Lousy do-gooders, making it hard for a man to make a dishonest livin'. I'll get you yet, Quaker. And Tuck. I got ideas. Plenty of them.

Days later, Felicity woke in the night. She froze, her heart pounding. What had wakened her? She heard voices. She rose from her bed and went to the window.

Parting the curtains, by moonlight she saw two men in her front yard.

Both carried what looked to be rifles. They shook hands and one walked away. The other moved into the shadows around her house. She went back to her bed and sat. Her back still burned, but it was healing without infection. And except for the itching, this was a true boon.

But she didn't like the fact that her home and her children had to be guarded like this. Where would this all end? And how did God want it to end? Was she to be doing something more than she was?

Felicity wondered about the poor man still in custody for the attempted kidnapping. The police chief wasn't happy with her or Tucker since neither of them would say that the prisoner was the kidnapper.

The man had no money for a lawyer and the police chief refused to release him, saying that the man was a material witness in an investigation. The chief was certain the man was the guilty party. The prisoner was the perfect scapegoat—a stranger and black.

Felicity would send Midge with a basket of food for him and try to think of some way to help. She was afraid that if she merely paid his bail or had her lawyer defend him, he might be set free only to suffer abuse outside the jail. Until he could be cleared, he was safer where he was.

Would she ever get used to men patrolling around her house every night? *I would much rather depend on thee, Lord. But sometimes Thee uses human hands to carry out Thy protection.*

Felicity attempted to lie back down and sleep, but she could not stop her mind, and her thoughts—of the fire, of Camie and of Ty—kept her up until dawn.

On Saturday morning, ready for baseball practice, Felicity strolled out into the perfect early November, Indian-summer day. Indian summer, that last breath of summer before winter, had lasted for over a week. At least, that's what Vista and Abel had been happily commenting on for days. Weeks had passed since the fire. Her shoulders had healed and she was feeling herself again. And Thanksgiving would soon be here.

The days fit for baseball were drawing to a close. But today would be perfect for it. Ty and the others should be here soon. She tried to quell her anticipation of seeing Ty again.

Thoughts of Ty brought thoughts of Camie. Felicity had prayed and thought and prayed, and knew no more about who had tried to kidnap Camie than she had the night Tucker had saved her. She didn't know why God had not pointed out who the would-be kidnapper was yet. But she was certain justice would be done—as long as she prevented injustice from being done.

Midge had visited the prisoner still in custody, taking extra food. The man had refused to give his name, much to the police chief's irritation. And the man never said anything to Midge except for "Thank you, miss." What was he hiding?

The bright sun warmed her face, distracting her thoughts. Donnie and Johnny, who'd become best friends over the past few weeks, ran to catch up with her at the tree where they usually sat. Soon everyone had arrived and Felicity, with Donnie and Johnny, settled in to watch another ball practice.

Baseball practice had attracted more and more children so that today, after a time of practice, they might have enough numbers to play a ball game. Eldon Partridge and Ty had the children in parallel lines and were having them practice catching and throwing the ball between the two lines. The sight filled Felicity with deep satisfaction.

"Hi!" Donnie called out, "Hi, lady."

Felicity turned to see who Donnie was waving at. Eldon Partridge's wife was approaching them. Felicity grimaced inwardly, dreading the woman's arrival. "Good morning," she said as cheerfully as she could manage.

"Good morning. I wonder…may I watch the baseball practice with you?"

Of all the words that might have come from this woman's lips, Felicity could not have anticipated these. "Of course! Thee is always welcome here."

"I'm Martha Partridge. My husband says that you don't use titles like 'Mrs'."

"Friends do not."

Martha Partridge had brought a thin cushion, which she put on the grass. She sat, carefully arranging her skirts. She smiled. "I haven't sat on grass for so long."

Felicity imagined that to be correct. The woman didn't seem like the type to enjoy watching sporting events.

Still, Martha watched the children tossing the balls back and forth. And Felicity did likewise. Finally, Martha cleared her throat. "Percy truly enjoys this new game."

"Baseball is a good game for teaching many skills and sportsmanship. How to win or lose like a gentleman or—" Felicity grinned "—a lady."

"I was never allowed to run and play with the boys." Martha sounded wistful. "Mother didn't want me to be what she called a hoyden."

"I'm sorry," Felicity said sincerely and then covered her mouth with one hand in embarrassment.

Martha chuckled. "I am sorry, too."

Felicity smiled. "My parents let me run and play. My best friend was a boy on the next farm. He was always getting us into trouble." Memories of childhood days with Gus tugged at her heart. The limestone grave marker set for him in the Pennsylvania cemetery also pulled at her heart. If only she had been able to love him the way he'd wanted her to—romantically. When would thoughts of him not bring regret?

"You were fortunate." The lady looked down and plucked a blade of grass. "I was wrong to take such a negative attitude toward…"

"My work here with children?"

Martha nodded.

"Would you mind if I asked thee why thee has had a change of heart?"

The woman bent her head and plucked another blade of grass. The children playing ball were calling to each other with eager voices. "The night of the fire, I woke and all I could think of was the chance that the children might be hurt. Or die. It made me think. Children are children. I didn't want anything to happen to Percy or to your children."

Felicity rested a hand on Martha's, truly touched. "Yes, children are precious gifts from God."

Martha looked up, smiling. "And Percy, my son, is so much happier. He used to hate to go to school. I didn't know that the other boys made fun of his clothes. Why didn't he say something?"

"Boys don't like to talk about such things. They think they must handle it themselves. They don't want to be thought…" Felicity's voice faltered.

"Tied to mama's apron strings?" Martha finished for her and shook her head, grinning.

The throwing practice ended. Both women turned toward the game. Ty was calling everyone to count off to form two teams. Some of the children were dancing up and down with excitement. This would be the first time they tried to play a game.

There were many strikes, outs and foul balls chased. Sitting near Felicity, Johnny yelled encouragement. "Hey, Eugene, hit that ball!" Eugene missed and Johnny groaned.

"Katy, hit ball! Hit ball!" Donnie's face glowed with excitement. He hopped up. Felicity noticed that the child was no longer thin. His toothpick legs had filled out and were now sturdy. He jumped up and down like a healthy, happy boy. Tears of joy filled her eyes.

"What's wrong?" Martha asked.

Felicity shook her head, unable to speak.

Katy managed to hit the ball so that it bounced a few times. But she ran as fast as she could. And with all the fumbling by the other team, she made it to first base.

Donnie screeched and jumped up and down. Johnny joined in. Felicity realized that she had risen, too. Martha stood beside her, grinning. Felicity suddenly thought that in some indefinable way, her best childhood friend Gus was there with her, jumping up and down, cheering her on. Tears flowed down her face. She turned her head to hide these.

Gus had been her best friend. But now Ty was the one working beside her, helping these children. She wiped away her tears with her fingertips. Ty had become her champion.

Breathing in the crisp autumn air the week before Thanksgiving, Ty walked from the courthouse to the Barney house. The cases against petty thieves and drunks had petered out early. At only a half hour after the luncheon break, he'd adjourned court. He drew in the clean, fresh air and lengthened his strides. As soon as he'd taken off his judge's robe, he'd known whom he wanted to talk to—Felicity Gabriel.

The two of them had been so busy with work, with baseball, with children, that they hadn't had a moment to do anything concrete about her campaign to change Illinois law. He knew when he announced the purpose for his visit this afternoon, she would spend precious time with him—uninterrupted. The children were all still at school and the house would be quiet.

He found himself smiling. Last night when he left, Camie had said good-night to him without being told to for the very first time. He had read about people who had their hearts warmed. Now he knew that sensation was real. He'd walked home last night, his heart no longer aching. Hope had taken root there. Someday his daughter would let him swing her up into his arms and squeal with happiness.

Hearing the scrape of rakes dragging leaves into piles, he turned up the path to the Barney House. He was greeted by a sudden spate of industrious hammering. Then a sawing sounded. So much for a quiet house. Instead of just repairing what the fire had damaged, Felicity had decided to go ahead and enlarge the dining room. He grinned, waved at the carpenters at work and walked around them to the back door.

"Come in!" Vista called when he knocked.

Ty stepped into the warm kitchen. "I didn't want to make you come to the front door. Is Miss Gabriel at home?"

"She's in her den. Midge has taken the little boys for a walk. And the new maid is busy cleaning." Vista held up her hands, covered with bread dough and flour. "Would you mind showing yourself in, Judge?"

"Not at all." He passed Vista and walked down the freshly scrubbed and painted hall. The outside wall with the bow window had been replaced by a canvas partition, keeping out the wind and the sawdust as the carpenters worked, and muffling the sounds of hammers and saws.

Ty sauntered to the den on the opposite side of the staircase. He halted at its open door. Felicity was bent over papers on her desk. In this rare private moment, he let himself gaze at her. Though she always dressed in modest gray without any lace or intricate tucking, she couldn't hide the fact that she was a very pretty young woman. How had she stayed single? The answer of course was that she had probably turned down proposals. He liked that; he didn't like that.

"Felicity." Her given name was off his tongue before he could call it back.

She glanced up and one of those blazing smiles burst over her face.

He walked in, feeling the pull toward her and for once, not resisting it. "Do you think we might actually have an uninterrupted conversation?" he teased.

The smile sparkled now, bathing him with the warmth of sunshine. He moved to the chair next to her, not across from her. He wanted nothing between them today. "I came to go over the rough draft of my letter to the senators and representatives in the state legislature. I wanted to know what you might want me to add. The legislators are back in session for two weeks."

She glowed in the dim afternoon sunlight. "Wonderful. What shall we—"

The sound of heavy footfalls stopped her. She looked past Ty. The builder appeared at the door.

"Miss, I'm going to have to drive to the lumber yard to see if our order for more quarter-sawn oak for the floors and trim has been finished."

"Excellent," Felicity said. The man hurried away.

Ty thought about closing the door, but of course that would be most improper. The subtle scent of roses came to him from the lady. He drew it in. "I wrote a rough draft last night. I need some information that I know you must have—" he grinned at her "—committed to memory."

"Indeed?" Her glimmering smile turned mischievous.

He loved that quality in her—as if she still retained some of the fresh joy of childhood. He pulled a few folded pages from his pocket. He smoothed them out and then sat back and began reading, "Dear Senator, I am the justice of the peace for Altoona. Prior to the war, I acted as a circuit court judge. As I go about my duties, I am often powerless to rule in a manner I think best for delinquent children under the age of reason…" He read to the end.

"That is an excellent letter, Ty." She reached for it and their hands touched. Neither of them moved. The air around them became charged. He closed his hand over hers. The letter fluttered to the desk and Ty could hardly breathe.

Extricating her hand, Felicity picked up the dropped letter and gazed at it. Within seconds, her prim façade had been put back into place.

He took a deep breath, trying to reestablish their

usual rapport. It wasn't easy. "I was thinking that it might be advisable to prick their vanity."

"Vanity?" She gave him a measuring look.

He was careful to sit up straight again, not lean toward her. "Yes, I thought we might mention what is being done in other states and even England. I think that our state representatives won't want to be thought backward."

"Ah." She nodded, grinning.

He loved the quick intelligence she always showed. "So why don't you tell me more about those women you've mentioned? I can't remember their names."

"Mary Carpenter and Elizabeth Fry." A sudden extra-bright shaft of sunlight gleamed on her wayward curls, which had pulled free of her plain, tight bun. Ty tried to look away.

"You said we should include our own Dorothea Dix. So the representatives will have a precedent for action. The problem, of course, is that special treatment for children will necessitate the raising of funds through taxes for—what did you call them?"

"Reformatories." She tapped the end of her ink pen against her lips as if prodding her thoughts.

Silence settled between them, quiet and companionable, nothing like any moment he'd ever spent with Virginia, who had always been playing one of three parts: injured party, trusting maiden or her most accomplished role, shrew. He pulled his mind back to the present, recalling the very first time Felicity had come to his house. His daughter had sensed Felicity's sincere goodness and had gone to her willingly. *I should have realized then how special this woman is.*

Felicity continued tapping the pen tip against her soft lips.

Ty leaned forward, fascinated by her perfectly shaped mouth. Fascinated by this woman whose every thought was to help others. Such a tender heart he'd rarely known. "Felicity," he whispered. Her eyes connected with his as if she could not look away. His hand drifted up and he brushed her cheek. Once. Twice.

His mouth was dry. He cupped her chin with his open palm. He waited, expecting her to pull away or shake her head. Yet she stayed still, very still, watching. He leaned closer, closer. He couldn't breathe. He pressed his lips to hers. Soft. Exhilarating. Heavenly.

The front door banged open. They jerked apart. "Miss! Miss!" The familiar voice of Donnie echoed in the hall and was joined by Johnny's. "Miss Fesisity! Miss Fesisity!"

Ty leapt up just before the two little boys shot into the room. They crowded around Felicity. "We got peppermints! The man at the store gave us peppermints!"

Midge hovered in the doorway and curtsied. "We were walking through town and the man at the general store came out and gave the boys each a peppermint drop."

Both boys thought that this was the signal to stick out their tongues streaked with red. "See?" Donnie helpfully pointed to his tongue.

Felicity shook with laughter. "Peppermint tongues! How sweet!" She clapped her hands.

Giggling, Midge captured two wrists, one from each of the sticky-handed boys, and shepherded them out. Donnie turned back. With his free hand, he waved at Ty. "Hi!"

Ty waved back at him, unable to do more than that. He was still reeling from the kiss he had bestowed upon Felicity, unsure what to do or say next. When he finally looked back at her, he noted the pink rising up in her pale face. He took every ounce of strength he had not to lean over and kiss the beautiful Felicity again.

Chapter Nine

If possible, Felicity could have shrunk to the size of a white button mushroom. She had just let Tyrone Hawkins kiss her. No one had ever kissed her before. At twelve, Gus had tried and been sternly rebuked. And he'd never tried again—even when he proposed marriage. *What was I thinking?* Felicity realized that she was trembling.

She sat down in her chair and folded her hands to keep him from seeing them shake. The rigid wood of her desk chair forced her to sit up straight, reassuring her that she was still a mature and intelligent woman, a woman of strict principles. A woman who never planned to marry and did not engage in flirtation.

Felicity tried to still her inner mutiny and draw breath normally. "Your suggestions are very apt. I will write you a list of reformers here and abroad, and what measures other states and England are taking toward dealing with youthful offenders."

"Fine. Excellent," he said, sounding distracted. Flustered. He sat down where he had been before the boys—so fortunately—interrupted them. "And I've already made a list of everyone in Illinois who might be influential or favorably disposed toward these changes."

Reading the signs of his own discomfiture, she hoped that he was just as shocked as she. If so, this... amazing, astonishing kiss, no, this lapse of decorum wouldn't be repeated. Even as she thought these words, she felt her face increase in temperature. Her face must be bright crimson now. But she could not be sorry. *I have been kissed by a wonderful man.*

Both of them kept their focus studiously on the list of names he was showing her. But before Felicity's eyes, the letters jigged up and down. She couldn't stop her inner shaking, the heady sensation.

Then she heard a door slam with unusual vehemence. She rose. *What now?* "Please, thee must excuse me. I don't allow door slamming in the house." He rose out of courtesy. She reached the door and halted there. "Jack, I didn't know you were here."

The older man came up the hall toward her, looking upset. "Miss Gabriel, I dropped by to give a message to Vista."

"Oh?" Felicity tried to read more from his somber expression.

"I didn't think I was doing anything wrong." He stopped and stood, bending his hat with both hands.

"What has happened, Jack?" she asked. "I heard a door slam."

"That was Vista. I give her the message and she just turned and ran into her room and slammed the door."

"What kind of message was this, Jack?" Felicity asked, her mind whirling with possibilities.

Jack did more damage to his cloth hat. "You see, I been meaning to go down to the jail and visit the man who they say started your fire." He nodded toward the opposite side of the house where the carpenters still pounded nails and sawed boards. "But with one thing and another, I didn't get there till today."

"Why did you want to visit him?" Ty asked.

Jack looked over at him. "Hello, Judge, sorry I didn't see you there. I went because I thought he might need help. Our congregation doesn't have much money but we'd try to help, you know. And my granddaughter Midge told me he wasn't a rough man, but a polite one. So I went to see him." Jack pursed his lips and then said, "The man told me his name and asked me if I knew a woman of color by the name of Vista."

"Vista?" Felicity parroted Jack, tingling with unpleasant surprise.

"Yes, miss. I didn't want to disappoint the man. So I came straight here and talked to Vista in the kitchen. I told her that this man wanted to see her. That's why he came to Altoona and asked for the Barney house. He said that he'd heard that she was working for Mrs. Barney. When I told Vista his name, I was afraid she'd faint. I took her arm but she pulled away and ran into her room and slammed the door."

When Jack fell silent, Felicity stared at him. Vista had run away and slammed her door?

"The man gave you his name?" Ty asked. "He wouldn't give it to the police. Why would he give it to you?"

Jack began to rotate his hat brim within his hands. "He said he been waiting for them to let him go. He didn't want to be known to have been in jail before he got to talk to Vista again."

Felicity questioned, "What did thee think of this man, Jack?"

"I think he's an honest man, miss."

Felicity nodded thoughtfully. "I am of the same opinion. When I saw him that day he appeared frightened and sad, not defiant and guilty."

"You can tell if a man's guilty by just looking at him?" Ty said skeptically.

"Not always. But much can be read from a man's stance and in his eyes," Felicity replied.

Ty didn't look as if he believed this, but she couldn't let that sway her.

"Perhaps I should go to Vista." Felicity looked to Jack for advice.

"That's why I came to get you, miss." Jack stopped mangling his hat.

Felicity nodded decisively. "Do not worry, Jack. Thee has done right, not wrong. I thank thee." She turned to Ty.

The full force of his effect on her gusted against her

like a blast of wind. She clung to her self-control. "I must bid thee good day, Tyrone."

"I understand." He paused, looking confused. "I will take what we have worked on and I'll bring another draft. May I?"

"Please. I am very pleased with our progress and thy support." She knew she should offer him her hand, but she couldn't risk that. Touching him might undo her.

Ty hesitated, glancing at Jack and Felicity. Then he excused himself.

"Miss, the prisoner told me I could tell you his name, as well as Vista."

She heard Ty close the front door behind him. "What is his name?" she asked, shrugging away her sudden sense of loss.

"Charles Scott." Jack bobbed his head, donned his hat and departed without another word.

Felicity stood alone in her den, listening to the voices of Donnie and Johnny, who must have gone outside to play. This day had dawned like any other. Nonetheless, it had turned into an extraordinary day. Tyrone Hawkins had kissed her.

Felicity gripped the edge of the pocket door to steady herself. Center herself. She closed her eyes and prayed, "Holy Spirit, guide me. Show me the way Thee wants me to go." She whispered that to herself several times. A measure of composure returned.

Her first inclination was to go to Vista and try to talk to her. But she hadn't lived with Vista these past months without realizing that her housekeeper was an intensely private woman. No, she would let Vista come out when she felt she could face others again.

Felicity walked to the kitchen. Midge was just finishing shaping the yeast dough into six loaves of bread. "Midge, thee is taking over the kitchen while Vista is indisposed?"

"Yes, miss. I thought I better." The young woman looked confused and worried.

Felicity patted her shoulder. "We will not bother Vista. When they come home, I will watch the children. Does thee think thee can go on with preparing supper?"

"Yes, miss. We're just having the soup here in the pots and bread."

Felicity nodded her thanks and patted Midge's shoulder once more. "We will do what is in our power and let God take care of the rest."

Midge assented to this and began putting the loaves in the buttered pans.

Felicity walked to the back door and went outside to give Donnie and Johnny a few moments of attention.

Ty's unbelievable kiss lingered on her lips. She fought the urge to touch them—as if touching them would make the kiss feel real. *Ty Hawkins kissed me.* And this had opened a door to completely new and radical feelings. She glanced at the window of Vista's room.

Yet in spite of this lightness, her heart was heavy for Vista. What had driven her into her room?

* * *

The next morning a subdued Vista came out of her room and cooked breakfast and went about her duties. She offered no explanation for her absence the day before. And uncertain what was best, Felicity asked for none. What had brought about this marked change? Should Felicity intervene or continue to give Vista her privacy?

Vista appeared to have retreated within herself. She went about her duties but no smile touched her mouth or eyes. Even the children became serious in her presence. They were no doubt accustomed to her giving them orders and urging them to eat more. Her silence had communicated itself to the children, who went quietly off to school without the usual last-minute hectic rush to find papers and books.

Felicity walked to her den and sat at her desk. Her mind was quickly overwhelmed with the memory of Ty's kiss here in this room just a day ago. She pressed fingertips to her mouth. She felt the touch of his lips on hers. Closing her eyes, she savored the remembrance. If one was going to get only one kiss in a lifetime, was it better or worse that the kiss had the power to shake, tempt her?

She rose without any answer. *I can't sit here. I have work to do.* She marched to the hall tree in the foyer and put on her bonnet and gloves. She let herself out the door and crept down the steps—she wanted to walk to town, not be driven by Abel. With a wave to the carpenters, she scurried down the street. Soon she was approaching the jail, a place she didn't really want to go. But if Vista refused to reveal why she was upset, perhaps the prisoner would.

She stepped inside and approached the desk where a man sat, reading the morning newspaper. "Good morning."

The young officer dropped the paper to the desk and sprang to his feet. "Ma'am, what may I do for you?"

"I've come to visit a prisoner. The man who is accused of burning the Barney house. If thee pleases."

"You're that Quaker woman."

She nodded.

He stared at her as if trying to make up his mind.

"Prisoners may receive visitors, may they not?" she asked.

"Yeah, I mean, yes, ma'am." Still, he made no move to take her to the man.

"Will thee please take me to the prisoner?" She looked around at the barred windows and row of rifles hung on the wall.

"Ladies don't usually come to the jail," the young man stammered.

"No doubt thee is correct, but I am a lady who does unusual things." She smiled. "Please."

Shaking his head, he reached for a large ring with two keys. He waved her to precede him through the door to the inner hall, the keys clanking. "Now, ma'am, you can't give the prisoner anything we haven't looked at first. And you can't touch him. You just got to stand outside the cell. And I got to stand back and watch you."

"As thee wishes," she agreed. This was her first visit to a jail, though her father had gone to the nearby jail whenever he could to minister to the prisoners. She was pleased to see that everything here was clean and neat.

"Hey, you, stand up," the jailer called out. "This lady is visiting you, so watch your manners."

The prisoner rose from the bare cot where he sat. He approached the bars with caution.

"Good morning to thee." She greeted him with what she hoped was a warm smile.

"You're the lady Midge told me about." Holding the bar with both hands, he studied her.

She lowered her voice to almost a whisper. "I hear that thee came to town to visit someone who lives at my house."

He nodded.

"Can thee tell me anything else?" she asked.

He gripped the bars more tightly. "No, ma'am. This is a private matter."

She nodded. "I will send Midge again with more food. Does thee need anything else?"

"No, ma'am, I thank you," he said.

Felicity bubbled with unasked questions. But here in front of this guard, she didn't feel comfortable in trying to pry from this man what he did not want known. She bid him farewell and allowed herself to be escorted out to the office area.

The police chief walked in, halting at sight of her. "Miss Gabriel?"

She nodded and offered him her hand. And hoped he wouldn't ask her any questions.

"What brings you here, miss? Did you finally decide that our prisoner is the one who broke into your house?"

"No, I did not. I do not think I will ever be able to make that identification. I just came to see him for myself now that I am better. I must bid thee good day." She smiled and walked out, thankful that gentlemen could not insist on answers from ladies. She walked briskly down the wooden sidewalk, wondering at this new puzzle.

Puzzles, secrets and plots. These were not what she had expected in this new place. But since no one would tell her what they knew, she had to make do with what she had and start unraveling the mysteries. Or the children might suffer. Or Vista.

That afternoon she sat at the kitchen table with Tucker and a pile of books. A savory stew simmered in two large pots on the nearby wood stove. Tucker was reading aloud about the writing of the Declaration of Independence. Usually Vista would have been there, busy making cookies or something else for the children for after school. Her absence was louder, more prominent than her presence had been.

Tucker stopped, looked up at her and muttered, "Is Vista going to be all right?"

His question took her by surprise. She took a chance and laid her hand on his sleeve. "I hope so."

"What upset her?" he asked, still keeping his voice low.

"I don't know. Sometimes people have...secrets, troubles from the past. And sometimes something happens to stir everything up." A totally inept reply.

Tucker nodded solemnly. "I like Vista."

Felicity smiled. "I do, too. Now let's discuss what thee has just read."

The boy made a face. "What do I need to know this stuff for?"

"Someday thee will be a grown man and thee will vote. Thee must know the history of how our nation was established."

Tucker began punching the point of his pencil through the paper he had been practicing his penmanship on. "You should send me away."

This pronouncement shocked Felicity into gaping silence.

Tucker looked up. "More trouble will come. As long as I'm here."

"Will thee tell me what thee means?" she said.

He shook his head and began reading aloud about Thomas Jefferson.

Secrets, troubles from the past, puzzles and plots. Her mind hummed like a beehive in spring. She placed a hand on each side of her head as if holding in all the questions, buzzing within. *Lord, reveal whatever I need to know for the safety of the children Thee has put into my care.*

As Ty left the courthouse, he noted it was one of those austere November days. He had stayed away from Felicity for a few days—since the kiss. As much as he tried to put it behind him, he couldn't. Thoughts of Felicity plagued him in every undisciplined moment. Though he knew it impossible, he wanted her to be closer. But he wasn't a good candidate for marriage. And she had made it plain by her reaction that she was not going to kiss him again.

Still, when court had adjourned early, he hadn't been able to keep his feet from heading straight for her door. Around her large yard, the maple trees were already bare. Fragile bronze leaves flew from oak trees with every gust of wind. The harvest had been nearly finished outside of town. Wagons rumbled into town every day carrying grain in fifty-pound bags to be shipped south on barges.

At the Barney house, the children were playing in their new winter coats. Soon, snow would come and the baseball games would turn to sledding parties and snowball fights.

He approached the back door. Nearby, his mother was teaching three girls a rhyme while they swung a long rope in circles. Dee Dee was jumping. The neighborhood girls chanted, "Mabel, Mabel, set the table. Do it fast as you are able."

He paused, watching the children, looking for his daughter. He found Camie with Tucker, who was evidently helping her practice swinging the bat. He had his arms around her and was helping her hold up the heavy bat. Tucker glanced around and saw him. "Hey, Judge, come here."

Ty didn't appreciate the less than respectful tone, but decided not to take offense. Tucker had shown his true colors the night Camie had nearly been abducted. "What can I do for you, son?"

"These bats are too heavy for the little kids," Tucker said.

Ty nodded. "I've noticed that, too."

"Well, what are you going to do about it?" Tuck asked.

"What do you think I should do?" Ty countered.

"Get one of those carpenters—" Tucker pointed toward the workman busy at the side of the house "—to make us a few lighter, shorter ones."

"Yes, please," Camie added.

Once again, Camie had spoken to him. This still had the power to stop him. For a moment, he couldn't speak. "I'll do that, children."

He turned and walked toward the carpenters. His little girl was speaking to him. He snapped a tight control on his emotions. He couldn't let on that inside, he was dancing a highland jig. And Felicity Gabriel was the one who'd brought about this change. How could he not want to be near her?

* * *

That evening, Ty had been invited to stay for dinner on the chilly back porch along with his mother. The canvas curtains had been pulled down and tied. Though the night wind had calmed, it reminded Ty that the dining room must be finished soon, before the harsher winds of early winter blew in. After serving the two little boys on either side of him, he helped himself and then passed the heaping bowl of mashed potatoes to Felicity. He took special care not to touch her hand.

"I like mashed potatoes," Johnny told him.

"I must agree," Ty said. Johnny and his friend Donnie always made their preference for his company clear. They liked to sit one on either side of him. After months of feeling as if he were a monster in the eyes of his daughter and other children, this was healing something raw inside him. Of course, he would never admit it aloud but the admiration and approval in their eyes was a rare blessing.

Camie had taken to sitting near his mother and he could see that this was lifting her spirits, too. Was it possible that his child would soon be healed and come home?

He owed such a debt to Felicity. He tried to keep his eyes from drifting toward her, but he might as well try to change the way the wind chose to blow. He made himself look down at his plate.

"Ty," Felicity addressed him, "has thee made any

progress in persuading more influential men to write about changing laws governing juveniles?"

He turned to her. "Yes, the mayor and several on the town council will write letters. Also several other attorneys around the state."

"Excellent." She beamed at him.

He nodded and looked away from her vivid smile, afraid he might express more than he wished with his eyes. This woman didn't miss much.

"What kind of laws?" Tucker asked.

"Ty, why doesn't thee answer that?" Felicity said.

"Tucker, Miss Gabriel and I agree that children under the age of reason should not be held to the same standard and suffer the same punishments as adults." Ty kept his gaze on the boy, not letting it drift to Felicity.

"What would that mean? Kids could do anything and not be put in jail?" Tucker asked.

"No, but if a child fell afoul of the law, he wouldn't be sent to an adult prison. There should be a place where the young have a chance to change for the better."

"You mean like this place?" the boy asked.

"Yes, something like this," Ty replied, helping Donnie to another biscuit. "According to Miss Gabriel, they are called reformatories."

Eyes downcast, Tucker stirred his mashed potatoes. "That's a good idea. Is there one of those places anywhere close?"

"Why do you ask that?" Ty paused with his fork in midair.

"I think that's where I should go," Tucker said. "You know, a place like that. Away from here."

"No, Tucker, I don't want you to go," Camie objected.

Tucker reached over and tugged one of her braids. "Don't get excited, Braids." Camie appeared pleased by his teasing.

Ty looked to Felicity.

She mouthed, "Later."

He nodded and asked Eugene what he'd learned in school that day, though what he really wanted to do was press Tucker for more. Ty suspected Tucker thought he should leave because he was attracting danger. And if that was the case, Ty was no longer sure he wanted the boy anywhere near his daughter, yet how to protect the boy from himself?

Felicity led Ty to her den that evening after supper. She knew she should not be bringing him back to the very place where they had kissed. But she did want to discuss the letters to legislators and the hope of a re-formatory in Illinois.

I will keep a polite distance.

"What is behind Tucker Stout wanting to leave this place?" Ty asked without any preamble.

She stared into Tyrone's dark eyes. A mistake. She sat down behind her desk, making sure that her spine did not touch the chair. "I don't know. This is the second time that he has said that he should go some-where else."

Ty sat down. "Do you think it has something to do with that night?"

She knew exactly what he meant. "He has said that we would be safer if he weren't here."

"Troubling," Ty said.

"I think—I may be wrong, but I think he knew the man who broke in." Felicity straightened the papers on her desk.

Ty captured her attention with his fierce stare. "Why do you say that?"

"Just a feeling. But I know children and I've gotten to know Tucker. He's carrying some heavy load, some burden." She shook her head, dissatisfied with her own reply.

"I don't discount your intuition. You've shown great insight and wisdom, especially with Camie. Did you hear her talk to me tonight?" Ty's faced glowed with happiness.

Felicity had to repress the inclination to reach for his hand. *This man is dangerous to me, dangerous to my calling.*

He glanced away and reached into his pocket. "Here is the list of men. I sent each a letter, outlining what the problem is as we see it and the advances being made elsewhere, and appealed for their support."

She took the list and read the dozen names there. "Thank thee, Tyrone Hawkins. Thee is a good man."

He smiled at her and before she could do a thing to stop it, her attraction to him overpowered her.

As if drawn by an unseen string, she rose and moved toward him. He rose also. Both of them moved forward inch by inch. Felicity couldn't deny the thrumming of her pulse. He was going to kiss her again. And she was going to let him. But at the last minute, he stepped back, breaking their connection. "If you don't mind, I think I'll go spend time with Camie. I can never thank you enough for all you have done for her."

She hid her chagrin—chagrin at herself and him. "It has been my joy to help Camie. I hope that someday she will wish to go home and just visit here."

He bowed and left her so quickly that she stood where she was, pondering what had just happened.

She had intended to stick to their easy friendship. What had that to do with her wanting to hold his hand and moving toward him? For what? An embrace, a second kiss? *What's happening to me? I've never felt this pull toward a man before.*

Then she heard the door open and rapid footsteps coming up the hallway toward her. She pulled herself together. To her immense surprise and dismay, Alice Crandall appeared in her doorway.

"Good evening, Miss Gabriel. I saw through the window that you were here in your office. I didn't want to disturb your staff so I let myself in."

Felicity tried to read the woman's elegant face. All

she gleaned was a smooth façade. Felicity was certain Alice had come up with another ploy to get her own way. Suddenly she felt so very tired. But politeness dictated her response. "Won't thee have a seat and tell me what has brought thee here tonight?"

Ty came back from supervising the children washing up in the kitchen, and headed for Felicity's office. He wanted to take leave of her. It was a school night and Midge was getting the children to bed. As he came up the hall, he heard a familiar and unpleasant voice in the den.

"I think it's time you heard my side of the story, my late daughter's side of the story."

He stopped at the bottom of the staircase in the foyer. Her side? He almost turned away, not wanting to eavesdrop. But then he thought Felicity might be glad to have someone help her show Alice to the door.

"What story is thee talking about, Alice?"

"My daughter Virginia was a beautiful girl and she had the most delicate nature. I always took great pains to shelter her from the storms of life. She wasn't strong, you see."

If Virginia didn't get her way, she was strong enough to throw tantrums for hours that could be heard a block away. Ty fumed in silence.

"So many men courted her. She could have married ten times over, but she chose Tyrone Hawkins, her one true love."

Virginia's one true love was herself. Ty began chewing the inside of his cheek, a habit that living with Virginia had caused.

"Alas, she chose the wrong man," Alice complained.

"Indeed?" Felicity commented, sounding unconvinced.

Just try to pull black wool over this woman's eyes, Alice. Ty rested a hand on the staircase railing.

"Tyrone didn't seem to understand my daughter's fragile condition. Then the war started. Virginia had just miscarried. I nearly lost her that time."

"I am very sorry to hear that," Felicity said sincerely.

"Tyrone didn't care at all," Alice moaned. "He enlisted as soon as she was able to leave her bed. Virginia begged him on her knees not to leave her when she needed him so."

Ty remembered that awful scene. Virginia had enacted it in front of a roomful of Alice's cronies. In steamy waves, anger began rising in him.

"As a Friend, I do not participate in or support any war. But this war had a moral aspect. Slavery was what broke our nation apart—"

"I have no interest in politics," Alice interrupted. "I only know that my frail daughter needed her husband and he left her. She wept for weeks and would barely eat a morsel. And then Virginia found herself with child. She wrote to Tyrone telling him he must come home or she might not make it through the pregnancy."

Ty was blazing now. He remembered those tactics

all too well. If Virginia didn't get her way, she'd starve herself and then go out in public and faint. *She should have taken to the stage.*

"Then Ty finally came home on furlough," Alice said. "I thought he'd see the state Virginia was in, but no, he did not. He went back to war."

"I don't believe that soldiers are allowed to quit the army for that reason," Felicity said, sounding unimpressed.

"We have friends in the state house and the U.S. Congress. We could have arranged an honorable discharge for him," Alice insisted.

Both Alice and Virginia had lived in a dream world of their own. Facts and reality were not allowed. Facts and reality were expected to obey their whims. Ty gripped the carved walnut finial on the railing until his knuckles were white.

"I sincerely doubt that," Felicity said, putting his thoughts into words. "And I doubt that any man would want one under those circumstances."

"You are a cold woman," Alice snapped. "I saw that from the first time we met. No one will ever make me believe that Tyrone Hawkins's callousness wasn't the cause of my daughter's decline. I have said it before and I'll say it again. Tyrone Hawkins killed my daughter."

"That is a serious charge," Felicity said. "What I want to know is why Camie is so afraid of the night. Can thee tell me?"

"It doesn't lie with me," Alice said. "She was never

pampered and spoiled at my house. After her mother died, I put her in the care of a nurse. And I told her not to coddle the child. That only feeds a child's disobedient nature." Alice huffed loudly. "If Camille wanted to cry herself to sleep every night, that was her choice. In time, she would have learned that those tactics don't work in my house. So I've come tonight to appeal to your better nature. My granddaughter needs discipline and I can give her that. Her father killed my daughter, and he and his mother have ruined that child."

Ty realized he was gripping the finial so tightly that soon he would snap it from the railing. He heard a chair pushed back in haste.

"I am very glad that thee has come to give me thy side of the story, Alice Crandall," Felicity said, her voice loud and firm. "It is plain to me that thee would do anything, say anything, to get what thee wants. And from what thee has said, thy daughter was the same. I am very sorry that thee lost thy daughter. Nevertheless, no power on earth would prompt me to give even a stray cat into your care."

A second chair was shoved back and hit the den wall. Ty took a step forward, then halted.

"You are a woman without conduct," Alice accused. "I will do whatever I can to ruin you and this orphanage. I will have my granddaughter back."

"No, thee will not," Felicity said.

His mother-in-law shouted a vile epithet and then charged out of the den. She saw him in the foyer and cursed him, too. "You killed my daughter!" Then she stepped out and slammed the door so hard that the glass in the windows rattled.

Ty hurried into the den. Felicity was flushed and shaking with obvious outrage. He threw his arms around her and pulled her to him. "There, there, don't let her upset you."

"That woman," she said. She shuddered in his arms. "I'm so sorry for you, Ty, and for Camie. That awful woman."

Her warm sympathy and outrage on his family's behalf overwhelmed his good sense. He stroked her hair and cradled her in his arms. "Alice is not important. And Virginia is gone."

"Someone like Alice Crandall, entrenched in her own self will, can be dangerous." Felicity lay her head in the crook of his neck. "I couldn't believe what she was saying to me, obviously misrepresenting the facts. She must have no conscience left."

She doesn't. Ty kissed Felicity's cheek.

"I can't imagine living with someone like Virginia." Felicity looked into his eyes. "I know I shouldn't speak ill of the dead, but how could she torture thee just because there was a war on?"

"It doesn't matter now." *Because you are here. And you are nothing like Virginia.* He tucked her closer within his embrace.

Felicity suddenly broke from his arms. "Thee shouldn't be holding me."

Had she even noticed he had kissed her? Part of him wanted to take her into his arms and kiss her until she could think of nothing but kissing him back. Another part ordered him to stand back. Alice Crandall's visit had not changed their circumstances. Just because Felicity turned to him and he had turned to her in a moment of stress meant nothing.

The sound of many footsteps forced Ty to distance himself further from Felicity. The children crowded in the doorway. "Story time! It's time to read us a bedtime story!"

She smiled at them. "Have you all brushed your teeth?"

Nodding, the children grinned. They scampered toward the stairs and clattered up them.

Ty took a deep breath. "My mother and I will be leaving then, too."

"I bid thee good-night."

He didn't look at her as he left the room. His mother was donning her hat and gloves in the foyer. He took his hat and coat off a peg and offered her his arm. Although he heard Felicity's soft footsteps behind him, he did not turn around.

I will not be ruled by my ephemeral emotions. He just had to convince himself of that—and soon.

A few weeks later, the cutting winds of December had come. Felicity donned a sweater and heavy shawl, and walked between Camie and Tucker on their way to town. Camie was skipping and Tucker kept trying to hide his smile.

Camie had been kept home for the morning because

Felicity felt it would do her relationship with her father some good if Camie saw Ty in his respected role as judge. Tucker was going to get new shoes today. His old ones were on the verge of falling apart. And he was the last of the children to get his pair.

"We got a late start this morning, so Tucker, we'll stop at Mr. Baker's store for your shoes first. Then you can take them home and I'll take Camie to the courthouse so she can see what her father does every day."

Tucker looked around Felicity. "Braids, don't you know what your dad does?"

Camie stopped skipping and gripped Felicity's hand tighter. "No."

"Of course not," Felicity said. "She's been too young to go to court and see her father. She wouldn't have understood."

"I wouldn't have understood," Camie parroted.

"I guess." Tucker began to whistle and kick a pebble along.

Felicity tried not to let her spirits take flight just because she was going to see Ty again. See the man who had kissed her—who might kiss her again. Caution whispered in her ear but she refused to let it tamper with her bliss.

Felicity reveled in the bright, cheery sunshine and disregarded the sharp wind, reciting Browning to herself. "God's in His Heaven; All's right with the world." What could go wrong on a day like today?

Chapter Ten

Felicity led Camie up the steps of the courthouse, hoping this outing would be another bridge between Camie and her father.

"This is a big place," Camie said, staring up at the ornate building topped with a dome.

"Yes, and it is also a very serious place. We must not talk and we must sit very quietly." In spite of her cautious words, Felicity tried to keep her rising anticipation in check. "Thy father will be the most important man in this courtroom."

"He will?" Camie said, sounding awed.

"Yes. Thy father holds a very important position." She was smiling, not only with her mouth but with all of her. "He is the one who decides who is guilty of breaking the law and who is not. And he is the one who decides what must be done to persuade people to do right, not wrong."

"Oh," Camie said.

Felicity was going to be free to sit and watch Ty and no one would think it unseemly of her.

Felicity squeezed Camie's hand to reassure her. "He is a very wise and good man." Camie looked puzzled at this.

As they walked to the courtroom, Camie looked around her and kept up with Felicity. The bailiff looked surprised to see her with a little girl. But she merely nodded her greeting and led Camie to a seat in the visitor's area. Felicity had timed their visit just right. At the end of the midmorning recess, the court was now about to resume. The bailiff called everyone to rise. Ty entered and took the judgment seat.

He looked startled to see them, but an irresistible smile spread over his face. Every bit of Felicity wanted to rise from the hard bench and go to him. Instead, she smiled and bent to whisper to Camie why everyone had risen as her father entered.

The court proceedings were quiet and few. Though Felicity was certain that most all the conversation was far above Camie's understanding, the little girl watched with evident fascination.

When the lunch recess was announced, Felicity led Camie to her father. "Good day, Ty. As thee can see, I brought thy daughter along so that she could see where thee works. And know what an important man her father is." She beamed at him, flushed with pleasure.

"I don't know how important I am," Ty replied, sounding uncomfortable with her words. But he smiled, too, his face lifting into happy curves. "Hello, Camie. Why aren't you in school?"

"Miss Felicity said that I could stay home this morning. She said that she wanted me to learn something else." Camie spoke up without hesitation, though she still clung to Felicity's hand.

"And what was that?" Ty stooped down.

"She was teaching me about what you do. That you decide who's done right and who's done wrong."

"Well, I'm impressed, Camie. Well done." Ty's voice betrayed how deeply this simple exchange was affecting him.

"I wonder if Camie might see thy office." Felicity glowed with satisfaction over Camie speaking to Ty.

"Would you like to see my office, Camie?"

Camie nodded vigorously.

Ty offered her his hand. Camie took it. And Felicity rejoiced on. Despite all the unanswered questions about the fire and near-kidnapping plaguing her present life, she saw that progress with reuniting Camie and her father had been made. Perhaps by Christmas, Camie would be home with her father and grandmother, where she belonged. A touch of sadness trickled into Felicity's mood. She banished it as unworthy.

With evident pride, Ty showed off his daughter to the county prosecutor, and several law clerks. Camie sat in the big chair at his desk and asked many questions about the room.

Finally, Felicity excused them. "I must get Camie

to school. Her lunch is there and she wants to eat with Katy."

Ty walked them down the steps of the courthouse, and paused. He took one of her hands and one of Camie's. "Thank you for coming."

Felicity read the gratitude in his dark eyes. She nodded, suddenly unable to speak.

"I…" Ty started.

A colleague hailed him to go to lunch. Ty hesitated, then squeezed her hand. "Thank you. Thank you for everything." He kissed Camie's forehead and then hurried away.

Felicity felt warm and cozy inside. Her hand quivered from his touch. She understood his hesitation here in public. That made it hard for a man to put his feelings into words. She hummed to herself as she and Camie walked down the cobbled streets, the cold wind hurrying them along, but it could not touch her inner glow. At the school, Felicity explained to Camie's teacher where they had spent the morning. At the teacher's request, she promised she would ask Tyrone if a few of the older students might visit the court and observe how a court worked. This conversation was not lost on Camie, who looked proud that her father was someone who impressed her teacher.

When Felicity reached home, she walked up the steps and into the foyer where she took off her bonnet and gloves. She entered the warm, welcoming kitchen, hoping that Vista would be feeling better today.

Still subdued, Vista looked up but said nothing.

"Am I in time for the noon meal?" Felicity asked, her happiness tempered by her friend's sad look.

"I see Abel coming." Vista nodded toward the back windows. "And Midge is at the pump washing Donnie and Johnny's hands. They been playing in the last piles of leaves all morning."

"Excellent." Reassured by Vista's being able to perform her usual routine, Felicity went to the back door. She opened it to welcome Abel and the others into the kitchen. Now that the dining room was enclosed, they usually took their meals there. But when the children were at school and there were only the few of them, they sat in the cozy, warm kitchen. "Abel, isn't Tucker coming to eat?"

"He never come back from goin' to the store with you," Abel replied, looking surprised.

Felicity halted where she stood, Tucker's words suddenly ringing in her mind: "You should send me away—more trouble will come as long as I'm here."

A feeling of dread stole over her as she sent up a silent prayer for Tucker's safety—she knew instantly something was very, very wrong.

Had he run away to protect her and the children?

By the time the children had returned from school, Felicity's nerves were fraying. She could remain idle no longer. She had to find Tucker.

He had been so happy to have new shoes for the coming winter. He'd been so proud of them. Why would he run away? She was in the foyer when someone sounded the brass knocker. She opened the door and there stood Ty. Relief washed through her. Help had come. "Ty, I'm so—"

"I have bad news for you," Ty said in a cheerless tone, his expression shuttered.

"Tucker," she breathed. "He's been hurt."

"No." Ty wouldn't meet her eyes. "He's back in jail."

Felicity gaped at him. Her ears filled with a humming.

Ty took her arm. "Here, sit down on the steps. You look faint."

She sat on the hard step and looked up into his face, so full of concern for her. "What has happened?"

Ty's face twisted with displeasure. "I'd give anything not to have to tell you this. Tucker snatched another purse. Just like he did to you."

"No." She knew this could not have happened. "No."

"The facts are very straightforward," Ty said gently. "Hogan was there again and nabbed him. I'm very sor—"

"Hogan was there? Isn't that odd?" she asked.

"No, Hogan's beat is the wharf and that's where this happened."

Felicity rose, her pulse racing. "Where is Tucker?"

"He's in jail, as I said. And since he has violated the terms of his probation, he will be sent to the state prison as soon as possible to serve his year sentence."

"Tucker did not steal anything." As she spoke these

words, the truth of them glowed within her. "I must call on Mrs. Barney's lawyer."

Ty caught her sleeve. "Felicity, that will do no good. Tucker will come before me tomorrow. He'll be asked what his plea is." His voice begged for her to understand. "But no matter the outcome, I must go through with the terms of my previous sentencing. He has broken his probation by stealing—"

Felicity looked into Ty's troubled eyes and knew without a doubt that he was wrong. "I absolutely refuse to believe this. Tucker is not the same boy he was when he came to me over three months ago. He has changed."

Ty shook his head, looking miserable. "Old habits die hard."

"Why would he steal?" she asked, sizzling with sudden irritation. "We had just been to Baker's to buy new shoes. He has everything he could need or want. This doesn't make sense, Ty." *Can't thee see that?*

They stared at one another. Felicity read sorrowful disbelief in his face. She ached over it. "Ty, thee can't tell me that thee thinks the boy who saved thy daughter would do this?"

He flung out both hands. "How can I argue with the facts? Hogan brought him in and gave a full account of what he saw."

Felicity stood straighter. "Then Hogan is lying."

Ty couldn't believe his ears. Felicity had always been so much more logical than most women. This unexpected irrational thinking snapped him like the end of a whip. "That doesn't make sense," he said, trying not to let his disappointment show in his voice.

"Did anyone else see this purse-snatching?" she demanded.

"Yes, the man who lost his purse came to the station with Hogan and preferred charges." Did she think that he was happy about this failure? He tried to soften his tone. "There is no doubt of Tucker's guilt—"

"Yes, there is doubt," she insisted. "Tucker told both thee and me that he should leave this place for our safety. And we know that someone tried to steal thy daughter from this house. Something isn't right here in Altoona. Not right at all."

Fuming silently, Ty folded his arms and shook his head. Why couldn't she accept the facts? "No. There is no proof of any connection between—"

"Miss Felicity!" Camie ran into the hall. "Miss Vista says that Tucker isn't home. Where did he go? Oh, hello."

His daughter had just greeted him. He wanted to pick her up, but was afraid to take any action that might upset her. Then the full impact of Tucker's dilemma hit him. A cold brick settled in Ty's stomach. Camie loved Tucker. *And I must send him to prison for a year.*

Felicity glanced into his eyes. "Camie, there has been a misunderstanding—"

"There has been no misunderstanding." Aggravation with Felicity's denial unraveled his nerves. Didn't she know that he would have given anything not to have to be the one telling his daughter this? But even when sad or hurtful, truth and reality must be faced.

Felicity gripped his sleeve. "No," she whispered.

Putting off the inevitable never won anything but more unhappiness. As he had this morning in his courtroom, Ty stooped down to speak to his only child. "I'm afraid that your friend Tucker tried to steal something. He won't be coming back here."

Camie stared at him openmouthed. "Not ever again?"

Her crestfallen expression cut him in two. "He may come back but it will be a long time. He has to go to jail."

"But Tucker is a good boy. He wouldn't steal," Camie insisted and looked up. "That's right, isn't it, Miss Felicity? We're good children and we wouldn't do anything like that."

"I believe so," Felicity admitted.

"Camie, I don't want to send Tucker to jail—" Ty said.

"No! I don't want Tucker to be in jail." Camie's voice was rising shrilly. "Miss Felicity, I want Tucker back!"

"I will do my best—" Felicity began.

Camie turned to him. "You're the judge. You tell those people at the jail that Tucker is good. Miss Felicity said you decide who has done right and who had done wrong. You can tell them."

He tried to reach for Camie.

She pulled away. "Tell them!"

"That's not the way it works," he said, knowing that his words were futile. How could he make his little girl understand the complexities of the law?

Felicity knelt down beside him. "Camie, dear, it looks bad for Tucker now. But we must have faith that we can prove that he is innocent. Now go and stay with Midge. I must go talk to my lawyer so he can help Tucker."

Camie looked to him again. "But you said my daddy was the judge and he decided."

"I will do everything I can to prove that Tucker is a good boy." Felicity patted her shoulder.

Camie looked into her father's eyes. Her face and voice turned hard with accusation. "Why isn't my daddy in jail? He killed my mama."

Ty couldn't swallow. Shock riveted him to the floor.

"Camie," Felicity objected, "that isn't true. Thy father didn't kill thy mother. She died of influenza, a disease. Thy grandmother Louise told me that."

"My other grandma told me." Camie's face was turning a dark red. "She said my papa killed my mama. She told me."

Ty clenched his fists, holding in a shout of rage. *That woman.*

Felicity folded Camie into her arms. "Camie, people say things like that when they are angry or upset. But when thy mother died, thy father was far away at the war. He couldn't have had anything to do with thy mother's dying." She stroked Camie's cheek.

Camie's eyes filled with tears. "I want Tucker back.

He protects me. Not even the bad man hurt me. Tucker stopped him. Tucker's my friend." She turned and shouted at Ty, "He's not bad!" With that, Camie whirled around and pelted toward the kitchen.

His daughter's footsteps echoed within his heart. Ty stood rooted to the floor. He knew his wife and Alice had portrayed him in a bad light, but he'd never thought that Camie would take Alice Crandall's vitriol literally. He had always blamed himself for upsetting Camie his first night home. He arrived late on a stormy night. In the midst of thunder and lightning, he'd bent over her bed. She had wakened and screamed.

I always thought it was the scar on my cheek. But it wasn't that alone. It was Virginia getting revenge on me through her mother. Virginia—petty, willful and cruel to the end and beyond. He felt nauseated at the thought that his daughter had screamed each night because she thought he was going to kill her in her sleep. *Dear God, help.*

"Ty, I'm so very sorry this has happened," Felicity said, touching his sleeve. "But I think Camie has the right of it. Tucker did not steal that man's purse."

Ty stared at the floor. Why couldn't Felicity understand that cruel reality had to be faced? With a harsh edge to his voice, he said, "Hogan reported what he saw and I have a man willing to testify that Tucker stole his purse. What am I supposed to do in the face of such evidence?"

"They must be lying," Felicity stated. "I know Tucker. I know that the boy I walked to town and bought shoes for had no reason to steal and had no intention of doing so. Will thee help me find out what is wrong?"

Her insistence on denying the facts turned his stomach to curdled milk. "I am the judge. I cannot take any interest in this or any case beyond what is presented by counsel before me in a court session."

"Then I will have to find out the truth myself." She tightened her grip on his sleeve. "I will do what I can to calm thy daughter and help her see that thee is only doing thy duty."

He tried to pull together a smile and failed. Tugging free, he walked out the door and down the stone path. Why did this have to happen just when he was beginning to have hope that Camie might come home?

"Ty," Felicity called after him, "don't forget— 'Trust in the Lord and do good. And evildoers will be cut down like grass.' Don't despair."

He kept walking. He couldn't swallow her reassurance. He'd wanted Tucker to break away from evil, hoped he would. But evidently the habit of theft had been too powerful for the boy to break.

Why had he thought that leaving Camie here was a good idea? It had just shoved another wedge between them. He recalled Camie repeating Alice's vicious words and he was instantly filled with rage. When would he ever stop paying—or worse, when would Camie stop paying—for his poor choice of a wife?

* * *

In her bedroom later, Felicity rocked Camie, patting her back and crooning a wordless melody softly. This was the first time that Camie had been afraid of going to sleep with Katy and Donnie. And Felicity couldn't blame the little girl. Felicity herself wished someone was there to hold her and soothe her fears. She forced the memory of Ty's strong arms from her mind.

"I want Tucker to come home," Camie whispered, her throat raw from weeping.

"Tucker will come home." Felicity rocked her.

"But my father says he's going to make Tucker stay in jail." Camie touched Felicity's cheek. The little girl's eyes were red from crying.

"Everybody makes a mistake from time to time." Felicity kissed the small hand. "Thy father has been misled, lied to. I will do everything in my power to show him that. Thy father is a good man. He will change his mind."

"My father isn't a good man," Camie said.

"Camie, I'm sorry to have to say this." Felicity stiffened inside with harsh outrage. "But thy grandmother Alice is not a person thee should listen to. She does not always tell the truth."

"Grandma Crandall is a fibber?" Camie nestled closer.

"She thinks she—" Felicity found herself at a loss for words to explain a twisted mind to a little child. "Camie, some people a person can trust. Others cannot be trusted. I am afraid that thy grandmother Alice is a person who cannot be trusted. I'm sorry to say that, but it would be wrong for me to let thee believe her lies."

"Can I trust my Grandma Louise?" the little girl asked, looking up.

"Yes, thee can trust her." Felicity hugged her tighter. "She tells the truth. She loves thee very much and thy father does, too."

"I want Tucker to come home." Camie yawned.

"Camie, I have always followed a promise of God. I trust in God and do good. Thee must trust God to take care of Tucker, too."

Camie sat up. Katy was standing in the doorway. "Camie, can you come to bed now? Donnie is worried about you."

Camie glanced up at Felicity seriously. "I better go to bed. Donnie is a little boy and needs his sleep."

Felicity nodded and let Camie slip from her lap. Katy held out a hand and the two girls walked away together. Doubt assailed Felicity. She was going to do her part. But digging into sin to expose the truth was always dangerous. She would have to follow her own advice and trust God to do the rest. But would Ty be able to do the same?

The next day, wearing her warmest shawl, Felicity stood outside the cell in the jail. Tucker wouldn't meet her eyes.

"Tucker, I wish thee would tell me what really happened yesterday. I know thee didn't steal any purse."

"The cop nabbed me, okay?" Tucker shrugged. "Forget me. I'm just unlucky."

"Camie is heartbroken." Felicity rested her hand on a bar.

Tucker hunched up a shoulder.

"Will thee tell me the truth?"

Tucker snorted. "The truth is what the cop says, right?"

Felicity glanced into the other cell and saw that Charles Scott was listening to them. Felicity knew that neither this boy nor this man deserved to be in custody. Yet how to prove that? "I have hired a lawyer for thy arraignment today. And I will be there."

The officer arrived to take Tucker to court, effectively ending their conversation. With a sigh, she followed them to the courthouse, her mind spinning wildly, trying to come up with a way to break through the wall of lies someone had constructed around Tucker.

She seated herself behind her lawyer, John Remington, and prayed as Tucker pleaded guilty. Looking unusually forbidding, Ty sat in the judgment seat. After the bailiff read Tucker Stout's previous sentence and the terms of probation, Ty asked Tucker, "Do you have any explanation for what has happened?"

Tucker shrugged.

"Your Honor," the prosecuting attorney said, "the man Tucker stole from is here in court and ready to testify."

Felicity followed the prosecutor's gesture and looked

at the man he was indicating. Felicity's mind began to buzz. Where had she seen this man before? And then everything clicked into place in her mind.

She had to speak to Willie and Butch. They knew Tucker from before, no matter what they all said. And Felicity knew in her heart that those two boys held the key to saving Tucker.

The next morning, Felicity sent all the children to school except for Willie and Butch. In the foyer, she drew on her gray wool shawl, gloves and bonnet. Vista stood beside her doing the same while Willie and Butch waited.

Fear bubbled within her. Today she was going to do something very risky, perilous even. If there were any other way to make the men in this town see reason, she would not be forced to this extreme action. But she had finally questioned the truth out of Willie and Butch. Now she must put this knowledge into action so that the truth could be made visible to all. *Father, protect me and Vista—but more importantly, protect the children.*

"Now boys, thee knows what I want thee to do?" *What I'm forced to ask thee to do, so thee and the rest of the children will be safe.* So much was dependent on her success today. Surely God would be in this with her.

The boys looked at her warily. "Yeah."

"You mean 'Yes, Miss Felicity,' don't you?" Vista scolded.

This note of normalcy eased Felicity's tight worry one tiny notch. "Thee two are the only ones who can help me show the truth about what really happened to Tucker."

"Yeah, but—" Willie began and then corrected himself, "Miss Felicity, we don't want to go back to St. Louis. We like it here."

"Thee will not go back there. Ever again," Felicity said with an assurance she didn't feel. "And the danger that has hung over both thy heads and Tucker's will be done with, broken." *Lord, let these words be true.*

"Okay, we'll do it then, Miss Felicity," Willie said with evident resolution. Still, both boys looked scared and worried.

Felicity smoothed her dress, preparing to go into the battle for truth and justice. "Now start out and Vista and I will follow thee. Don't look back and try to behave as naturally as thee can."

Willie and Butch walked outside and headed for town. When they reached the corner, Felicity nodded to Vista. The two women started out, following the boys at a discreet distance. As Felicity watched the boys, she questioned her plan. Was she putting their lives in danger? What if something went wrong? Regardless, it was too late to turn back now. All she could do was stay on her guard—and pray. For all of them.

From the bushes near the house, Camie watched Willie and Butch leave home and head in the opposite direction from school. And more troubling, she saw that Miss Felicity and Miss Vista were walking to town, too. Camie had dawdled on the way to school with Katy, feeling that something was very wrong. Did it have to do with Tucker? Was Miss Felicity taking Butch and Willie to see Tucker? This had made her decision. She wanted to visit Tucker. She turned to Katy. "I forgot something. I'll catch up with you."

When Katy was around the corner, Camie turned toward town, following Miss Felicity. Camie sensed something important was happening. Worry tingled through her. She walked near the full bushes that edged most yards in case she had to hide, but Miss Felicity didn't look back.

Heart thumping, Felicity was praying as hard as she could. The sharp wind flapped her bonnet ribbons while she hovered near enough to hear but not be seen, Willie and Butch would make contact with the man she'd seen in court yesterday. They had said they knew where the man they called Dalton would be, somewhere here around the wharf.

As planned, Vista would hover farther behind in case she needed to run for help. Felicity wished that she could have turned to Ty, but Ty refused to consider that Hogan might not be honest. And neither would her lawyer. So she must depend on God.

Drawing in cold air, she wondered if she had the courage to confront the men responsible for such evil. The Lord had said it would be better for a man who corrupted little ones to have a millstone tied around his neck and to be cast into the sea. *Dear Lord, protect me, Vista and these children. Let us catch the evil ones in the act. Then Ty will believe me.*

Soon, deep in the noisy, busy wharf area, Felicity and Vista hung back farther. Willie and Butch were looking for Dalton. Felicity glimpsed Hogan and turned to look at a street vendor's wares, hiding behind her bonnet brim. Willie and Butch walked up to Hogan and within a few minutes, Hogan nodded with a satisfied smile and waved them toward the wharf. Then he turned and went the opposite direction.

Felicity turned to Vista, gave her a nod, and walked in the same direction that the boys had gone. She tried to look nonchalant, smiling and nodding at acquaintances. The quay was stacked with all sorts of boxes and huge cloth bags of grain. The workers were calling to each other and singing a work song. The wharf was crowded with people who weren't aware of the drama taking place.

Willie and Butch slipped into an alley and then inside a shack that was shielded by bags of grain piled high, ready to be shipped.

Her heart beating was so loud, Felicity wondered why even in this tumult no one heard it. She drew near to the ill-fitting shack door. Immediately she knew that her intuition had been accurate. She heard a rough voice saying, "You seen what happened to Tucker, did ya? He'll do a year in jail for crossin' me. I'm going to go back to St. Louee today and I'll take you boys with me. And you better tell the others there not to cross me or—"

A muffled outcry came from behind Felicity. She whirled around and found Hogan with a hand clamped over Vista's mouth as he held her tightly. "Get inside, Quaker," he ordered in a low tone. "I've had enough of your interfering."

Struck mute, Felicity could not have cried out if she tried. But would she have been heard anyway? And she and Vista were hidden from sight by the bags of grain piled high all around them.

"Move," Hogan ordered. "Or else I snap her neck."

Felicity walked into the shack, shrieking silent prayers for help to come. Now.

Camie had followed Miss Felicity and Miss Vista all the way to the wharf. The women hadn't looked back once. Everything was so noisy and busy. People pushed past her. Then she heard what sounded like Miss Vista shriek with hurt, like the time she had caught her finger when shutting a kitchen drawer. Camie hurried around a pile of bags. She glimpsed a man pushing Miss Vista into a bad-looking place.

Camie couldn't move. She couldn't cry out. What was happening? She couldn't catch her breath. She closed her eyes. What should she do?

She needed to find out if Miss Vista and Felicity were being hurt. Creeping around the big piles of bags, she was able to get near enough to the shack to catch some of what a man inside was saying: "…toss her in the river…tired of Quaker meddling…losing me money."

Toss her in the river? Icy fear inside, Camie turned and zigzagged through the high piles of wares and workers carrying big sacks. She ran right into a man.

"Aren't you the judge's daughter?" he asked, taking her shoulder in his hand.

Camie looked up. It was the nice man Jack who had brought Eugene and the other children to Miss Felicity's home. "Yes, please, I need help." She grabbed his big hand. "Please."

"What's the problem?" Jack demanded. "I seen Miss Felicity and Miss Vista going this way."

"A man grabbed Miss Vista and had his hand over her mouth. I heard him say he was going to toss the Quaker in the river." Camie's words rushed out. Would this man believe her? "Something's wrong. Please, what should I do?"

Jack looked around. "You say a man forced Vista in there?"

Camie nodded, silently calling help, help!

"I seen you yesterday going to court with Miss Gabriel. Your daddy's there now. Go get him. Now. I'll keep watch here in case they take the ladies away."

Camie spun around and started running. She ignored everything around her till she saw the stairs of the big courthouse. She ran up and inside. She knew right where the courtroom was. A man tried to stop her but she ran around him and with both hands, pushed open the door.

She saw her father in that high seat and headed straight for him. "Papa! I need you! The man's going to hurt Miss Felicity and Miss Vista! Help me!" Gasping for air, she ran around hands that tried to stop her. Her father met her at the front of the court.

"Camie, what is it?"

"Papa!" She threw her arms around his waist and looked up at his face. "Someone is going to throw Miss Felicity in the river! I heard him say it. Jack told me to come and get you! Help! Please! *Help!*"

Horrified, Ty gazed down at his terrified daughter. "Someone's going to hurt Miss Felicity and Jack told you to come and get me?"

"Yes!" Camie began to tug him to go. Tears were streaming from her eyes. "Yes!"

Coming out of shock, Ty didn't know what had happened but Jack would. "Court's adjourned!" He took his daughter's hand. "Take me to Jack!"

As they ran out of the courthouse, Camie clung to his hand. Ty tried to ask more questions but his daughter would do nothing but run. Soon, she slowed and turned to him. She pressed her index finger to her lips, telling him to be quiet.

As they came around a pile of grain sacks, Jack rose. He held his finger up just as Camie had. The concern on Jack's lined face punched Ty in the gut. Something was wrong, very wrong. *Dear Heaven.* He pushed Camie behind him. "Stay," he whispered.

"I been listenin'," Jack whispered. "And your little

girl's right. Something's going on in that shack. I heard voices and sounds of someone in pain. Your girl said Vista is inside. And I seen Miss Felicity go this way first."

A steel band snapped around Ty's lungs. "How many men inside?"

Jack held up two fingers.

"There's two of us," Ty stated.

Jack nodded.

"I'll go in first." Ty turned his head. "Camie, stay here." Then he started forward, kicked down the flimsy door and rushed in. In the dim light, he saw that Hogan—*Hogan*—was tying Felicity's hands behind her back.

Hogan shouted and another man wheeled around—the man who'd testified against Tucker.

Ty didn't hesitate. He slammed his fist into Hogan's jaw. The man went down, but reared up. He swung at Ty. He missed. Ty barreled into him and bashed his fist into Hogan's eye. The man yelped. Then Ty hit him with an uppercut and a left hook. Hogan staggered and fell, unconscious.

Ty swung around to see about the other man but found that Jack had knocked him unconscious, too. Ty moved to Felicity and pulled out his pocketknife to cut her bonds. She ripped the dirty gag out of her mouth and threw her arms around his neck. "Thank God thee came. I was praying."

Jack had taken care of Vista's bonds and she was rubbing her wrists as she wept. Jack wrapped his arm around her and helped her up.

"How did this all come about?" Ty asked, fresh shock crashing over him.

"I think we better get these two tied up and taken in first, don't you, Judge?" Jack suggested.

Ty nodded. "You're right."

Then Jack squinted. "Boys, is that you? Willie and Butch?"

Ty looked over and found the two boys cowering in the corner of the littered, dirty shack. "Boys, are you all right? Did anyone hurt you?"

"No, we're okay," Willie said, his lower lip trembling.

"Now that you're here," Butch added. "We were afraid Hogan and Dalton were going to throw Miss Felicity in the river. And make us go back to St. Louis."

"I don't understand any of this, but first things first." Ty pulled a length of rope from the floor that had been used to tie the women.

But before he could tie Hogan's hands, the man reared up and punched Ty right on the jaw. Lights flashed in front of Tyrone's eyes. He felt weightless as he fell.

Chapter Eleven

"**I** don't care how ridiculous it sounds!" His head still throbbing, Ty shouted at the chief of police in the jail's office. The small room was crowded with everyone who had been in the shack on the quay. With his hands tied behind his back, Dalton looked downward while Jack still gripped his arm.

"Hogan tried to kidnap Miss Gabriel and knocked me unconscious," Ty declared, anger at himself rising, searing inside. "Then he took off. You need to get your men on the street to catch him. He can just jump a boat and be gone down river!"

"You're not making any sense," police chief Kidwell retorted. "You come in here with that Quaker woman and the man Tucker Stout robbed with his hands tied up—"

"Tucker didn't rob anyone," Ty objected, clenching his fists. "I tell you Hogan and this man are working together. They are the ones who should be in jail."

Showing signs of rough treatment, Felicity held up both her hands. "Please let us sit down and start at the beginning. But first, this man needs to be taken into custody." She pointed to Dalton. "He took my house-keeper and me against our wills and tied us up. He threatened us with harm, even murder. And we will both swear out a complaint against him."

Kidwell didn't look happy about this.

"Are you going to believe this crazy woman?" Dalton demanded. "I didn't do nothing."

Ty fought the urge to backhand the liar.

"I'm another eyewitness along with the judge, Miss Gabriel," Jack spoke up. "He tied up both the ladies."

"Yes," Camie, who was clinging to Felicity's hand, agreed. "He's a bad man."

Still looking disgusted, Kidwell motioned to an-other officer. "Put him in a cell."

"Not with Tucker!" Felicity cried out. "He might try to hurt the boy!"

Ty chafed at these delays. Why didn't Kidwell get it?

"Put the boy in with the black prisoner and put this man in the other cell alone." The officer did as he was told. "Now, Miss Gabriel, will you please explain to me what has happened?"

Felicity sat down in the chair that Kidwell showed her to. She pulled Camie onto her lap and motioned for Willie and Butch to come in and stand by Jack and Ty. "This isn't going to be easy to sort out."

"It isn't?" Kidwell heaved himself onto the chair behind his desk.

"No. Has thee read the book *Oliver Twist*?"

Kidwell looked startled. "My wife read it to our children. What has that got to do with this?"

Felicity took a deep breath. "The man the other officer has just taken to a cell is a man like Fagan."

Kidwell's eyebrows rose. "He's corrupting children? Teaching them to steal for him?"

Ty paced, trying to keep a cap on his furious, billowing rage.

"Yes, and evidently Hogan has been working with him." Felicity added.

"That's a serious charge." Kidwell looked at her with narrowed eyes.

"If I couldn't prove the charge, I wouldn't make it." Felicity lifted her chin.

"Will you please take action?" Ty demanded, his fury pushing him. "Hogan is a dishonest cop. He's been working with Dalton. I didn't believe it either till I saw it with my own eyes."

Kidwell threw up his hands. "What are all these children doing here?"

Ty's anger was a pot about to boil over. He clenched and reclenched his hands. The urge to choke sense into Kidwell threatened to overpower him.

Felicity put a hand on Kidwell's desk. "I know it's hard to believe that a long-respected policeman has been two-faced. But please dispatch officers to catch Hogan. From what the boys have told me, Dalton allows children who steal for him to live in a St. Louis warehouse. I'm afraid Hogan may go there and hurt or take the children away with him. They could testify against him and Dalton. I fear for those children." Her voice faltered. "Please, don't delay."

Felicity's simple, direct words appeared to work. Kidwell rose and began barking orders to the other officers in the station.

"And thee should talk to these boys and Tucker," Felicity said.

"Let's do that right now," Kidwell said.

Ty took Felicity's arm and helped her walk back to the cells. As they approached, he saw that Dalton was talking in low, harsh tones to Tucker.

"Shut up, Dalton!" Kidwell roared. "You're finished." Then he unlocked the door of the cell where Tucker and the black prisoner were.

Felicity spoke up, "Tucker, was this man Dalton the one who tried to kidnap Camie?"

Dalton growled a curse and a warning.

"Yeah," Tucker declared, glaring at the man in the other cell. "I recognized him that night—even with a sack over his head."

Dalton shook the bars with his hands, promising to pay back Tucker for this.

Kidwell barked, "Shut up or I'll have you gagged. Come on out, you two." Kidwell motioned to them. Both Tucker and Charles hesitated.

"It's all right, Tucker," Felicity said. "We know the truth. And we need your help. Hogan is at large and he might go across the river and hurt the other children.

Will thee show the police chief where they are? He wants to see to their safety."

Dalton cursed Felicity and tried to reach her through the bars.

Ty wished he could get his hands around the man's throat.

Kidwell roared. "Somebody manacle his hands behind his back and gag him!"

Dalton's face hardened and he turned his back on them, still muttering to himself.

Tucker slowly approached Felicity, pausing in the opening. "You know everything?"

Felicity hugged him. "Yes, Hogan and this man were caught in the act." She turned and gestured toward the two boys. "Willie and Butch helped me."

Tucker let out a gust of a sigh. And then he leaned his head against the bars. "It's over then?"

Ty spoke up. "Yes, it is. I'm very sorry we doubted you."

Tucker shrugged. "Dalton and Hogan knew how to work things. That day Miss Felicity come to town, they set me up to get caught purse-snatching as a warning to me."

"A warning?" Kidwell asked.

"Yeah, Dalton would get drunk and beat the kids. I stopped him and so they set me up."

At this Ty wished he and Jack had beat on Hogan and Dalton a bit longer.

"It's over now," Felicity repeated. "Will thee go with the police chief? He has children of his own and doesn't want anything to happen to thy friends across the river."

"Hogan might go there but he might not. He knows that I know where they are," Tucker said.

Charles Scott stepped out of the cell, looking around like he couldn't believe what had just happened.

"Before you leave," Kidwell said to the man as he led them back to the office, "I'd like to know what your name is and why you were asking about the Barney Home."

No one answered. Ty looked at the troubled faces around him. Finally, the man replied, "I'm Charles Scott, sir. And I thought I knew someone who lived at this woman's house." He pointed to Felicity.

"You knew this woman lived at the Barney house?" Kidwell asked.

"Yes, sir, she was pointed out to me. And I…"

"And you?" Kidwell stared at Scott.

"I followed her one day, trying to see what kind of woman she was, sir." Scott wouldn't look anyone in the eye.

Felicity looked thoughtful. "Was that the day I took the children to school?"

"Yes, ma'am, I apologize."

Felicity gazed at him. "That's all right, Charles Scott. No harm was done."

Ty realized that Vista had not come with them to the cell area. And she was no longer in the police office. Why had she disappeared rather than face this man?

"Mr. Scott," Jack said, "you should come home with me. We'll get things straightened out soon."

Kidwell apologized to Charles and thanked Jack. The two of them left.

"Please take Tucker across now," Felicity urged. "I'm sure he can show thee the place and convince the children to come here. I want them to be safe and cared for at my home."

Kidwell sucked in air. "This is bad business. I hate to think that adults would corrupt or hurt children. I have five myself."

Felicity nodded solemnly. "It grieves my heart, too." She pulled Tucker into another quick hug.

Relief weakened Ty and he leaned against the wall. When he'd seen Felicity tied up and gagged, scorching anger had rushed through him. Now, in the pit of his stomach, a chunk of ice hardened and radiated icy waves, freezing him. Would Felicity ever forgive him for thinking she was just another emotional woman? *I was a fool. A fool not to believe Felicity.*

Ty entered the court, still reeling from the day's astounding events. Since court rarely convened after dark, it was odd to see the candles in wall sconces lit. But with December came the early darkness. And today, reconvening court was necessary in the cause of justice, justice that had been denied. Ty's own incompetence left a sour taste in his mouth. *Why didn't I suspect Hogan?*

The prosecutor was at his place, looking stunned.

John Remington, the defense lawyer, appeared startled but pleased. Tucker Stout sat beside him.

"I think we can take care of this legality fairly quickly," Ty began. "Mr. Remington?"

"Your Honor, in light of facts which I can enter into the record, I ask that my client be released back into the custody of Miss Gabriel."

"Does the prosecutor have any objection to this?" Ty asked.

"No, Your Honor." The portly prosecutor looked stunned, but his words came out calm and clear. "Though the facts, which will become apparent in a subsequent trial, are still unfinished, we feel confident that Tucker Stout should be in Miss Gabriel's custody."

"Granted. This court stands adjourned." Ty rapped his gavel and watched as Felicity sprang to her feet and clapped her hands. The chunk of ice in his midsection had almost rendered him numb. There was a breach between him and Felicity. How could that be healed? He stopped in his office, shed his black robe and then set out to do what he must to protect the children and the ladies at the Barney Home. Hogan remained at large.

After bedtime that evening, Felicity opened her front door. Ty stood there. She recalled the moment he'd kicked down the shack's door and burst in to save her. For a second, her arms rose of their own accord, as if to wrap around his neck.

Interrupting this, her neighbor Eldon Partridge,

who stood just behind Ty, said, "Miss Gabriel, we are going to start patrolling your house again until Hogan is arrested."

She swallowed and clasped her hands together so they wouldn't reach for Ty again. "Does thee feel that is necessary?" She wished that Ty would say something. A disagreement lay between them. She wanted to tell him that she understood. But for some reason, she found she couldn't speak of this. Men took the protection of females very seriously. And Ty must be regretting his not believing her. She tried to form the right words.

"We do think it's necessary," Eldon insisted. "Two men will keep watch, one front and one back, all night. We've just let everyone know to start up the same schedule."

"But it's so much colder now," she cautioned. "I will leave the front and back doors unlocked so the men can come in out of the cold," Felicity said, looking to Ty, hoping he would speak to her.

"I don't think that is advisable," Ty said grimly, not looking into her eyes.

"Most of us have served in the army," Eldon reminded her. "We can handle four hours of cold. Now don't you women worry. You're protected." The man actually saluted her. Then grinned.

Felicity tried to think of more to say, but could only say, "Thank thee." Ty was already turning away, so she shut the door, trying to ignore the feeling of being rejected by Ty. She stood for a moment in the foyer, looking up the grand staircase. The house had finally settled down for the night, hours later than usual. All the children save Tucker were in their beds sleeping—safe.

Felicity couldn't recall ever feeling like this before. It was hard to find words to describe all the turmoil and emotions that she was experiencing—shock, sadness, joy, vindication, fear, exhaustion. She'd wanted Ty to fold her in his arms, warm the chill she couldn't shake. Rubbing her chilled arms, she made her way down the hall to the warm kitchen and found Vista sitting there.

"Good." Vista rose. "I was hoping you'd come here. I can't settle down. Too much…too much." She shook her head. The kettle on the stove whistled. She turned to it. "I got the pot ready for chamomile tea. That might help us calm down."

Felicity couldn't speak. Too many words clamored to be spoken. She sank into the nearest chair and watched Vista prepare the tea. Finally, a large cup was set before her. She sighed. "Thanks."

Vista sat across from her. "I keep going over in my mind what all happened today." She shook her head again. "I can't believe it. I can't believe we followed the boys and put ourselves into such jeopardy."

"I knew it was dangerous." Felicity sipped the hot tea laced with honey. "But I couldn't get Ty to believe that Hogan had dirty hands. It was the only way to break Ty's confidence in Hogan. We had to catch him and Dalton in the act of doing what they were to the children. I know it was risky." Felicity laid her hand over Vista's. "But we had to do it. Or the children would suffer. Ours and others."

Vista nodded. "I know. It's just that it's hard. It's hard to think that two men would use children like that. I've seen a lot of evil in this life so it shouldn't shock me. But it does."

Felicity agreed, nodding her head.

"Miss Felicity?" an unexpected voice called.

Felicity turned to see Camie in her nightgown, rubbing her eyes. "Camie, what is it?"

"I woke up. I can't get back to sleep. I'm scared. What if that bad man comes here?"

What if that bad man comes here? Felicity opened her arms wide and Camie climbed onto her lap. "Thee doesn't need to be afraid. Men are patrolling around the house like they did before. No bad man will be able to get inside."

Camie clutched her. "Good." But the child still looked fretful.

"What is it, Camie? Thee can tell me."

"I keep thinking about my papa. Why did my grandma say such bad things about him? He's not a bad man. He fought that real bad man today and saved you and Miss Vista."

"Your father is a good man," Vista agreed.

Suddenly hot around her prim collar, Felicity was glad Alice Crandall wasn't here right now. If she were, Felicity wouldn't have been answerable for what she might say to the self-centered, coldhearted woman.

Felicity couldn't ever recall wanting to box someone's ears before. Keeping tight control on her words, Felicity said, "Camie, as I told thee, unfortunately thy grandmother Alice is not a person who can be believed."

Camie nestled closer and whimpered. "When my papa came home from the war, I was so afraid. Grandma Alice said he killed my mama and he would kill me, too. And so I was afraid to go to sleep 'cause my mama went to sleep and never got up."

No child should ever have to live with such fear. And this little one had been terrorized her whole young life. Had her mother, Virginia, spared one thought for her precious child?

"Evil," Vista murmured. "Evil."

"Camie, once and for all," Felicity said, tightening her hold on Camie, "thy father is a good man. He did not kill thy mother. Thee must let thy father know that thee is glad he came home from the war."

Camie looked up into Felicity's face and touched her cheek. "When I ran to him for help, he came right away. I believe you. My papa is a good man."

Felicity drew in a deep breath, holding in how much Camie's gentle touch meant to her. "Good. Thee were very brave to do what thee did." She kissed Camie's cheek. "I should scold thee for following us, but in the end, thee did what God had planned. Now thee is a brave, big girl so thee can walk upstairs and put thyself to bed again. I must not baby thee."

"I can go by myself." Camie slid from her lap, but turned back for one more hug. "I'll go see that

Donnie is covered up. Sometimes he gets uncovered and gets cold."

Felicity smoothed back Camie's dark hair, smiling. "That would be a good thing to do. We must take care of the littler children."

Camie waved to Vista and left the kitchen. The two women listened to her footsteps fade away.

"How could a woman be so evil?" Felicity asked, resting her head on one hand. In that moment, Alice Crandall's malice oppressed even her spirit.

"It's bad, all right. Alice Crandall is a captive of sin. A slave of sin."

Felicity shook her head. Why did people do evil? She'd never understood the desire to hurt others.

"I been a slave of sin, too," Vista murmured.

Startled, Felicity looked up. "What?" Vista had never revealed anything about her life.

"Charles Scott came looking for me and I wouldn't go to him." Vista traced the rim of her cup with one fingertip and then she pulled out the locket she wore under her collar. "Mrs. Barney give this to me and told me to hope for the future. I have hid this locket, hid from hoping. I never thought I'd see Charles again."

"Thee *does* know Charles Scott, then?" Felicity smoothed a wrinkle in the starched tablecloth, giving Vista some space to speak freely.

Vista nodded with a moody expression. "I didn't want to look him in the face."

Felicity sipped her hot tea, trying to find a way to

help Vista free herself from whatever weighed on her. "Why didn't thee want to see Charles?"

"Because seeing him would bring it all back on me." Vista's voice became vehement. "All the slave days of my life. All the sorrow. I felt like I was suffocating all over again. It's hard—" Vista clenched her hand "—so hard to think of the past."

"Were thee in love with Charles?" Felicity was startled by Vista's sudden flare-up and her own audacity in asking these plain questions. But who knew when this very private woman would open again?

Vista nodded slowly. "We were childhood sweethearts."

This phrase echoed inside Felicity. "Childhood sweethearts," she whispered.

"When I was around fifteen, Charles wanted to marry me." Then Vista fell silent.

Memories of Gus Mueller's proposal before he went off to war played through Felicity's mind. "Thee didn't want to marry him?"

Vista stared down into her cup. "It wasn't that. I *wanted* to marry him. But as I got older, I just couldn't bear being a slave. It was like being smothered alive. Being a slave made it impossible to simply marry Charles and settle down to life together."

Felicity thought deeply on Vista's words.

Shivering suddenly, Vista took a sip and then put down her cup. "How could I marry him if I could be taken from him at any time? My mother said I should find whatever happiness I could. That life was short anyway. But I wasn't like her. I wanted my life to be *mine*." Vista wrapped both hands around her cup. "And I was a pretty girl, a very pretty girl, and that's not good if you're a slave."

Felicity said nothing. What was there to say about such things? "Thee ran away and came here?"

Vista nodded. "Mrs. Barney hid me for a long time. Finally, the slave-catchers gave up and left. She smuggled me out of town. Then, in new clothing, I come back with a new name and a story to tell of living near Beardstown, Illinois." Vista sighed. "She hired me as her housekeeper. Her former one had just retired. I was happy here. I didn't let myself think about the past—it just made me sad. So I taught myself *not* to remember."

Felicity squeezed Vista's hand, glad Vista had trusted her, confided in her. "I don't know what it feels like to be a slave. But I understand wanting to be free. I was fortunate to come from a family that didn't deem girls as less than boys. I am one of seven sisters and we all have been blessed with a mission to live for. After I volunteered at an orphanage, I knew I wanted to devote my life to children."

Vista gave her a small smile. "I didn't have any mission for my life. I just wanted to be free. And I didn't want to remember."

"That's understandable," Felicity said.

Vista looked away. "But it made me a coward. I should have been brave and gone to see Charles."

"None of us can be brave all the time." Felicity touched Vista's wrist.

"You're brave all the time," Vista said.

Felicity shook her head, smiling sadly. "I was afraid this morning. And I'm afraid now. I'm afraid Hogan will try to hurt the children in St. Louis or try to pay me back."

Vista looked into Felicity's eyes. "You ask me if I loved Charles. What about the judge? Do you love him?"

Hearing the words out loud stung Felicity. "I don't plan to marry," she said without even thinking about it.

"Planning is different than feeling, different than being," Vista observed. "I think the judge wants to make up with you. I think he's sweet on you."

Felicity said nothing. Her mouth had betrayed her once and she wouldn't let it do that again. Marry? No. That wasn't the plan for her life. If she married, her first loyalty would have to be to her husband, children and their home. No time for orphans in that life.

Ty's face lingered in her mind. But that should mean nothing. She closed her eyes and held back tears.

Felicity awoke with a start, lifting her head from her arms folded on the kitchen table. Someone was knocking hard on the door. She'd sat up waiting for Tucker's return and she had fallen asleep sitting in the kitchen at the table. Stiff and groggy, she rose. Vista came out of her room off the kitchen. "Didn't you go to bed last night? You said you were when I left you."

Felicity stretched her spine and tried to wake completely. "I'm fine," she muttered.

"Not if you slept at the table all night. I'll go get it." Vista seemed herself again as she bustled out of the kitchen.

Felicity went to the sink and from the bucket there, splashed some water onto her face. She heard loud exclamations coming from the foyer. She turned and hurried there.

Charles Scott had come. He'd lifted Vista off the floor and was holding her tightly. Then Vista kissed Charles. And though she knew she should, Felicity found she couldn't look away, couldn't hold back a wide smile.

Jack remained in the doorway, looking pleased with himself, too.

Felicity waited till Vista finally ordered Charles to put her down. Then Felicity went forward, beaming. "Charles Scott, I'm so glad to see thee."

Charles bowed slightly. "Ma'am, I spent the night at Jack's house. But before I left town, I wanted to try once more to see Vista."

Felicity studied Vista's face. She looked happy but shamed and uncertain, too. "Vista, why doesn't thee take Charles to the parlor? Thee will have privacy there."

Vista nodded. Not looking at Charles, she led him by the hand.

"I'll be leaving now," Jack said.

Felicity went forward, her hands out. "Thank thee for thy help yesterday. Thee showed great courage."

Jack smiled and bowed himself out. Felicity had barely gotten halfway up the steps and the brass knocker sounded again.

She opened the door and there stood the police chief with a crowd of ragged children and a beaming Tucker.

"Miss Gabriel, Tucker and I did go over to St. Louis on the ferry late yesterday," Kidwell said. "We found these children in that warehouse. Tucker explained everything to them and they came with me. The police chief in St. Louis has his men searching for Hogan, too. He said I could leave these children at the orphanage in St. Louis, but I figured they belonged with you. We got back so late that they spent the night in my house."

Felicity looked at all the grimy, frightened faces lifted toward hers. Her heart expanded with love for these little ones. How could she have doubted her calling, even for a second? She opened her arms wide. "Welcome, children. Welcome to thy new home."

The new children had been scrubbed mercilessly clean in the new bathing room off the kitchen with its indoor pump and stove for heating water. Felicity had sent Midge to town to buy more clothing. The number of children had doubled overnight. Twenty children now lived in the Barney house. The bedrooms were filling up and Felicity was grateful for the larger dining room. All day Camie and Katy had shown the newcomers how things were done here. Katy was quite the little leader.

Now sitting around the dining room table after supper, the new children clustered together and eyed her with uncertainty. Felicity wished she had slept more last night and thought longingly of bedtime.

The brass knocker sounded. The new children looked apprehensive. Felicity went to the door. She opened it to a huge evergreen tree filling the doorway. "Hello, Miss Felicity!" Jack called from somewhere on the other side of the tree. "The men in my church thought you could use a Christmas tree. We went out on a member's farm and cut this one down for you."

"Come in!" Sudden gaiety zipped through Felicity. *A Christmas tree!* The children were clapping and calling out in excitement.

After some consultation, it was decided that the tree should be set up in the grand foyer where it was visible from the dining room table and the parlor, but away from the warmth of the fireplaces in both rooms. Jack and Charles then set the tree in a bucket of water and braced it with rocks and blocks of wood to stand straight.

Soon the children and Felicity sat around the table, some stringing popcorn and others stringing cranberries. Vista and Charles were in the kitchen baking gingerbread cookies to hang with ribbons on the tree. The fragrance of nutmeg, ginger and cinnamon wafted through the house. A few snowflakes drifted by the windows. All was happy inside.

Outside, however, Hogan was still at large, so two

men would be patrolling again tonight, a pebble in Felicity's shoe. Over and over, she glanced at the window with a sense that she was watching, waiting for something, someone.

The brass knocker sounded. When Felicity made to rise, Tucker hopped up. "I'll get it."

Felicity had to smile. Tucker was a different boy. The burden of worry had been lifted from him. Willie and Butch showed the same new confidence. They encouraged the new children who were beginning to smile a little.

"It's the judge!" Tucker announced. "And his mother, Mrs. Hawkins."

The new children shrank visibly. Tucker reassured them, saying, "He's okay. He's the one who punched Hogan."

"Thank you, Tucker," Louise said as she took off her bonnet, smoothed her hair before the mirror on the hall tree and then entered the dining room. "Jack stopped to tell us that he had delivered your Christmas tree. We brought some red and white Christmas candles and candleholders. My, the tree is a magnificent one."

"Hello, Grandma Louise," Camie greeted her. "I'm stringing cranberries for the tree. Hi, Papa."

Ty followed Louise in, carrying a wooden box. Camie hopped up, kissed Louise and hugged her father. Felicity couldn't ignore Ty's response to this spontaneous affection. She glanced away, not wishing to embarrass him. She realized she was disappointed that she couldn't show him the same gratitude for rescuing her. But that would be most improper.

After exchanging greetings, Ty set the box on the table and lifted the lid. "I'll go ahead and start clipping the holders onto the boughs."

"Can I help?" Tucker asked.

"Sure." Ty and the boy went to the tree and began clipping the small candleholders on the branches, fiddling with the candles so that they would stand straight and not burn nearby boughs.

Felicity couldn't take her eyes from the two of them, working so well together, all antagonism gone. When the job was done, Tucker and Ty returned to the dining room.

"When is Camie going home?" Tucker asked out of the clear blue.

Felicity held her breath. This was something she had wondered about but had not had the courage to bring it up. Now taking her cue from Tucker, she turned to Camie. "When does thee want to return home?"

Silence. Camie stopped stringing cranberries and looked around the table. "Do I have to go home?"

"Well, yeah," Tucker replied. "This is a home for kids who don't got family. But you have a dad and a grandma right here." He motioned toward them.

Felicity prayed silently for reconciliation.

Camie started kicking the rungs of her chair with her heels. "I didn't think about that."

"We'd like to have you come home," Louise said,

her voice strained. "I know it's hard to leave Katy and Donnie, but you would still see them every day at school, and you could visit here, too. And they could visit you at our house."

"I could come home," Camie said, "but I would miss sleeping with Katy. I don't like sleeping alone."

"Maybe you could stay. You don't got a mother," Katy added. "You're half orphan. Does that count?"

"I want Miss Felicity to be my mother," Camie said.

Felicity shimmered with surprise.

"That makes sense," Tucker said with a grin. "I think your pa should marry Miss Felicity. I think he's sweet on her."

Felicity's face warmed. "Tucker, this is not—"

"Yes, I agree," Louise said, grinning. "My son is sweet on Miss Felicity. And I think she would make a wonderful mother for Camie."

Refusing to look at Louise or Ty, Felicity cleared her throat. "I am the mother here. This is my place to care for children."

"But why couldn't you take care of the children here in the daytime and then come home with me in the evening?" Camie asked, picking up the large needle and beginning to string cranberries again.

"That makes sense," Katy agreed.

Felicity shook her head, blushing furiously. "No, children, no husband would want a wife who did that. If I were a married woman, I would have to devote myself to my own home. I would have no time to care for the children here."

"I don't know about that," Vista said, coming in with a plate of gingerbread men, Charles following her. "Charles and I have decided to marry and I don't know why we couldn't live here and be house parents, do you? And Midge and her cousin who's going to start after the New Year will be here, too. If your husband hired help at your place, you wouldn't have much work to do at home."

Felicity was completely flustered. Why didn't Ty say something? "This is a most improper conversation. I made a decision long ago that my calling is to care for orphans and children who are being mistreated—"

"I think that's an admirable goal," Louise said. "But I don't think that should prevent you from marrying my son."

Ty spoke up at last, an amused look on his face. "I think that this is something Miss Felicity and I should discuss privately." He rose. "Will you come with me into the den, please?"

Felicity stared at him as if she'd never seen him before. But courtesy dictated that she at least refuse the man in private.

Once inside the den, Ty closed the pocket door. Felicity felt his gaze upon her. Her nerves began to hop. "Ty, I'm so sorry—"

Pulling her close, Ty silenced her with a kiss.

She gasped for air. "Ty, please—"

He kissed her again, more insistently. This man had given her her first kiss here in this very room. But that tender touch was nothing like the kiss he was giving her now. His arms clasped her to him and his lips persuaded hers to part.

"Felicity," he whispered.

She felt each syllable as his lips touched hers. She trembled against him, against her will. "Ty," she murmured breathlessly, "thee mustn't kiss me."

He gazed down into her eyes, grinning. "Don't you like my kisses?"

That put her in a quandary. In all honesty, she did like his kisses. She had often wondered why a woman would let a man kiss her—she was getting the full explanation for that here and now. But it wasn't proper for her to encourage him. "Ty, I will not marry. I have a mission—"

He interrupted her again with a kiss, pulling her even closer to him. She tried to think but her mind was dancing, reeling.

"I'm sorry," he murmured next to her ear. "When you said that Hogan was dishonest and lying, I should have believed you. Don't hold that against me. Please."

"Of course I won't." Felicity tried to step out of Ty's embrace but found she was backed up against the desk and had nowhere to go.

"Felicity, until Camie spoke up tonight, I thought we could never be together. I've behaved so foolishly."

Felicity tried to interrupt and was ignored again.

"Now I realize I can't face that empty house without you. Camie loves you and needs you. I need you and I love you."

"Thee loves me?"

Ty kissed her nose. "Yes, doesn't *thee* love me?" he teased, using her plain speech.

"That's beside the point."

"I will hire a full-time housekeeper again and have a maid and laundress at our home." He lifted and kissed one of her hands. "You will be free to spend your days here at the orphanage. I don't see why you can't do both." He kissed her other hand. "We'll work together to protect orphans and get the Illinois laws for juveniles changed. I'll be a help to you. I promise." He squeezed her hands. "Your mission will become ours."

Felicity felt herself weakening. "Ty, thee is so persuasive. But I already refused to marry my childhood sweetheart, Gus, because I'd committed myself and my life to my mission. He went off to war and died. His mother blames me for her losing him and any possibility of a grandchild. How can I have turned down Gus, my best friend, only to accept thee? Can a sensible person change her whole life plan just because of love?"

Ty chuckled. "You have always talked sensibly, Miss Gabriel. But those are the silliest words I've ever heard from your lips. People change and grow. You will not dishonor Gus's memory by pursuing your own happiness." He reached up to touch a strand of her hair. "I never knew real love till I met you. Love changes everything. You of all people should know that. See what love has done for Tucker and Camie? See how Vista glows now that Charles has come back into her life? How can you say that love shouldn't change anything? It changes everything—and for the good."

She looked at him, openmouthed. *Love. These three abide—faith, hope and love—but the greatest of these is love. How could I be so foolish?*

She rested her cheek against his shirt. "Truly will we work together for the children?"

"Yes, a thousand times, yes. And we will make a home for the children here and for our children in my house. I will do everything in my power to help you." Ty looked down and stroked her hair. "Do you love me, Felicity Gabriel?"

The past fell away and Felicity smiled. "I do, Ty. And I will marry thee."

Epilogue

Hogan had not been seen since the day he was exposed for what he was. With Charles living on the premises, the Barney house was no longer guarded by the men of the neighborhood. They had a lovely Christmas, and today, the afternoon of the first day of 1868 in the parlor of the Barney house, Felicity in a new dark blue dress with white cuffs and collar faced Ty in his best suit and said, "I do." Ty echoed her promise of lifelong devotion, and kissed her so sweetly, he brought grateful tears to her eyes.

Then Vista, wearing a lovely new red dress, faced Charles in a new black suit. The pastors from both Jack's church and Ty's officiated at the two weddings. After the wedding, neighbors and friends of Felicity and Ty's and from Vista's church sat around the large dining-room table and sipped punch and nibbled the beautiful white cake that Martha Partridge had baked and decorated herself. The shared friendship and shared joy of this day enfolded Felicity in a blissful cloud.

Surrounded by the general gaiety, Felicity looked around. A shy but beaming Vista came to her and whispered, "Is it time for us to toss our bouquets? The children keep asking."

Felicity nodded. Both of them carried bouquets of pinecones and short pine boughs, and holly with red berries. They walked to the front porch. All the young women and even little girls gathered below them on the walk, calling for the bouquets, their breath floating white in the chill air.

Felicity watched Vista turn her back and toss the bouquet. When Midge caught Vista's bouquet, everyone's shrieks of excitement filled Felicity with a billowing, limitless elation. When Felicity did likewise, her eldest sister, Mercy, caught hers. Both of them had stared at each other in shock.

Mercy had worked as a nurse side by side with Clara Barton throughout the war and Felicity was very proud of her. Beside Mercy stood Indigo, the little orphaned slave whom Mercy had adopted and who was now near in age to Midge. And showing signs of becoming a lovely woman. Mercy and Indigo were on their way to begin Mercy's life's work far away in the West. Mercy had just graduated from the Female College of Medicine in Pennsylvania and was now a qualified physician.

As everyone hurried back inside, Felicity watched

as Mercy handed Indigo the bouquet and slipped out of the limelight. Felicity didn't believe in omens, but then she hadn't believed that she would be a married woman on January 1, 1868, either.

When Ty came and put his arm around her, Felicity squeezed his hand. Camie stood beside her. Ty kissed the tender skin below Felicity's ear and whispered, "I love you, my bride." Her cup of joy overflowed. Ty's words came again—love changes everything for the good. Maybe love was in Mercy's future too. *Lord, let it be so.*

* * * * *

Dear Reader,

Felicity means happiness. And I think that my heroine lived up to her name. She certainly brought happiness wherever she went—even though she stirred up the status quo. It's hard for us to believe now the conditions prisoners—especially children—were subjected to in the 19th century and before. Many years passed before these were changed by people who followed Felicity's advice from Psalm 37: "Trust God and do good." And it's hard to believe that in many places around the globe, these same conditions still exist. Just in case you're wondering, Charles Dickens's book *Oliver Twist* was first published in 1838 and the term *cop* was in use from around 1850.

On a personal note, in this book, I did something fun with the names. Almost every name in the book is a name popular in my family. I used the names of my grandparents, aunts, uncles and cousins. I'll let you try to guess which ones are family names and which ones aren't.

This was the second sister in my *Gabriel Sisters* series for Love Inspired Historical. The third, Mercy's story, will come out December 2010. Hope you will be able to read all three.

Merry Christmas!

Lyn Cote

QUESTIONS FOR DISCUSSION

1. Felicity believed that she had a mission for her life. Do you have a mission for your life?

2. Why did Gus Mueller's mother hold a grudge against Felicity?

3. Have you ever met someone like Alice Crandall? Do you have any idea how a person becomes this way?

4. What kind of wife was Virginia?

5. Often we think we know why someone feels and behaves the way they do. What did Ty think had made his daughter fear him? And what was the truth?

6. What was the attitude of people in the 19th century toward orphans? Why?

7. What had caused Vista to be a very private person?

8. What was Felicity's reaction when Tucker snatched her purse? Would her reaction be thought unusual today or not?

9. Why did Martha Partridge change her mind about Felicity and her children? Have you ever had this experience? Did something open your eyes and make you reassess someone and their motives?

10. Ty was obviously suffering from Post Traumatic Stress Syndrome. How did his PTSS affect his behavior and reactions?

11. Camie suffered from night terrors. How did Felicity help Camie overcome this?

12. Felicity's guide for life was "Trust the Lord and do good." How did she live this?

13. Why did Felicity think she could not marry?

14. What changed her mind?

15. Who was your favorite secondary (not hero or heroine) character in this story and why?

Here is an exciting sneak preview of
TWIN TARGETS by Marta Perry,
the first book in the new six-book
Love Inspired Suspense series
PROTECTING THE WITNESSES
available beginning January 2010.

Deputy U.S. Marshal Micah McGraw forced down the sick feeling in his gut. A law enforcement professional couldn't get emotional about crime victims. He could imagine his police chief father saying the words. Or his FBI agent big brother. They wouldn't let emotion interfere with doing the job.

"Pity." The local police chief grunted.

Natural enough. The chief hadn't known Ruby Maxwell, aka Ruby Summers. He hadn't been the agent charged with relocating her to this supposedly safe environment in a small village in Montana. He didn't have to feel responsible for her death.

"This looks like a professional hit," Chief Burrows said.

"Yeah."

He knew only too well what was in the man's mind. What would a professional hit man be doing in the remote reaches of western Montana? Why would anyone want to kill this seemingly inoffensive waitress?

And most of all, what did the U.S. Marshals Service have to do with it?

All good questions. Unfortunately he couldn't answer any of them. Secrecy was the crucial element that made the Federal Witness Protection Service so successful. Breach that, and everything that had been gained in the battle against organized crime would be lost.

His cell buzzed and he turned away to answer it. "McGraw."

"You wanted the address for the woman's next of kin?" asked one of his investigators.

"Right." Ruby had a twin sister, he knew. She'd have to be notified. Since she lived back East, at least he wouldn't be the one to do that.

"Jade Summers. Librarian. Current address is 45 Rock Lane, White Rock, Montana."

For an instant Micah froze. "Are you sure of that?"

"'Course I'm sure."

After he hung up, Micah turned to stare once more at the empty shell that had been Ruby Summers. She'd made mistakes in her life, plenty of them, but she'd done the right thing in the end when she'd testified against the mob. She hadn't deserved to end up lifeless on a cold concrete floor.

As for her sister…

What exactly was an Easterner like Jade Summers doing in a small town in Montana? If there was an innocent reason, he couldn't think of it.

Ruby must have tipped her off to her location. That

was the only explanation, and the deed violated one of the major principles of witness protection.

Ruby had known the rules. Immediate family could be relocated with her. If they chose not to, no contact was permitted—ever.

Ruby's twin had moved to Montana. White Rock was probably forty miles or so east of Billings. Not exactly around the corner from her sister.

But the fact that she was in Montana had to mean that they'd been in contact. And that contact just might have led to Ruby's death.

He glanced at his watch. Once his team arrived, he'd get back on the road toward Billings and beyond, to White Rock. To find Jade Summers and get some answers.

* * * * *

*Will Micah get to Jade in time to
save her from a similar fate?
Find out in TWIN TARGETS,
available January 2010
from Love Inspired Suspense.*

Love Inspired
HISTORICAL

INSPIRATIONAL HISTORICAL ROMANCE

Drake Amberly, duke of Hawk Haven, came to the colonies for revenge—to unmask the spy who killed his brother. Yet he finds himself distracted from his mission by the beautiful and spirited Elise Cooper. But as Drake's pursuit of the "Fox" brings him dangerously close to Elise's secrets, she must prove to him that love and forgiveness are all they need.

Look for
The Duke's Redemption
by
CARLA CAPSHAW

*Available January
wherever books are sold.*

www.SteepleHill.com

Steeple
Hill®

LIH82828

REQUEST YOUR FREE BOOKS!

2 FREE INSPIRATIONAL NOVELS
PLUS 2
FREE
MYSTERY GIFTS

Love Inspired.
H I S T O R I C A L
INSPIRATIONAL HISTORICAL ROMANCE

YES! Please send me 2 FREE Love Inspired® Historical novels and my 2 FREE mystery gifts (gifts are worth about $10). After receiving them, if I don't wish to receive any more books, I can return the shipping statement marked "cancel". If I don't cancel, I will receive 4 brand-new novels every other month and be billed just $4.24 per book in the U.S. or $4.74 per book in Canada. That's a savings of over 20% off the cover price. It's quite a bargain! Shipping and handling is just 50¢ per book.* I understand that accepting the 2 free books and gifts places me under no obligation to buy anything. I can always return a shipment and cancel at any time. Even if I never buy another book, the two free books and gifts are mine to keep forever. 102 IDN EYPS 302 IDN EYP4

Name	(PLEASE PRINT)

Address	Apt. #

City	State/Prov.	Zip/Postal Code

Signature (if under 18, a parent or guardian must sign)

Mail to Steeple Hill Reader Service:
IN U.S.A.: P.O. Box 1867, Buffalo, NY 14240-1867
IN CANADA: P.O. Box 609, Fort Erie, Ontario L2A 5X3

Not valid to current subscribers of Love Inspired Historical books.

Want to try two free books from another series?
Call 1-800-873-8635 or visit www.morefreebooks.com

* Terms and prices subject to change without notice. Prices do not include applicable taxes. Sales tax applicable in N.Y. Canadian residents will be charged applicable provincial taxes and GST. Offer not valid in Quebec. This offer is limited to one order per household. All orders subject to approval. Credit or debit balances in a customer's account(s) may be offset by any other outstanding balance owed by or to the customer. Please allow 4 to 6 weeks for delivery. Offer available while quantities last.

LIH09